Susanna Chelton Sheehy

Elden Publishing, LLC
P. O. Box 421803
Atlanta, Georgia 30342

Book cover designed by Christy Bishop
Layout designed by J. L. Saloff

Fonts: Gavinha, Bookman Old Style, Worstveld Sting,
    Art Nouveau Flowers

First Edition

Sheehy, Susanna Chelton
    Marking Time: A Novel

10-Digit ISBN: 0-9789271-0-9
13-Digit ISBN: 978-0-9789271-0-3
LCCN: 2006911173
Copyright: Txu1-271-845

Printed on Acid Free Paper in the United States of America

For everyone in the world
who is facing the challenge and excitement of
the second half of life.

One

"I'll plant a garden." Victoria Vandor startled herself with her own voice. "I used to love to work in the yard."

"Who are you talking to, Victoria?" a high-pitched voice said from behind her.

Victoria turned slowly, dreading the sight of her nosey neighbor, Dolores Crisp, but there she stood.

"I'm talking to myself, Dolores, something wrong with that?"

"Of course not, dear, we all know about the depression," Dolores said, with a sympathetic tilt to her head.

Lord help me, Victoria thought. "I'm feeling much better now." She couldn't believe the efficiency of the neighborhood grapevine. Why do they think I've been depressed? It's not like I've been hospitalized or anything.

"Oh, my God!" she gasped, taking another look at her yard. "The ivy has taken over the trees. The smaller ones are bending under the weight of it."

"I've been so worried that one of them might fall on somebody," Dolores said.

Wincing at the reminder that she wasn't alone, Victoria said, "The undergrowth is so thick I'd need a machete to walk through it. It's pure Georgia jungle.

I guess that's how they knew I was depressed. This place is a disaster."

"That's right." Dolores smiled sweetly. "It wasn't hard to figure out."

"I wonder if I can still do the work. I used to like the physical labor of it, feeling the muscles at work. But at my age, can you regain those muscles?"

"Of course you can, dear. You're not that old."

Dolores was still there. Why didn't she go away? Victoria looked at her. "I wasn't talking to you, Dolores. I was talking to myself."

Dolores stepped back a bit, as if she were afraid insanity was contagious.

"I'm just planning my garden. I talk to myself when I'm planning." Victoria smiled.

"Well, Victoria, the neighborhood will be pleased if you clean the place up," she said, then, startled by the flash of fire in Victoria's eyes, took another step back. "Of course, nobody has really been saying anything about it. We're very forgiving neighbors. I mean...what I meant to say is—"

"Never mind, Dolores, just leave me to my thoughts."

"If there is anything I can do to help, you know where I am." Dolores moved off in the direction of her house and Victoria was alone again.

"Deliver me from helpful neighbors." She laughed. "I'm still talking to myself, maybe I am nuts."

"What I need is a plan," she said to her reflection in the mirror.

"You talking to me?" Joe asked, as he poked his head out of the bathroom door.

She looked around to find her husband with a toothbrush in his mouth and white foam running down his chin. "No, I was talking to myself," she said, turning back to the closet and stepping inside. "I'm going to plant a garden, but first I need to sketch it out. Do you know if we still have any of those gardening books in the basement? Remember I used to have a whole collection of them?"

Her question was met with silence. "Joe?" She looked out of the closet door. The shower was on and she could hear Joe's smooth baritone coming from the bathroom.

She shrugged and went into the closet to get dressed. "There's really nothing to wear in here. The only thing that fits is my work uniform. Yuck! I can't possibly wear stretch pants and T-shirts." Her hand went automatically to her bulging belly. "Jeans just don't work that well at my age."

"I'll have to do something about this." She patted her soft belly and reached for a pair of loose fitting cotton pants with an elastic waistband and a large T-shirt.

"Are you going out?" Joe asked when they were both back in the bedroom putting on their shoes.

"Yes, I'm having lunch with Jane and I thought I'd do some shopping. There is nothing in my closet that fits any more," she said. "Joe, how long have I been this fat?"

"You're not fat," he said without a glance in her

direction. He was looking at his reflection in the mirror over the dresser, and running a comb through his hair.

"I used to be so slim," she said more to herself than to him. "What happened?"

"You're fifty-four years old, Vicki. You're not supposed to look like you did twenty years ago." He kissed her cheek and left the room.

"Well, that makes me feel a lot better."

"Over here, Tori," she heard Jane call from the corner of the restaurant. It was one of their favorite places to have lunch. Victoria felt good every time she walked into the place. It smelled like brewing coffee and freshly-baked bread. She waved at her friend and hurried across the room.

"I was starting to think you were going to stand me up," Jane said. "I've had a hard time talking you into going out lately."

"I'm just so busy these days," Victoria said to her best friend. She and Jane had known each other since birth, well, since *Victoria's* birth; Jane was five years older.

"What's keeping you so busy, Tori? Tell me about it." Jane folded her hands in front of her on the table and looked into Victoria's eyes.

"Well, you know, work and..."

"And what...what do you do in the evenings and on your days off?"

"What is this, Jane, the third degree?"

"Something like that." Jane sat back. "We've been as close as sisters all our lives and lately I'm beginning to think you're avoiding me."

Victoria picked up her menu and opened it.

"Don't try to ignore me, Tori. I'm not giving up. The last time we went out to lunch you told me all you did in the evenings was read trashy novels, remember?"

"Yes." Victoria put the menu down. "And you said it sounded like depression."

"That was months ago, and we haven't had lunch since, even though I've asked you about a dozen times." Jane reached across the table and put her hand on Victoria's. "Talk to me."

"I don't know what to say, Jane. I guess it is depression. Everything was going so well and I was so happy until the kids got into their mid-teens. Then everything just fell apart, and I can't seem to put it back together."

"You mean because they'd gotten into so much trouble?"

"Patricia didn't get into much trouble," Victoria corrected. "But Ellen was awful. She even got arrested a couple of times. I never pictured myself sitting in a jail trying to bail my kid out."

"I know that was tough on you, Tori, but she's doing all right now, isn't she?"

"Yes, but she has to live all the way across the country from me to do all right—Patricia too. What did I do so bad that they don't want to be close to me, Jane?" Victoria swallowed and took a deep breath.

"You didn't do anything wrong. They just need their independence."

"Except when it comes to money, of course." Victoria took a sip of water and looked at the menu again.

The waitress came to the table to take their orders.

"I'll have a turkey burger on a seven-grain roll," Jane said. "And the oven fries, extra mayonnaise on the side, and we'll want the crème brûlée for dessert, so you might as well put two in now."

"Just one," Victoria said. "And I'll have a salad with grilled chicken with the light vinaigrette, and put the dressing on the side, please."

"No crème brûlée, Tori? It's your favorite."

"I'm so fat, Jane. Look at me." Victoria patted her belly. "How come going through menopause had this affect on me and you're still thin as a rail?"

"I'm five foot ten and I've never had any children. You're five foot two and you've had two children. I'm sure that has something to do with it." Jane smiled at her. "And besides, you aren't fat. You just need to firm up a little."

"You know something silly?" Victoria leaned forward and lowered her voice. "When I realized that I had gone through *the change* I felt really sad because I couldn't have any more children." She sat back. "Can you imagine after the disaster I created with the two I had." She picked up her napkin and dabbed at her eyes.

"Your kids aren't a disaster, Tori," Jane said. "And we all feel that way about menopause, even those of us who've never had any kids. It's the end of a chapter in our lives." She leaned forward and looked into Victoria's eyes. "But it's the beginning of a new chapter."

The food arrived and they ate in silence for a while.

"I'm glad you talked to me today, Tori. You need to talk about these things and who better to talk to than someone that loves you as much as I do?"

"I guess you're right, but you know what? I think I am working out of this depression. This morning I decided to clean up my yard and plant a garden. In fact, after lunch I'm going to the book store to buy a book on gardening in Georgia."

"That's great, exactly what you need, a challenge."

Two hours later Victoria walked back into her house and put down her packages. Running shoes. Why did I buy those? Joe's not going to believe how much I spent on them, she thought. "Maybe I shouldn't have let the sales guy talk me in to $65 shoes," she said out loud.

"What did you say, Vicki?" Joe said, as he came through the doorway of the kitchen. "I was working in the office and didn't hear you come in."

"I was talking to myself. I think it's becoming a habit."

"I know. Dolores Crisp called to tell me she was worried about you. Said you stood in the front yard and talked to yourself," Joe said, and then laughed. "The neighbors must really love us, a yard that looks like jungle and a nutty woman who talks to herself."

"How does she know I was talking to myself? I may have been talking to the Faeries."

"Vicki, are you all right?" He patted her bottom and kissed her cheek.

"I'm fine. In fact, I'm excited. I'm going to plant a garden."

Joe stopped in the doorway on his way out of the room. He turned around and gave her a questioning look. "Plant a garden in this mess?" He waved his arm at the forest beyond the kitchen window. "You'll have to tear up the jungle first."

"That's true." She looked out the window, feeling discouraged. Why did she get so excited? she thought. I can't plant a garden in a mess like that. "Wait a minute, Joe. No wonder I don't believe I can do anything any more, with support like that."

"You're right, I'm sorry. I hope you enjoy it. I have to get back to work." In a minute Joe was talking on the phone. She could hear his voice from the other room.

"No more interest than that? Oh, well," she said under her breath, putting the kettle on to boil for tea.

Victoria sat at the kitchen table. She could see the reflection of her husband of thirty-two years in the glass door that led to the back yard.

When did his hair get so gray? she wondered, and pondered his reflection. When did his neck start to sag? And his belly...well, it's flatter than mine, but it hangs over his belt. She poured the boiling water over her tea bag. How long have I been in this rut? I don't remember us getting old.

She thought about her conversation with Jane at lunch. The truth is the kids just distracted her from any goals or dreams that she may have had. Now that her children were grown, she was right back where she'd started.

I can't remember myself, she thought. I don't know what I used to do for fun, nor do I remember my dreams. And now I'm so much older, what do I do, just mark time until I die, or do I try to do something only to find out that I'm too old?

The backs of her eyes ached with tears. "I'll plant a garden, a beautiful garden," she said.

"Are you talking to me, Vicki?" Joe called from the other room.

"No, just talking to myself."

"I can't believe this. I followed the directions in the book perfectly. The recipe for potting soil is exactly what was called for and the stupid seedlings are all dying. It looks like water is just sitting on top of the soil and not sinking in." She was talking to herself again, but she had decided she liked this new habit.

After reading her gardening book from cover to cover, she was eager to plant her garden, but since it was early spring, and the soil couldn't be turned yet in Atlanta where they lived, she really couldn't work outside. First thing to do was try to start some seeds.

She set up a potting table in the basement with all the supplies she would need.

"The soil isn't right," Joe said from behind her.

"Ah," Victoria jumped. "You startled me. I didn't hear you come in."

"Look," he pointed. "The water doesn't sink in. It just sits there for a minute then falls through to the tray under the pot."

"I know, but I followed the directions perfectly for potting soil."

"I know," Joe laughed. "Remember I followed you from one nursery to another collecting the ingredients? I didn't even know there were recipes for potting soil."

She looked down at her pots. "You know what? I need to take a course. I'll never get this by myself."

"That's a good idea. I'll bet you can find a course at the nursery down the road." He turned to go back to his office. Joe worked from home, which was nice because he was around all day, but he was so involved in his work, that he really didn't provide much company. Victoria thought it would probably be a relief to him if she took a course. She'd be out of his way for a couple of hours, at least.

She went up to the little workspace that was set up in the fourth bedroom, the one they used as a guestroom. She'd found one of the girl's old desks in the corner of the basement and had brought it up.

"This room is in bad need of a paint job," she said.

Victoria hadn't had the energy to do much for a while now. Patricia, the younger of her two daughters, left four years ago, and Victoria hadn't even painted over the poetry on the bedroom walls. Both of her daughters' rooms were exactly the way they had left them.

She sat down at the desk and took a look at her sketches of the garden she was planning. "I can't draw, either. Maybe I should just quit and go back to what I was doing before."

She thought about her dead-end job. It didn't stimulate her in any way. Still, it gave her focus. That was why she stayed. She would continue to go to work, she thought, but couldn't read another trashy novel.

"No, I'm not going back to that. I can't. I'll die."

She thought about the last time she'd had lunch with Jane. When she confided this secret life to her, Jane had said, "Tori, that's depression, and it doesn't go away unless you make it."

"No, I'm not depressed," Victoria insisted. "I'm just in a slump."

"Call it what you want, Tori. It doesn't go away unless you make it."

"A course in drawing is also a must," she said. "This slump, or depression is going away."

Victoria pulled into the parking lot of the assisted living complex where her mother lived. She tried to get over to see her mother once a week, but she hadn't been there for a couple of weeks. It was sometimes hard to spend too much time with her. She was getting grumpy as she aged.

"Wonder what this will be like?" she said to her-self as she picked up the little plant she brought for her mother.

She could hear the television blasting as she stood in the hall outside the door of her mother's ground-floor apartment. She knocked twice, louder each time then called out to her. She hated to unlock the door and walk in unannounced, but more and more these days she had to do that.

"Mom," she called out as she went into the small living room where her mother had her TV. "It's me, Victoria. Sorry to just walk in, but I knocked. I guess you didn't hear me."

Her mother looked up at her, startled. "That's okay. You know you're always welcome." She smiled. Victoria couldn't help but notice how small her mother had gotten. Her white hair was thinning too. Her mother had always been proud that her hair had remained thick and curly even as she grew old, but it had become wispy in the past year or so.

"I'm watching *Jeopardy*. You'll have to wait for a commercial," her mother shouted over the volume. She waved her hand as she turned back to the TV.

Victoria went into the kitchen, watered the plant, and then carried it out to the window that looked out onto the balcony. In front of the balcony was an open grassy area that joined to the other apartments for a common lawn. There were spots for gardening and benches to sit on and pathways that wound through shrubs and trees. It was a nice spot. Just beyond the balcony, a cat chased something in the grass.

"Now I can talk. It's a commercial," her mother shouted over the noise.

Speaking loudly, Victoria said, "Turn down the volume on the TV."

"What?" Her mother cupped her ear.

Speaking even louder, Victoria said, "Mute the sound. Where's the remote, Mom?" She looked around the room. The noise was deafening with the TV and the shouting.

"I can't hear you," her mother shouted, and picked up the remote control from the seat next to her. She searched around for the mute button and pressed it. The silence that resulted was heavenly.

Victoria sighed. "What a relief," she said.

"What were you saying?" Her mother was still shouting. She was going progressively deaf.

"Mom, why won't you wear your hearing aid?" Victoria had taken her to the ear doctor to get one.

"It's uncomfortable. Besides, I can hear fine. You just mumble," she said as she turned back to the TV.

"I suppose that's why the TV was blasting when I came in," Victoria said. "Mom, you can watch TV any time. I'm here to visit you now, let's go outside for a few minutes. It's a beautiful day." Anticipating an objection, she picked up the sweater on the peg next to the door and walked over to her mother's chair. Taking her by the arm, she urged her up.

"I don't want to go outside. I've been outside already today."

"Humor me, okay, Mom? I want to go outside. I want to look at your roses." Victoria put the sweater over her mother's shoulders. "Put on this sweater. It's just a little cool out. I wouldn't want you to catch cold."

"The cat's cold?" her mother shouted. "How do you know that cat is cold? Where did that cat come from anyway? He chases my birds away from the feeder."

"I didn't say the cat's cold. I said I wouldn't want you to *catch cold*." Feeling frantic, Victoria ushered her out the door.

"I don't think cats can catch colds. Anyway who cares? I hate cats." Her mother picked up her cane on the way out the door. They walked together over to the small flowerbed she had planted roses five years ago when she first moved in here. Victoria did most of the work on it now. The work had become too much for her mother. She did a little of the pruning, and of course supervised anything Victoria did in the garden.

Seating her mother on a stone bench next to the garden, Victoria started to pull some weeds that were coming in around the edge of the bed.

"I think there will be a lot of roses this season. The buds are forming already," she said. "You really know how to grow roses, Mom. I can't make them do much in my yard. I wonder why. I always try to follow your rules. I should know how by now. You've certainly coached me enough."

She worked quietly for a while. Then hearing a steady breathing sound behind her, she turned in time to witness the first snore, chin propped on her cane, her mother was sleeping.

Fearing she would fall, Victoria moved to the bench and sat down beside her. She gathered her mother into her arms. She could feel tears brimming in her eyes, and there was pressure in her throat.

The shoulders under her hands felt small and frail. Just like everything in her life, her mother was drifting away from her. What would be left?

"Oh, Mom..." she said out loud.

"What?" Her mother lifted her head. "What are you doing now? Don't get all over me like that." She pushed them apart with her elbow. "You always were a clingy little thing." She must have noticed the tears in Victoria's eyes. "Now don't get your feelings hurt. You know I love you. Let's go back in. I'm getting cold." They got up and walked slowly back to the apartment.

"The first thing I need to do is tackle the ivy." Victoria stood at the back of the house looking out over the back yard. It was heavily wooded, which she liked, but every tree in it was covered with ivy. It had gotten so thick on some of them, that she couldn't even see the foliage until the tops of the trees.

She pulled on her work gloves, picked up her garden shears from the table, and waded through the ivy to the first tree. Taking hold of the vines down low to the ground, she began to pull them off, cutting the thicker ones that she couldn't break. As she uncovered layer after layer of ivy, she reached a vine that had been there so long it was at least three or four inches in diameter.

"My shears won't get through that," she said. Prying the vine away from the tree with her gloved hand, she tried to break it off, lost hold, and rolled over backward. Tucking her shoulder, she did a backward somersault and landed on her belly in the soft ivy.

"That's right," she said. "I used to take gymnastics when I was young. It's starting to come back." She laughed at her conversation and got up to go inside.

"Joe, I need your help." She stood in the doorway of the small office Joe had made out of the storage room off the kitchen.

"With what?" he said without looking away from the computer screen, his fingers typing frantically.

"Some of that ivy has been there so long that the vines are like tree trunks. I can't get them off. I think you'll need to help me with the chain saw."

"The chain saw for ivy? Surely not, Vicki." He continued to work.

"I really can't do it myself. Please, Joe?"

He stopped and turned around. "Vicki, I know this is your day off, and it's nice that you have a day off during the week, but I'm still working. I can't just stop because you need help with your garden."

She looked at him and frowned. He had a point. "How will I get this done?" Joe turned back to his computer. "Where is the chain saw?" she asked. "I'll do it myself."

Joe turned around quickly. "You can't use that chain saw. You're too small. You'll hurt yourself."

"No, I won't," she said firmly. "If you can't help me, then I'll have to do it myself."

"Okay, wait a minute, Vicki. There has to be a solution to this." Joe stood and walked to the window. "It looks like you've gotten quite a lot of the vines off of that tree you've been working on."

"I have, but there are a few vines that are so thick, I can't cut them."

"Okay," Joe turned around. "You go out and get all of the vines you can off of all of the trees in the yard and on Saturday afternoon, I'll help you with the others."

Victoria laughed. "That was simple. I guess I let my frustration take over. Thanks, Joe."

"It's nice to hear you laugh, Vicki. You haven't done much of that lately."

Something was bothering her. "Oh, my God, what is it?" Victoria groaned. She looked at the clock on the bedside table. It read 1:00 a.m.

"The phone is ringing, Vicki, get it or move over so I can." Joe's voice was rough with sleep.

"Hello..." she said as she fumbled the receiver to her face. Her heart was pounding. Thoughts of possible disasters were rolling through her mind. Even her ears were ringing with anxiety.

"Mom, this is Ellen. Sorry to call so late. With the time change it's hard to get you any other time."

"Oh, that's all right, what's one more year off my life. Are you okay? Is there a problem?"

"Nothing serious, I'm just out of money. I only have one more quarter in school and I would really hate to take out another loan. I wondered if there was any way you and Dad could help." Ellen, the oldest at twenty-eight, had gone to college after running wild for four years. They'd told her that she would have to finance her schooling herself since she'd spent the money they had planned for college on legal fees and such. She had done very well. Victoria had been surprised when she told them she'd been accepted to Washington State University at Pullman, Washington. She had worked on campus at the school and supported her apartment, getting loans and scholarships for her education.

Not that she and Joe hadn't helped a lot. When she was doing so well, it was hard to say no. Whenever there was a shortage, Ellen would call and they would send her the money, even if it meant borrowing. They had a good bit of debt to show for it, but it was worth it if it would set Ellen up to be independent. She was following in her father's footsteps, and studying architecture. It could make her a good living in time.

"I'll let you talk to your dad. He really handles the money." Victoria had handled the money in the family until a few years ago. When she lost the energy to keep up with it, Joe took over the responsibility.

"She wants us to pay for her last quarter at school," Victoria said, as she handed him the phone.

Joe frowned. "Ellen," he said into the receiver. "Do you know the amount? How much will it be?" He paused, listening. "I'll have to get back to you; I need to see what I can do, move some things around in the accounts." He paused again. "Ellen, you need to give me a little notice on these things. If you can't wait a few days then we won't be able to do it." His voice was edged with irritation. Victoria could tell that he was trying not to show it...another pause. "I think we can, but, like I said, I'll have to look."

He handed the phone back to Victoria without saying goodbye. She took it reluctantly. "It's me again, honey."

"Is he mad at me? I thought you wouldn't mind

since I've done practically all of college by myself."
Ellen sounded tearful.

Victoria took a deep breath. She thought to herself, of course he's mad at you. You woke him up in
the middle of the night to ask for money, what do
you expect?

But she said, "He isn't mad, Ellen, neither of us
is mad. We're proud of what you've done. You just
have to understand that it's hard to wake up in the
middle of the night and think clearly. Dad will get
back to you tomorrow." She didn't have the energy to
fight with her now.

"I love you, Mom," Ellen said, her voice sounding steady again.

"I love you, too, honey." Victoria hung up the
phone and lay back on her pillow.

Joe sighed. "I guess I hurt her feelings. I should
have been more supportive. I'm just tired of it all.
You'd think at twenty-eight years old she wouldn't be
asking us for money any more."

Victoria was silent. Joe turned toward her in
the bed. "Vicki, are you okay? Don't you have anything to say?"

"I can't feel anything, Joe. I can't feel love for
her or anger or frustration. I don't know when the
feelings went away, but they're gone. I know that I
must love her. She's my kid. I carried her inside my
body for nine months for fuck sake."

Joe jumped startled by her vehemence.
"Swearing isn't like you, Vicki."

"I can't feel anything. I'm dead. I'm the walking dead. I'm a Zombie. I don't even miss her, Joe. I
don't miss either of them. What is wrong with me?"

She started to shake. Joe draped his arm across her waist.

"What about me, Vicki? Do you feel anything for me?" he asked quietly.

She looked at him. She could only see the shadows of his features in the dark.

"I don't know," she answered softly.

"I love you, Vicki."

Doing anything at work the next day was hard. Things had ended the night before with Victoria turning over and saying goodnight. She knew that Joe was confused and probably hurt, but she was in such distress herself. She just couldn't think about him too much. Sometimes she felt like she needed to get in her car and start driving. Not look back. Not think ahead. Just go and see where she ended up. Would it be any better? She wanted out, but out of what, her marriage? Why would she want that? Joe was good to her and she could remember loving him, even if she couldn't feel it now.

"Do I want out of my job?" she said.

"If you don't, I'll question your sanity." Jen, one of her co-workers, said.

Victoria jumped. "How long have you been there? I didn't hear you come in."

"Long enough to hear you talking to yourself. Is this something you do often?"

"As a matter of fact, I seem to be doing a lot of it

these days." Victoria laughed. "My neighbor caught me talking to myself in the front yard not long ago."

"Are you okay?" Jen asked. "You have been very quiet lately."

"I think it's just a life-stage problem. I'm sure it'll pass. Anyway, I've got to get this order in or we won't have anything to sell." Victoria went back to her work.

She worked at the grocery store in her area. Needing something to do when the girls first left home, she'd started out stocking shelves, and had worked her way up to assistant manager. It was not really an interesting job, but the pay was good and it was close to home. It had worked well to fill in the emptiness in her life for a long time. However, it was getting hard to go in each day. She just didn't care anymore. Everything that she did seemed like a chore. She worried sometimes that her lack of interest would show in her work, but no one had said anything. They had been happy with her work for a long time. Maybe they just hadn't noticed yet.

"I'm going to stop at Landrum's nursery on my way home from work," she told Joe when she called him before she left that evening. "I want to see what courses they offer. I shouldn't be very late. I'll fix us something to eat when I get home."

"Are you feeling any better today, Vicki?" Joe asked.

"I'm fine!" she snapped. His concern was getting on her nerves.

"I just worry about you, Vicki. You haven't been yourself lately."

"What are you worried about, Joe? That I might be going insane, talking to myself and forgetting to love family members?"

"Of course not, I'm just concerned. I'll see you when you get home." Joe hung up the phone.

Victoria felt guilty for snapping at him. "It's just that he's always hovering," she mumbled.

"Who's hovering, Victoria?" She jumped. She hadn't heard her boss approach.

"Just talking to myself, and yes I do that often." If she didn't get a hold of herself, she'd be in trouble.

At the nursery she got a schedule of the classes they offered. They even offered a course in garden design sketching. "Perfect!" she said, and looked around quickly. No one was in hearing distance. Good.

For the first time in years she felt excited about something. There was also a class on starting your own bedding plants from seed. There were several classes that looked good to her, but she couldn't take them all. These two would be a good start.

It was raining hard when she came out of the nursery. She was disappointed. The plan had been to go home, feed Joe, and go out into the yard to look around, and get her imagination going.

The road was slick. She wished, not for the first time, that she had replaced the tires on her car. She slowed to go around a corner, but the tires didn't hold. The whole thing happened so fast that she didn't have time to react. The car spun off the road, bounced down a steep hill, and collided with a tree.

"Ouch!" Victoria heard her own voice from what seemed to be a great distance. "Oh, great, I'm talking to myself again," she said as she slowly opened one eye.

"What hurts, Vicki?" Joe stood over her looking down. Had his cheeks always sagged like that when he looked down? Glad I didn't say that out loud. This constant stream of conversation she was having with herself was really fun. If only she could keep it quiet.

"My right arm, oh, no!" she gasped, as she tried to sit up. Her head pounded and she felt dizzy. "Where am I?" she groaned, dropping back to what seemed to be a bed.

"You're in the hospital. Your car slid off the road. I've been telling you to get those tires taken care of for months. They just couldn't hold the road. It scared a year off my life when the hospital called. You're as bad as the girls."

Joe was really mad, the jerk. When he yelled like that his face got all red and his cheeks puffed up. Victoria started to giggle, but the startled look on Joe's face made her stop. If I'm not careful, he'll lock me up. She moved again and winced. "I can't have a broken right arm! I'm going to start a garden sketching class next week."

"It's just a sprain." Joe seemed relieved that the giggling had stopped. He ran a hand through his hair leaving it rumpled. A small strand of hair stood straight out from the side of his head like a horn.

Victoria giggled again and sobered immediately at Joe's frown.

She put the palms of her hands to her temples. Her head throbbed. The pain in her right arm wasn't as bad as she'd thought at first. "I guess I just panicked."

"Are we awake? Do we have a headache?" A young man in a white coat came into the room.

"I'm awake and I have a headache," Victoria responded. "I don't know about the rest of us." She giggled again.

"Oh, a sense of humor, that's a good sign." the doctor said. "I'm Dr. Henry." He held out a hand.

"I can't shake your hand. I'm holding my head together," Victoria responded. "Dr. Henry what?"

"Dr. Charles Henry."

"That's two first names. You could turn your name around and it would still work, except, of course, it wouldn't be your name," Victoria prattled. "Since I'm old enough to be your mother, I could call you Dr. Charles...or then again, I could call you Hank."

Both men looked a little puzzled. In fact, the looks on their faces triggered another giggle.

"I'm concerned about her, Dr. Henry, she isn't herself. How bad was that head injury?" Joe turned as if to block the conversation from Victoria.

"I wasn't too concerned about it, but she does seem a little silly. It's just a concussion, but maybe we'd better keep her overnight." The doctor glanced her way for a second. She smiled sweetly.

"Dr. Hank, I'm right here, and I can hear what

you're saying. Why don't you talk to me?" She was indignant for a second, and then giggled.

"I think you should stay overnight, Vicki. You took a pretty good whack on the head. I wouldn't want you to get into trouble in the night."

"Don't call me Vicki. Only Joe calls me Vicki," she said in a commanding voice. Then, looking at Joe, she said, "And come to think of it, don't you call me Vicki, either. My name is Victoria. Vicki is a little girl's name." She focused on the troubled faces above her and giggled again. Putting her palms back to her temples, she winced as fresh pain shot through her head.

"I'll get you something for that pain," the doctor said soothingly. "Mr. Vandor, could I talk to you before you go home?"

"Thank you, Dr. Charlie," Victoria said weakly.

"Goodnight, Victoria."

"Arthritis in my hands? When did that happen?" Victoria said, as she picked up another shovelful of soil and tossed it into the cart. She had bought a small plastic cart. It was easy to use, but it was already falling apart. She winced at the pain in her hands. "Maybe I won't be able to do this after all." She stopped and looked at her progress.

She had decided to start with a patio on the side of the house by the kitchen. She had researched the project at the library the day after she had come home from the hospital. Her wrist was slightly inflamed and had recovered quickly. Her head still ached a little and there were bruises on her forehead and temple, but she had recovered enough to do some yard work. She felt a little guilty about taking time off work and then playing in the yard. "But not too guilty." She laughed.

Her research had taught her that she first needed to dig down about eight or nine inches so that she could put sand down before the paving stones. Sand would be easier to get flat and even. Then she could place the paving stones. If she wanted, she could grout between the stones. She hadn't decided whether to do that or not. "I'll decide that when I get there, if I get there." The digging was really hard. Even harder was taking the cart up into the woods full of dirt, and dumping it in the holes that Patricia's beagle had dug in the back yard years ago. "I'll be glad to finally get those holes filled in."

"Victoria..." Joe called from the back door.

She stopped and turned around. "Joe, I told you...you don't have to call me Victoria. Please don't hold what I said at the hospital against me. I was a little out of my head." Everything he did got on her nerves these days.

"I'll say," he chuckled. "I think Dr. Hank was a little traumatized." Joe walked out to where she was standing. "But, no. I think your name means something to you right now. Whatever this is that you're going through, if I can help by not calling you by a 'little girl's' name, I will. I never meant for it to be condescending." Joe looked sad.

"I never took it that way." She turned and started to dig again.

"I just heard from the insurance adjuster. The car is totaled. They don't want to pay to fix it. The damage is too bad. It makes me feel sick every time I think of you in the middle of that crumpled mass of metal."

Victoria stopped digging and looked at Joe. He did look a little pale. Why can't I feel anything for him anymore? she thought, being careful to keep it to herself. She said, "So, I guess I'll have a car payment again. Good thing I have a job." She thought of how much she really wanted to quit her job. Guess not.

"The insurance money will give us a good down payment. We can look around this weekend. In the meantime, I can take you to work and back."

"Thanks, Joe." She went back to digging. Joe walked to the back door.

"A pickup truck!" Victoria said enthusiastically. "That's what I want. It'll come in handy for my gardening." She turned and looked at Joe, excitement lighting her face.

"Okay, if that's what you want." Joe turned slowly back to the door and walked inside, shaking his head as he went.

Three

It was a beautiful morning. Victoria stood at the second-story window of her bedroom looking out at the new day. Joe was still sleeping. It was Saturday so he didn't have to get up for work. Even though he worked out of the house, he made sure to take Saturday and Sunday off. "Such an organized man." She sighed and went back to looking out the window.

She just couldn't seem to sleep late any more, even if she had nothing to do that day. She looked at the yard before her. The classes on garden design had started the week before and it was surprising how nervous she'd been. "You'd think it was my first day of kindergarten," she had confided to Joe at dinner the night before her first class. "I'm scared to death."

"What are you afraid of? The teacher won't be mean. I don't think they can punish adult students." Joe laughed.

"I don't know. It's silly." She paused, and said, "I guess this is just very important to me. I really never have been much of an artist. I don't know if I can draw a garden."

"You'll learn how in the class." Joe reached across the table and touched her cheek. "You'll do fine," he said.

She'd gone to class that evening and he was right; she'd done fine. The class was fun. The drawing was hard, but they were learning how to do things as basic as holding the pencil. They were doing exercises of drawing lines and circles. It was moving slowly enough that she felt like she was keeping up. In fact, some of her drawings were pretty good. As good as lines and circles can get, anyway.

Victoria reflected on Joe's support of her adventure. He's such a good man and he clearly still loves me. She felt ashamed. It was bad enough that she couldn't find feelings for the girls. Joe was supposed to be her soul mate. For years she had felt that he was her soul mate. She just couldn't feel anything at all, not for anyone, not for anything. The gardening was the closest she'd come to enjoying herself in ages. It was interesting that enjoying herself meant doing painful heavy digging and lifting.

She certainly didn't enjoy running. She'd been going out every morning since she bought her running shoes, except while she convalesced after her accident. One day she'd walk, and one day she'd run. Sometimes it seemed like she was getting better and other days it felt like she was carrying lead. "Why am I doing this?" she asked time and again. Her lungs hurt and her legs got sore every time she ran, just like they had the first time, but she said, "I have to admit, it feels good when I stop." She laughed.

"What did I do for fun before I had this family?" she said to herself.

"You always loved to garden, and you enjoyed hiking in the woods, too." Joe startled her. "You're talking to yourself again, or were you talking to me while I slept?" He laughed.

"No, I have some real good conversations with myself."

"When you were very young you liked to ice-skate," Joe said. "Your mother told me. You liked Gymnastics in high school, and you always loved animals." Joe rolled out of bed and went into the bathroom.

Victoria was still looking out the window when Joe came back into the room. He walked up behind her and put his hands on her shoulders. "I want you," he whispered, kissing her neck.

Nothing...I feel nothing, she thought. She said, "I know there hasn't been much sex lately. I'm sorry."

"I want you now. It's Saturday morning. There's no one in the house but you and me. Come back to bed with me." Joe's face was close to hers. She could smell the minty toothpaste on his breath. He picked her up in his arms and carried her to the bed.

"This is really romantic," she said. Why don't I feel anything?

He laid her gently on the bed and followed her down. He kissed her and she tried to respond. He slid his hand into the opening of her bathrobe and circled her nipple with his thumb, massaging her breast gently, kissing her jaw and moving down her neck.

Joe was a gentle lover. He'd always known just how to arouse her. He was doing all of the right things, but she couldn't feel it. He parted her robe and pushed it over her shoulders.

Victoria raised her hands to his face above her.

"You're a good man, Joe," she whispered. "I don't deserve you." She eased out of the robe and put her arms around Joe's shoulders.

He positioned himself between her legs and eased inside of her; still nothing. Victoria started to move with him—out of habit—or to make him believe she was with him? She didn't know, but she moved. She tried to make the sounds and movements of lovemaking, but the feelings were absent. What am I doing? she thought. Moaning when his rhythm increased, she tensed when he did and relaxed when he collapsed on top of her.

She lay still beneath him, feeling his heartbeat slow to normal again. A tear rolled down her cheek. This wasn't fair to him. He deserved a loving wife.

Joe rolled off of her and sat up. He swung his legs over the side of the bed and sat with his back to her, his head bowed. "Don't pretend, Victoria. I can tell the difference." He put his hands up to his face and rubbed his eyes. "When will this end, Victoria? I'm beginning to wonder if we're going to make it."

"I wonder, too, Joe. I don't know what to say." She sniffed. "I haven't hidden anything from you. I told you I couldn't feel anything. I don't know what's wrong with me. All I can do is keep going until something happens."

"I don't know if I can keep going." Joe got up and left the room. In a minute Victoria heard the shower start.

It had been another grueling day at the store. "I can't do this any more," Victoria said.

"Don't even think about leaving," Jen said. "We'd be lost without you."

"I'm burned out, Jen. I learned in management class that people who are burned out aren't just tired of their jobs. They really can't do them anymore. I'm only half doing this job. It isn't fair to the store."

"What are you going to do?" Jen asked, serious now.

"I don't know, but I've got to do something."

That evening after work, she stopped at the nursery to pick up the new schedule of classes. There was a sign on the bulletin board advertising for a full-time nursery attendant.

"That's what I'll do." Victoria looked up at the cashier. "Can I get an application for this job?" The girl went over to the office door and knocked. She returned a minute later with the application. Victoria went into the classroom to fill it out. She took it to the office herself and handed it to the manager.

"I would really like to have this job," she said.

"I was looking for someone younger. It requires some lifting and digging, some real physical work." The manager said, frowning.

"I can do that. I work in my own garden all the time. I've just finished putting in a patio. I had to do a lot of digging for that." She paused. He was still frowning. "Really, I'm strong. Look." She rolled up her sleeve and flexed her muscle.

She looked back at the manager, smiling with pride. He was smiling, too. He was a handsome man, about her age, maybe a little younger. He had brown hair with just the hint of gray, and crystal blue eyes. She felt a little tingle of something deep inside. Was it attraction? "Is that a natural color of blue or are those contacts?" She felt her face flame as she realized she'd said it out loud.

"What?" he asked, as he turned back to his computer.

"Nothing." I've got to get this talking to myself thing under control. "Well, what do you say? How about the job? I'll make you glad you hired me."

"Let me review your application. I'll call you in a few days." She stood there in the doorway, didn't make a move to leave. He turned back to look at her. "I'll call you either way." He turned back to his computer, dismissing her.

She walked out to her truck. "Well, that was uplifting. Too old, my foot!"

That night over dinner, she told Joe about it.

"I applied for a job at the nursery. I hope I get it. I just can't do that job at the grocery any more." She buttered her muffin and licked the extra butter off her knife.

"Just like that you made a decision that will affect both of us without even talking to me first?" Joe sounded angry.

Victoria was surprised. She hadn't thought he would object. Actually, she hadn't thought of him at all. "I didn't think you would mind. You know how burned out I am."

"No, I didn't know you were burned out. You haven't mentioned that to me. In fact, you haven't talked to me much at all lately." He stopped eating and stared at his plate.

"Aren't you hungry?" she asked.

"No, I don't have much appetite these days."

She glanced across the table at him. He looked a little drawn. His face showed signs of strain. He'd lost weight and she hadn't even noticed. "Do you feel all right? Are you sick?"

"Sick at heart, maybe," he said quietly. "How much does this job pay?" he asked, changing the subject.

"I don't know. Really, Joe, I'm concerned. Are you all right?"

"Well, it's nice to know you still care a little," he said. "I'm fine. Don't worry about that. What do you mean, *you don't know*? We have financial obligations that we share. We still have one daughter in school that we support, and another that still makes big demands. You should have discussed this with me."

"I guess I didn't think. But, Joe, I can't do that job any more. Sometimes I have to think of myself, too."

"You've been doing a lot of that lately."

"If you came to me, Joe, and said that you needed to change jobs, that you were not happy and needed to make a change, do you think I would object?" she said.

"No..." He paused. "I guess not, but I would have come to you and talked to you about it before I made a decision. You just announced the decision to me, like it was already made."

"It is," she said firmly.

"I see." Joe stood and walked out of the kitchen. She could hear him in his office moving things around. She got up and went into the room after him. He was packing his laptop computer into its case.

"What are you doing?"

"I'm going away for a few days. I just need to get out of this house for a while," he said.

"Where are you going?"

"I don't know yet, maybe to the beach. I'm not sure," he sighed.

"You'll let me know when you decide?" she whispered.

"I guess," he said. He paused as he passed her. "I love you, Victoria." He kissed her on the cheek and continued up the stairs to pack his clothes.

Joe had been gone for a week. He had called to tell her he was okay, but hadn't told her where he was. She missed him. The house seemed so empty without the sound of his keyboard clicking in the study. "I guess missing someone is feeling something. Maybe I'm getting back to normal," she said. Talking to herself seemed to be getting more frequent now that she was alone all the time.

"I know what I need. I need a pet. At least then I would be talking to the pet," she said. "Is that better or worse?"

She had always had pets. At first, just cats. When the kids got older, they wanted a dog. So they had a succession of dogs. The beagle had died a few years ago, at the ripe old age of sixteen. She hadn't replaced it. She'd been in the deepest part of her depression at that time. The death of the dog had hurt more than she could remember the others hurting. So in self-defense, she had decided not to get another pet.

"Maybe I'd better talk to Joe about it this time. It's his house, too." She looked out the window. "If he ever comes home…"

She had heard from the manager of the nursery a few days ago, who she learned was also the owner. He'd told her that she had the job if she wanted it. There would be a cut in pay, but she would just budget a little harder to make up for it. Turning in her notice had been hard. She'd given them two weeks notice, but had told Jeff, the nursery manager, that she would start work right away on her days off and weekends.

Her manager at the grocery store had offered to raise her pay if she would stay. They'd be surprised if they knew how little she would be paid at the nursery. She'd have to deal with Joe on that one as well.

"I was holding out to see if I'd get any more applications, but I didn't. So I guess you're it," the owner of the nursery had said.

"Well, that's flattering." She laughed. "I'll be the best employee you've ever had. You'll see."

"I hope so," he said, but he was laughing. He had an easy laugh. She enjoyed hearing it.

"I'm so excited," she said. "I just wish there was someone to share it with."

Since there wasn't, she found the chain saw and, being very careful, went into the yard and cut the thickest ivy vines off the trees. Because of her car accident, she and Joe hadn't been able to get to it. The ivy was beginning to die now and fall off the trees.

At some point she would have to figure out what she was feeling about Joe. They'd been so close over the years, but right now, she just couldn't feel close to him. Was it that she was tired after thirty-two years of marriage and twenty-eight years of raising the girls, and maybe a little bit heartsick? It all seemed so important when she started. Now she wondered if she'd spent her life on something that didn't matter to anyone but her. And what had she done for herself? Nothing really. All those dreams of being independent and successful came to nothing. She was the same as she had been before, but a lot older.

What about Joe? He seemed so satisfied with himself. Why shouldn't he be? He'd been a father to the girls, but he'd done other things, too. He was a successful businessman. He had accomplished what he'd set out to do. It certainly wasn't his fault that she hadn't, but somehow she resented him for it.

When they had met, she'd fallen in love with him right away. He was so good-looking and he seemed to be really attracted to her. Not just the way she looked, but he listened to what she said, too. Victoria knew she'd been a pretty girl. Young men and boys had always tried to put their hands on her.

She'd never let anyone touch her intimately until Joe. She'd never wanted to.

What would it be like to fall in love again? What was it like the first time? She could remember the trembling feeling in her chest. It almost seemed electric. She remembered the race of her pulse when he kissed her for the first time, the warm feeling that washed over her whole body.

Would it be like that again, now, at this age, fifty-four years old? Could she even attract a man? She remembered the way Joe's features seemed to take on a whole different glow when she looked at him. After she was in love, each feature separately had a beauty of its own, and the way they came together was wonderful. Would it be like that now, if she fell in love again? Why didn't she see him that way any more? Could she see another man that way?

There was no point in thinking about it; she'd never leave Joe. She'd been with him too long.

"I guess I'll never know."

"Still talking to yourself, I see." Joe came into the kitchen through the garage door.

"You're home." Victoria turned from the counter where she was peeling potatoes for soup.

"Yes, I'm home." He came over to her and turned her around.

"My hands are wet. Let me dry them." She tried to turn back to the counter. Joe took the dishtowel off the rack and dried her hands.

"I need to talk to you, Vicki. I'm sorry, Victoria. I've done a lot of thinking in the past week." Joe looked serious.

"About...?" Victoria asked.

"About you and about me. I know that you're working up to leaving me. I can feel it," he said.

"I'm not going anywhere, Joe. Where would I go?" Victoria turned back to the counter, ashamed that she'd had the thought. He turned her around again.

"Sit down here, Victoria." He guided her to the table. "I need to tell you something."

"What?" His expression scared her.

"I won't let you go. If you leave, I'll follow you. If you tell me to leave you alone, I won't." He went on. "I realized while I was away how much we've grown apart. I don't want that. You're the only woman I've ever loved. I dated some before I met you. None ever made me want to be with them forever, until you. When I met you, I felt like I'd been looking for you all my life." The words seemed to pour out. Victoria had a lump in her throat. Her eyes were swimming. "I know you say you can't feel anything for me. Maybe that's more my fault than yours. I guess I just got so comfortable with our life that I got complacent."

"I don't know what to say. I've always loved you, until lately, when I can't feel anything. But I don't know if I'll ever get it back, Joe." She sniffed. "I don't want to hurt you, but I just can't feel it any more."

"You will, because I'll win you back." He smiled at her. He got up, picked up his bag, and left the room. She heard his footsteps on the stairs.

"Shit, how will he win me back? What have I gotten myself into?" She followed him up the stairs.

The bedroom was bright. It was Saturday morning and she didn't have to start full time at the nursery until the following week. The sun was shining and spring was moving into summer. Victoria walked into the bedroom and sat on the bed while Joe unpacked.

"I got the job," she said.

He looked up, his expression unreadable.

"The one at the nursery. I gave my notice at the grocery store. I gave them two weeks notice, but I start at the nursery on my days off and weekends. I'm really excited about it."

"Good." Joe went back to his unpacking. "I hope it works out for you. You really have always loved gardening. You're good at it, too. I was really impressed with the patio, and you knocked out most of the ivy by yourself. I'll help you with those thick vines tomorrow." He smiled at her.

"I did them myself while you were gone."

Joe looked up at her. "How did you cut them?"

"With the chain saw." She smiled. "I may be small, but I'm powerful."

"You scare me to death sometimes, Victoria." Joe touched her cheek then continued to unpack.

"You're not mad about the job?" she asked.

"No. You do what you need to do. I like my job. I can't fault you for wanting to like yours."

"I will take a cut in pay," she ventured.

"I figured you would. We'll manage." He reached inside his suitcase and pulled out some papers. "While I was away, I met someone who does greyhound rescue." He put a pamphlet on the bed beside her. "I know that you said you didn't want another pet, but I thought maybe you would change your mind. You've always liked having animals around. This seems like a good cause to me."

"I was thinking I might like to have another pet," she murmured, as she picked up the pamphlet. On the front was a picture of two greyhounds. One was white with black spots, the other a pale fawn color. "They're beautiful. The yard is fenced. Would you like to have one, Joe?"

"Yes, I think I would." He turned and smiled at her. "She has a facility here in Atlanta. If you'd like, we could take a ride over and look."

"She who?" Victoria asked.

"The woman who gave me the pamphlet." He paused and looked at Victoria. "She was staying in the cottage next to mine at the beach. She had a couple of the dogs with her. They were really nice dogs."

"You stayed in a cottage at the beach?" Victoria asked.

"I think we should do things separately from time to time. I think part of the problem we're having is that we just never get away from each other," Joe said. "That was one of the other pieces of wisdom I came up with while I was gone."

"Okay. Does that mean I have to go away by myself now?" Victoria asked.

"Is something wrong, Victoria?" Joe looked puzzled. "Did I say something that bothered you?"

"No. I don't think so."

Four

Victoria was standing on a cement block beside the compost bin. There was a huge compost container the nursery used to make their compost in. It consisted of mostly decaying plant parts. It smelled pretty bad. The side of the container came up to just above her waist when she stood on the block. She'd been putting one of the stacks of plastic pots they used for starting stock up on a shelf behind the container. One of the pots had come loose and fallen into the bin. She just couldn't quite get down to it.

Balancing herself on her upper abdomen she lifted her feet off the block and reached a little farther. She could feel her feet flailing in the air as she struggled for balance. Just as she was about to lose the battle and fall into the festering mass of compost, something stopped her. "What is that?" she murmured.

"It's a hand on your ankle," Jeff said from behind her.

"Damn," she said softly.

"I heard that. What are you doing, Vic?" He had called her that from the beginning. She liked it.

"I'm reaching for a pot that fell off the shelf. If you hold on to my ankle just a second longer, I think I can get it," she called. He let her slide a little lower then stopped her. "Okay hold tight, I'm coming up."

When she came back up she turned slowly, trying to gauge the look on his face. Was it mirth or anger?

"It's pretty nasty in there. It would have been better to go in with a tool, or to have come and get me. I would hate to have to fish you out of that," he said. She thought she detected a little smile around his mouth.

"I like to be independent," she explained.

"Don't be so independent that you get hurt. That won't do anyone any good." Jeff turned and walked off.

Victoria looked at her new co-worker, Lillian. There was no question about the smile on her face.

"That was great. You should have seen what you looked like from here, with your butt hooked over the edge of that bin and your legs flailing wildly. But even better, you should have seen the look on his face when he ran over to get you. It was sheer terror. I think he has a thing for you," Lillian said.

"Very funny," Victoria said. Lillian had worked for the nursery for about a year. She was in the same job as Victoria and was training her, but she was a good twenty-five years younger, a sweet girl with a wicked sense of humor.

"I'm serious, only true concern could have produced a look like that." She chuckled.

"He's concerned, all right. He's afraid it was a mistake to hire me." Victoria sighed. "I hope I last at least a month. I argued with my husband over taking this job."

"Don't be silly, you're doing great. You only spilled about half the soil on the ground when we potted those seedlings this morning. Your hanging baskets were great, and we'll work on the terrariums together. It'll be fine. Really, just stay out of the compost bin and you'll do fine." Lillian was finding this just a little bit too funny.

"Don't worry. I'm not going near it again." Victoria went over to the wheelbarrow she was using to carry stock. "It's empty. I've finished that stocking you had me doing. What now?"

"We need to move a pile of sand in the back. Come on. Bring the wheelbarrow." Victoria followed Lillian out to the yard. She'd had a hard time getting the hang of pushing the wheelbarrow. It always wanted to tip over sideways.

"These things should have two wheels," she said to Lillian the first day on the job.

"It's much more maneuverable with just the one," Lillian explained. "You'll get used to it. A lot of it is muscle. Once you build the right muscles, you'll be able to stop it when it wants to go over."

They started to shovel the sand up off the ground and into the wheelbarrow. Not only did you have to balance the wheelbarrow when you were pushing it, but when you were putting things into it you had to be careful to distribute the load properly. Otherwise, it tipped and dumped the load out. This happened a number of times to Victoria, to Lillian's apparent delight. Finally, they had the sand loaded.

Victoria was a little out of breath from the exertion when they were finished. "Now what?" she asked.

"Now we have to take it over there to the bagging dock." She pointed to a small ramp that led to a landing with a device that held the bags open.

"What a great idea." Victoria smiled. "Let me." She stopped Lillian when she reached for the handles of the wheelbarrow. "I need the practice."

Victoria positioned herself between the handles and started to turn around.

"You'll have to back up first," Lillian said, as she started across the yard. "But step over that hose behind you."

Victoria tripped over a hose that she hadn't seen. With a squeal she fell over backward. The wheelbarrow went over on its side and the sand spilled out in just about the same place that they'd gotten it from.

"One important rule of thumb," Lillian lectured, extending her hand to help Victoria up. "Always look around for obstacles before you do anything in a nursery. Obstacles are everywhere."

"Well, at least the boss didn't see me do that." Victoria dusted off her bottom.

"Don't count on it. That's the window to his office right over there." She pointed to the window on the side of the building, where she could see Jeff's profile looking at the computer.

"Vic," Jeff called from the office door as she and Lillian came into the nursery. "Could I see you in here for a minute?"

"Uh-oh," Lillian whispered. "The Principal's office." She moved off in the direction of the potting shed.

"I'll do fine. I just need to get trained. Then I won't be so clumsy," Victoria said defensively, as she entered the office.

"What?" Jeff looked up from some plans that he had spread on the table. "Oh, you mean the compost bin. That's okay. I was just concerned about you. You didn't hurt yourself, did you?" he asked, furrowing his brow with concern.

"No, I'm fine." Maybe he hadn't seen her stunt with the wheelbarrow. She wouldn't mention it to him.

"That's not what I wanted to see you about," he said. "You recently took a class here in garden design. My aunt taught that course. She says you did very well. I'd like to have your opinion of these plans I'm working on for one of our customers." His brow creased as he looked down at the plans on the table.

"My opinion?" She sounded surprised.

"Yes, do you mind? I know that's not what I hired you for, but I'm having a problem here. I know something just isn't right, but I'm not sure what." He seemed to be really concentrating on the design.

"Well, I'll look, but I haven't done very much of this." Victoria's eyes blurred when she looked at the plans. She hadn't ever seen plans this detailed. "What does this mean?" she asked, pointing to a pattern of lines on the paper.

"That indicates a hill. The hill moves gradually down to this flat area where I plan to put a weeping cherry tree." He spoke to her like she knew something.

"What about drainage? It could get marshy here. That wouldn't do the roots any good," she commented.

"Yes, I thought of that. My concern is more with

this hill. I've put an oak-leaf hydrangea part way up. The tree will cast some shade, but the hydrangea won't mind that. There's something bothering me about this spot." He pointed to the slope between the tree and the shrubs.

"This bed is wrong, I think. It isn't tall enough. I think something that stands higher would be good, maybe iris or day lilies if you wanted perennials, or an annual bed that could be changed with the seasons. The contrast in size between the tree and the hydrangea isn't as severe that way." She finished feeling a little like she had said too much.

"Hm. That's good. What about this spot under the tree? I was thinking shade grass, but that requires so much work. The customer doesn't want too much maintenance," he puzzled.

"Will people walk there?" Victoria asked.

"Well, I was thinking of putting a bench under the tree, so people would need to get to it." He looked at her. "Why, what were you thinking?"

"I was thinking of dwarf Mondo grass. It likes the filtered sun. It can tolerate a little traffic, but not much."

"I could put in a stone path. That would work." Jeff studied the plans a little then looked at her. "Would you go over there with me and look at the space?"

"Okay. If that's what you want me to do."

"Your hanging baskets look great. I put them in the shop this afternoon for sale." He smiled. The shop was the space they used to sell potted plants and terrariums. "The terrarium needs work."

"Lillian said she'd help me with that. I've

never made one before." She was beaming from his praise.

"I'm sure you'll get the hang of it. We'll go tomorrow morning, first thing, so you can see how the morning sun hits. That's important for planning."

At dinner that evening, Victoria laughed as she told the story of her day. Joe listened to all she had to say and then said, "It's nice to hear you laugh. You haven't done a lot of that for the past few years."

"It's been a hard time for me. This is a tough life stage. No one can warn you about it, because there's just no way to describe it. It seemed like I finished all the projects that I started in my youth and I thought, what now?" She took a bite of her dinner. "I was just marking time until I die. But now I'm moving on. It feels good."

"I'm glad," Joe said. "Just take me with you wherever you go. Okay?"

"Of course, what else would I do?" It was a slightly awkward moment. She didn't really know if she was taking Joe with her. He was so satisfied with life the way it was. How could he be a part of her life when it was changing so much and so fast? She cared very much about him, but was she in love with him? She couldn't remember what that felt like. That was a problem. She didn't know how she would handle it.

"You must be thinking about something serious.

You have a very somber look on your face." Joe interrupted her thoughts. He laughed a little uneasily.

"Joe, maybe we should separate for a little while, until I get straight in my head about what I want out of life."

"No!" His voice was firm, but not angry. "I knew you were working up to that and I won't let it happen. Once you leave, you won't come back. I know you won't. Victoria, I married you for life. I love you and I will find a way to make you love me again."

"Joe, this isn't fair to you—"

"And leaving me after thirty-two years of marriage is fair to me, after we've raised our children and earned our freedom to enjoy each other? I can't be happy without you and I won't let you leave." Joe rose from his chair and walked around the table. He stood behind her chair. He pulled her up by her elbows and turned her around to look at him. His eyes were clear as he leaned toward her. His fingers bruised her upper arms as he pulled her closer to him. She felt a slow tingle start in her chest somewhere, or was it her throat? Her eyes filled with tears and she looked into Joe's eyes. He was so fierce. Had he always been this passionate about her? She shook her head and looked down.

Joe's hold on her softened. "Victoria, are you okay? You're not dizzy, are you?"

"No. I'm just confused. I don't know what I'm feeling any more." She pulled away from him, and felt suddenly cold. Sitting back down, she said, "I won't leave, we don't have to separate right now, but Joe, you can't keep me here against my will. If I decide to go, I'll go."

"I'll just have to convince you to stay then." He sat down in the chair beside her and put his hand on hers. "Do you still want a pet? Maybe this weekend we could go look at the greyhounds, unless you'd rather have a cat or even a puppy."

"No, I like the idea of a greyhound. I like to save things." Joe kissed her on the cheek and began clearing the table.

"Jeff asked me to look at some garden plans with him today. He seemed to be impressed with my ideas," she said. "Apparently the person who taught the course is his aunt, and she mentioned to him that I did well in the class. Tomorrow he wants me to take a look at the site of the garden." She grinned. "It's really pretty exciting. Maybe I should go back to school and study it or something."

"Is Jeff married?" Joe asked.

"I don't know. It's never come up. He doesn't talk about a family, though. There aren't any pictures around or anything." She wondered if he was. She hadn't thought about it before, but now she was curious.

"I don't know if you should spend too much time alone with him. You're a very beautiful woman, you know." Joe sounded worried.

Victoria looked up at him and smiled. "You're kidding, right?" She laughed.

"No, I'm not. You're vulnerable right now, and I'd hate to have to break your new boss's arms or anything." He laughed, but his eyes didn't soften.

"Joe, I'm sure I'm ten years older than he is. Besides, it's a professional relationship." Was Joe jealous?

He turned around to the sink and began rinsing dishes. "Well, just be careful," he said. "We really don't know this guy very well. Don't spend too much time alone with him until you're sure you can trust him."

The next morning Victoria was at the nursery early. She yawned as she went into the greenhouse to check her seedlings. Sleep had eluded her the night before. She was too excited about seeing the garden space. She got up early and went for a jog. Running was getting easier, but not much. Some days she could go three miles with very little trouble and other days she just couldn't move. "I don't know what makes the difference, but it's got to get easier sometime," she said. Today had been a good day. The running shoes had been a good buy. Her belly was flattening some and she had lost a few pounds. Her legs were solid muscle after the gardening and the running, and her arms were building muscle, too. "I may be old, but I can still be in shape," she said.

"Who are you talking to, Vic?" Jeff stood behind her.

"Myself." She turned and looked at him. "I talk to myself a lot, great conversationalist. How long have you been standing there?" She couldn't remember if she'd said anything else out loud.

"Not too long, ready to go?" He pointed to the door. "We'll take my truck." He waved her through the door before him. The truck was sitting right outside the door to the greenhouse. She went to the passenger door and got in. Jeff slid into the driver's seat and they were off. He chatted about the garden space. "I'm concerned about a few things. The space can be a little marshy, and the shade may be a problem in some spots. The customer is reasonable, but has a lot of ideas of his own. Unfortunately, most of them are unworkable."

"I'm sure you know more about drainage than I do," she said.

"You'd be surprised how often you think about things so hard you miss the obvious," he said. "It always pays to have someone who isn't saturated with the job look at it."

She was surprised at how comfortable she was with Jeff. She wanted to ask him if he was married, but couldn't think of a good way to bring up the subject. He looked out the window during a lull in the conversation, giving her an opportunity to look at his profile. He really was an attractive man. His features were sharp, but not pointed. His nose was straight, his lips a little wide, and his chin, strong. The gray at his temples was appealing. She couldn't see his eyes right now, but knew they were crystal blue. She looked out her own window before he could catch her staring at him.

"I think it's going to rain, so we won't get much work done here today. But we can have a look and that way we can make some plans," Jeff continued, as if he'd been thinking about it the whole time.

"You're a very focused person, aren't you?" Victoria said. "You don't leave a subject until it's finished."

"Did you have something else you wanted to talk about?" he asked. The question startled her.

"No." She could feel her face turning red. "Just making an observation."

They pulled into a driveway on the right. You couldn't see the house from the road. It was behind a group of trees, a forest really, mostly pine with a few hardwoods. The driveway wound through the trees. When they got past the forest the front lawn opened up. It was small, but the house was big. It had pillars in the traditional southern style. It was red brick, two stories, with a balcony all the way around on the second floor, and on the first floor a front porch that went the width of the house. The house was still under construction and workers were moving in and out of the doors.

"The yard is around back," Jeff said, as he followed the driveway to the left of the house. He pulled the truck to a stop at the side of the house and they got out. Victoria followed him along a path to the back door.

"It's beautiful," she whispered. The yard sloped downward from the terrace off the back of the house. It was not landscaped at all, but the natural foliage hadn't been disturbed by the construction. "You'll really want to work with what's already here as much as possible," she said, thinking aloud.

"That's what I was thinking. I do think some terracing on this hill would be a good plan," Jeff said from beside her. "I plan to put a step path down here," he said, as he walked down the hill. "On either side, the beds you were talking about, and here, the oak-leaf hydrangeas, then the weeping cherry, here. They're one of my favorite trees," he said, looking back at her.

Walking over to the edge of the clearing at the bottom of the hill, Victoria noticed wild blackberries growing. "Look." She pointed them out. "It's too early in the season for the berries, but come summer whoever lives here can make pie and jelly, and whatever else you use blackberries for." She turned to look for Jeff, but he was standing right behind her. She hadn't realized he was standing so close. She put her hand on his chest to steady herself, then, feeling awkward, looked up at him. He was smiling down at her. For a frightening moment, she thought he was going to kiss her. He just smiled and put his hands on her elbows to steady her.

"I didn't realize you were so close. I'm sorry," she stuttered.

"I didn't mean to startle you. You looked cute looking for berries, almost childlike." He continued to look at her with that soft smile. "I had an urge to kiss you, but I didn't know how you would feel about that."

Victoria stepped back from him, but he pulled her forward a little as he stepped back. "Watch out," he said. "Those bushes have thorns. Well, Vic," He leaned closer to her. "How would you feel about it?" His voice was almost a whisper now.

She stepped away from him and turned toward the truck.

"Don't be uncomfortable with me now." Jeff followed her. "We still have to work together." He draped an arm casually over her shoulders. "I would like an answer, though. Vic, how would you feel about a kiss?"

She stopped walking and looked up at him. "I...I'm not sure. Certainly guilty, but I really don't know."

"Guilty? You mean the husband. I was under the impression that things weren't going well in that area." He smiled down at her.

"Were you?" She wondered how he knew. "Well, no they aren't. But I am an honorable woman. I wouldn't cheat on him without separating first. I've always been honest with him." She walked around the truck and got into the passenger seat.

Jeff got into the car. "Are you planning a separation?"

"Not at the moment. We've talked about it, but no decision has been made." Victoria laughed. "This is a strange conversation. I've never talked to anyone about this before."

"Then maybe I have a chance." Jeff smiled. "But, even if I don't, it's nice that we're comfortable with each other. I'm glad you came to work here. I admire your work. Have you ever considered studying landscape architecture?"

"I've thought about it, but I'm not sure I want to go to school at my age." Victoria looked at Jeff. "How old are you, Jeff?"

"I'm forty-six. Why?"

"I'm fifty-four, eight years older than you."

"Who cares? I don't think it makes much difference at this stage of life."

When they pulled into the nursery parking lot, Victoria recognized Joe's car parked out front. Jeff pulled around back and she got out of the truck. Wondering why Joe was here, she walked into the building. Joe was standing at the checkout talking to Lillian.

"Is something wrong?" she asked, as she approached him. Joe looked at her. He had a worried look on his face, but he smiled. "I guess you've met Lillian," Victoria said.

"Nothing is wrong. I just wanted to show you something. Come out to the car." Joe took her hand and pulled her out the door. At the car, he opened the back door and pulled out a cardboard box. She looked inside. A brown and white puppy looked up at her with worried eyes. It was a short-legged dog, partly dachshund maybe, with wiry wisps of hair, and spots on its feet. It had gigantic ears that hung almost to the ground.

"I know you wanted a greyhound, but I had to drive to Villa Rica this morning to deliver some drawings to a customer and I found this little puppy on the highway. I had to stop for it, otherwise it would surely have been hit." Joe smiled at the little dog. He put his hand in and stroked its ear. "I thought

I'd give you a chance to keep it before I took it to the humane society."

"She's not going to the humane society." Victoria reached in and pulled the little dog out. "Her name is Ethel, and she's staying with me."

"How do you know it's a girl?" Joe asked, smiling down at her.

"I can just tell. Look at her, she's so feminine." Victoria held her up to look at her underside. "Yep, I was right." She turned to Joe, beaming. "Oh, thank you, Joe. I'm already in love."

"I'm glad. I kind of like her, too." He kissed her on the forehead. "Well, I guess I'll take her home and put her in a crate. We still have one somewhere, don't we?" Joe said, reaching for the dog.

"No, let her stay with me. I don't think Jeff will mind and that way we can get acquainted." Victoria turned to walk back to the nursery, then turned back and kissed Joe on the cheek. "Thanks, Joe. It was nice of you to pick her up. Some people would have left her there."

"What...is...that?" Jeff asked, as she came into the nursery carrying the dog.

"It's a puppy." Victoria was a little startled by his tone. "Isn't she cute? Joe found her on the highway."

"I don't like dogs, Vic. It can't stay here." Jeff went into his office.

Victoria followed him in. "How can you not like dogs? Look at her. She's adorable."

He looked down at her beaming face and his expression softened. "It's just that I really never have had much experience with dogs. I don't know what to do with a dog."

"You'll learn. They make great friends." She smiled at him. "I'll keep her out of your way." Her eyes pleaded. "Really, please let me bring her to work. That way I can train her and she'll end up being a great dog."

"We'll see, but I'm serious. The first time it digs up a plant, it goes." Jeff huffed and blew out his cheeks. She was reminded of Joe when he gets irritated with her.

"She's a *her*, not an *it*, and *her* name is Ethel." Victoria patted Jeff's arm. "Thanks, Jeff, I know I'm demanding, but I'll make it work."

The little dog followed her around all day. It was so much fun having her there. In fact everything was fun. Her life was taking a turn for the better. There was no doubt about it. She enjoyed this job so much. It didn't pay much, but she would change that when she got better at it. And the design work that Jeff was letting her get involved with was really exciting. She'd take another course, maybe this time at the Botanical Gardens. She'd heard they offered some good classes.

The days were going quickly. "Time really does pass faster when you're having fun."

"I love the way you talk to yourself," Jeff said from behind where Victoria was designing a row of hanging baskets.

"Maybe it's something that happens with age." She laughed. "I don't remember talking to myself when I was young. Or maybe I just didn't get caught before. Look at my terrariums over there." She pointed to a shelf with three glass houses on it. Jeff went over. Ethel followed at his heels. "Ethel, come." The little dog responded promptly, returning to Victoria and sitting at her feet.

"You're doing a good job of training it," Jeff mumbled.

"*Her*," Victoria said, smiling to herself. He was really not a dog person, but he was trying. She never felt awkward after their talk about a kiss. They were becoming good friends. He never brought it up again, but she thought about it often. Her feelings were confused, but she really didn't feel romantic toward him. Of course, she didn't feel romantic toward Joe either. What a puzzle.

"What?" He looked around at her, bemused, then at the dog. "Oh, right, her. Anyway these terrariums are really good. You've learned a lot since you've been here. I want you to start helping me with garden design." He walked back over, leaned down and touched the top of the little dog's head with the tip of his finger. He really was trying.

"I'm not sure how to start," she responded.

"I'll teach you my way and you can work from there. I would also be willing to put you through some classes, maybe at the Botanical Gardens."

"I was just thinking I would take one. I'll go this weekend and get a schedule." She looked at him. He was smiling at her. "Why are you so good to me, Jeff? I'm not that valuable an employee."

"I think you're valuable. And besides, I like you." He brushed her cheek with his hand as he walked by her and out the door.

"I think you've got a problem." Lillian stood in the doorway to the work yard.

"What?"

"He's in love with you." Lillian came into the room. She had become a good friend. It was hard for Victoria to believe how close she'd become to this person, who was not even the age of her oldest child.

"Don't be silly." She returned to her work. "I'm a lot older than he is. I don't think I really attract men anymore anyway."

"That's dumb, Vic." Jeff's nickname for her had caught on. All of the staff called her Vic. "You have to know that you're pretty."

Victoria laughed. "I could have been described that way twenty years ago, but I don't think I can be described that way now." Turning back to her work, she couldn't help but glance at her reflection in the window.

"Really, Vic, age looks good on you. The things about aging that mar beauty for most people look good on you. Maybe it's because you're so thrilled by life. Even just simple things like ugly little dogs make you glow. You'll be attractive to men until the day you die. Isn't that obvious? Not only do you have a really sexy husband, but your boss, who's pretty hot in the looks department, also has a thing for you." Lillian moved off to continue her work.

"Thrilled by life?" Victoria muttered to herself. Wasn't it just recently that she told Joe she was dead inside? She couldn't feel anything. No, that was months ago and she'd changed her life. It was early spring when she had started her garden, and now it was early summer. It was hot outside, her garden was still underway, but she knew it would take years to get it the way she wanted it. It would always be changing. Just like her life.

Yes, her work life had changed for the better. Maybe it was time to work on her home life a little. She had to decide what to do about Joe. She had to get back in touch with her children, too. They hadn't just ceased to exist when they left town, but she hadn't thought of them—either of them—in months, hadn't heard much from them, either. It was time to touch base.

Suddenly, it seemed very important to talk to them.

Joe was in Augusta overnight for a business meeting, so when she got home she grabbed a sandwich and sat down to call the girls. First she called Patricia, the baby at twenty-three.

"Hi, honey, this is Mom," she said when Patricia answered.

"Mom, I've only got a minute. I'm getting ready to go out. Is everything okay?"

That's typical. The girls really never had time to talk to her. That was why she'd stopped calling. She realized now that it was up to the mother to stay in touch. The girls had so much going on in their young lives.

"Everything is fine. I was just missing you. I won't keep you, but promise you'll call when you have some time to update me on your life."

"I will. I'll tell you now, though, that I am having

boyfriend problems. This guy I've been seeing has a really bad temper. The problem is I really think I'm in love with him." Her voice broke as if she might cry.

"Oh, honey, I'm sorry. Bad tempers worry me. He doesn't seem violent or anything, does he?"

"Oh, Mom, of course not. I probably shouldn't have told you that." She sounded irritated. "Listen, he's here and he hates to be kept waiting. We're going for a hike. I'll call when I can talk more. Bye."

The phone was hung up before she had time to say goodbye. "Well, that wasn't comforting," she said aloud. Luckily there was nobody there to hear her. With Joe away, talking to herself wasn't so dangerous.

She called Ellen, her elder daughter. "Ellen, this is Mom."

"Hi, Mom, I'm glad you called."

Well, that was a switch.

"I wanted to talk to you about graduation. I'm not going to go to the ceremony."

"Oh, honey, I wish you would. Dad and I would be so proud. We'd love to come out there and visit. See where you've been all this time." They'd never been out there. Ellen hadn't seemed to want them, and since she'd paid for most of it herself, they couldn't insist.

"No. It's my spot. I really don't want to share it with you," she said.

"Well that hurts. Ellen, why aren't we close? I really do love you, you know."

"I know, Mom. I didn't mean to hurt you, maybe someday, but not now."

"Have you decided what you're going to do

now that you're graduating? Will you come back to Atlanta?"

"No. Not for a while anyway. I've found a job in Seattle. I'll start it in July. I'm going on vacation with some friends first. Have you talked to Patricia?"

"I just talked to her and she worried me. Has she told you anything about this new boyfriend she's seeing? She told me that he has a bad temper." Victoria was concerned.

"He's a real jerk. I don't know why she gets herself mixed up with such losers. I hope she breaks up with him, but she thinks she's *in love*. Can you imagine? The guy hits her."

"Does he really, Ellen? How can she let that happen?" Victoria was really upset now.

"There's nothing you can do, Mom. She says she isn't going back to Atlanta when she graduates either. She's staying there to be with him. Now, what's she going to do in that little college town? But, like I said, there's nothing you can do. Believe me, I've talked till I'm blue in the face."

"Well, at least she keeps in touch with you," Victoria said.

"Yeah, well, gotta go, Mom. I've got things to do. Bye." Again, the phone was hung up before she could say goodbye.

"I told them both I loved them, but I'm still not sure that's true." That hadn't helped much at all. No wonder she never called.

Victoria went upstairs to her bedroom and looked around. She really hadn't done any decorating in years. The bedspread was faded and the carpet was worn. The room didn't reflect her personality at all. It really didn't reflect Joe's either. Did they just not have personalities, or did they just not care? She looked at the bed. They hadn't had sex in ages. The last time was disappointing. "I guess neither one of us wants to feel that way again."

Lillian had said that Joe was sexy. "I used to think you were sexy, Joe," she whispered to no one. Was he still sexy? She tried to visualize him in her mind, but she couldn't call up an image. She would have to look at him when he got home.

She looked at her own reflection in her mirror as she began to undress. Lillian had said that age looked good on her. She hadn't thought about how she looked in years. She was watching herself in the mirror as she took her cloths off. She knew that she had been pretty when she was young. Her platinum-blond hair was natural. That was pretty rare. It had never gone dark. When she was young, she had wished that she had some curl in her hair like her mother, but instead, it hung in a thick straight sheet of white gold to her shoulders. It was so straight that there really wasn't any other way to wear it. She had tried to wear it short a couple of times, but it was so thick and straight that it stood up like a brush. That hadn't worked. She knew that there was gray coming into it, but with the pale color, it wasn't very noticeable.

Her eyes were blue and her skin was very fair. It was clear, though, no freckles. The lines that had formed around her eyes and mouth were not severe, but seemed to define the features. They bothered her a little, but she had to admit that the aging process hadn't hurt her much.

She had always been a full-figured woman, but she'd been diligent about having the proper breast support. Even when she was young and the style had been to go braless, she didn't. It had paid off. Even after nursing two babies she didn't sag much anywhere. The running, and heavy work in the garden and now at the nursery, had firmed her up. The belly that had bothered her still bulged, but not nearly as much. There were stretch marks from having babies, but that was sort of a badge of courage.

The phone rang. She checked the caller ID. It was Joe.

"Hello," she answered.

"Hey, Victoria, is everything okay?"

She told him about her conversations with the girls.

"So both girls are graduating this month, and we're not invited to either graduation?"

"Well, I don't know about Patricia. She didn't have time to talk. I guess she'll let us know." Victoria sounded sad.

"Don't let it get you down, sweetheart. Things are going well for you. What are you doing now?" he asked.

"I'm looking at myself in the mirror, naked." She wondered what he would think of that.

"I wish I was looking at you naked." He laughed.

"Do you really, Joe? I'm a lot older than when we started." She laughed too.

"You'll always look beautiful to me."

"I wonder if I would look beautiful to another

man?" She wished she hadn't said it as soon as it was out.

"You would," he said. "But I hope you don't find out."

"I'm sure I never will. When are you coming home?" She changed the subject.

"I'll be home by dinnertime tomorrow. How's Ethel?" he asked.

"She is so sweet. I just love her. She's smart, too. I'm getting her really well trained. Jeff even commented on it today. He's really not a dog person, but he's trying. He touched her today with the tip of his finger, like he's afraid to get dirty or something."

"It's nice of him to let you bring her to work, especially since he doesn't like dogs." He paused. "Apparently he likes you."

"We've become good friends. Lillian and I are good friends, too. Even though she's so young, and I'm not." She laughed.

"We're not old, just older. I'll see you tomorrow, Victoria. I love you."

"See you tomorrow." She hung up.

The next morning on her run, she noticed that her mind had wandered to the workday ahead. "That's the first time I've been able to do that," she said to herself, glancing around self-consciously. Most of the time she ran, she couldn't think of anything, but the discomfort of running. She'd been in bad shape when she started. It was always a struggle to make herself go. At first, going a half-mile had seemed impossible. Now she was on her third mile and wasn't even thinking about stopping.

"How many months have I been running?" she asked herself. "I started in late February. It's early June now."

"A little over three months. Doing pretty good." She patted herself on the back.

She noticed that she was running up a hill that she had always walked up before. "I'm definitely making progress."

When she got to work, Jeff was looking for her from his office door.

"Vic, I've got that schedule of classes. I had it faxed to me. Here's what I want you to take." Apparently he had everything planned out. There were three classes in six-week sessions. They met once a week, but there were to be computer exercises in between the classroom work.

"This is really serious." She felt a little nervous. Her stomach fluttered uncomfortably. "Jeff, I haven't worked on a computer before. I mean other than at the store, and that was just with simple programs. I haven't done Internet or anything like that."

"You're kidding?" He looked surprised.

"No, I just never needed to. I guess I should have anyway." She felt a little ashamed.

"You don't write your daughters e-mail? I would never communicate with my aunt if it wasn't for e-mail." Jeff laughed.

"Your Aunt has e-mail?" Victoria felt deflated. It must have showed on her face, because Jeff patted her on the shoulder.

"Don't worry. You'll have no problem with it. I can help, and I'm sure Joe can help, too," he reassured. "Anyway, you can take them one at a time or you could take these two classes together, and then this one," he said, pointing to the class schedule. "I want you to start right away because you need to be ready for the garden show next spring. I'm taking you with me." He went back into his office.

"Wait, wait, wait." Victoria followed him in. "What are you talking about?"

"Every spring there's a garden show. Next year it's in Washington, D.C. I want you to come with me." He stopped and looked at her. "I mean, if you want to. I would love for you to help me. We'll have a display with our name on it. We go every year. I usually do it alone, but next year I want you to come."

"I don't know." She looked distracted. "I've really never done anything like that."

"You'll love it. I always have a good time. It's a great competition." He looked back at his computer.

"Competition?" Her voice caught in her throat.

Jeff looked up at her. "I'm not trying to stress you." He laughed. "It's good for business because our name is there, but it doesn't matter if we win anything." He got up from his chair and walked over to her. He pulled her against his chest and put his arms around her. His chin rested on her head. His shirt smelled of detergent and man. She couldn't believe how comfortable it was. "Don't look so scared. If you don't want to go, you don't have to." He held her slightly away from him and looked in her eyes. "I guess I got excited about it and went a little fast. Let's start over."

Victoria swallowed and looked up at him from under her lashes.

"I would like for you to take these courses to learn how to design and plant a garden. It will help you here at the nursery, and if you like it, you could help me with the garden show next year, if you want to." He brushed her forehead with his lips. "Is that better?"

Her face was blank for a moment, then, she smiled. "It was better before you kissed me. Now I'm really scared." Turning, she left the office.

"Vic, think about it. I think you can do a great job." Without turning around, she waved a hand at him.

In the propagation house Victoria leaned against the wall. What was happening with Jeff? He did seem to be interested in her, she thought. He had held her when she felt afraid and kissed her forehead. Joe probably wouldn't like that.

"What am I doing here?" She enjoyed the attention she received from him. Surely it was innocent. He couldn't be interested in her, but there was just a little feeling of guilt. "He's a baby!" She looked around to be sure she was alone. He may be younger, but he was not a baby.

"I wonder if I'm playing a dangerous game." She smiled a smile that she could feel had the devil in it. "I should be ashamed."

"Yes you should," Lillian laughed. "I can't wait until I'm your age and can talk to myself without feeling weird."

"Oh, don't kid yourself. I feel weird, but only when I get caught." Laughing, she turned to the table where the seedlings were lined up ready to be planted. She started scooping the soil out of the mixing tub into trays and pots. There were the $4.99 pots and then the trays of six, for $6.99.

"So, what are you ashamed about? Dangling two men on a string?" Lillian put on her gloves.

"I feel stupid even thinking that, at my age. I didn't do that when I was young. I'm sure I'm just flattering myself to think Jeff feels anything for me, and Joe just does because he has to."

"Well, I've worked here much longer than you, and I can tell you that I've never seen Jeff treat another employee the way he treats you. And we've had other women work here."

"You don't think he might really believe I have some talent for the work?"

"You know I don't mean that." Lillian laughed. "You're deflecting."

"Explain that, psychology student," Victoria said.

"Trying to change the subject, you don't want to see what's really happening. Maybe you're having too much fun and don't want to give it up. I think you should take it a little more seriously." Lillian sounded stern.

Victoria looked at her. "You're not as humorous about this as you have been in the past. What's the matter?"

"I'm just starting to think someone could get hurt." She looked down at the pot she was filling with soil.

"Over me?"

"Yeah."

"Vicki, Victoria," Joe called from the office. "Could you come in here for a minute?"

"What do you need?" She appeared in the doorway from the kitchen. "I'm getting ready to go out into the garden. I've got some planting I wanted to get done before I go to lunch with the girls."

"We can't afford for you to go to lunch with the girls." Joe scowled at the computer screen. "We just aren't making ends meet. I need for you to sit down with me and go over the budget."

"I can't do it right now, Joe. This is my only day off this week and if I don't get this planting done today, it'll be too late to put in new plants without them burning up in the sun," she insisted.

"Vicki, this is very important. I don't want to go into debt." He looked up at her worried. "I'm trying to be supportive of you. I can see that this job change has been good for you, but it's been hell on our finances. We'll have to make some changes."

"Joe, don't worry yourself to death," Victoria said. "Maybe I should take over the finances again."

"No, I think we should do it together. We need to be a team," he said, obviously controlling his temper. "Now please, sit down here with me and help with this."

"All right," she said. She took her seat beside him and they proceeded to work on the budget.

It had been a grueling morning, and she hadn't gotten her planting done. Maybe she could do it after lunch. Joe had eliminated a number of things from the budget. Most of them were her indulgences. "I guess that's only fair, since I'm the one that reduced the income," she said to Lillian and Jane. They were sitting with her in the café, having lunch. "I insisted on coming today since we had already made the plans, but I'm not going to be doing much more of this. It's not in the budget," she said sadly.

"Well, if we have to, we'll take turns treating you to lunch," Jane said.

"Speak for yourself. I'm a starving student, remember," Lillian said. "Not only that, but I have the same job as she does, and I don't get paid any more than she does either. Maybe from now on we can picnic." She laughed.

"That's right. We'll all have to pack our own lunch, though. I can't afford to feed anyone but myself." Victoria laughed.

"Doesn't Joe make pretty good money? Didn't you tell me he was an architect?" Lillian asked.

"He does, but it's a fluctuating market, so some times are better than others. Before I went to work, we'd put some money away from the good times for expenses in the slower times, but since I went to work, we've gotten out of the habit of doing that. I'm sure we'll get back to it, but it was kind of a sudden job change. We didn't have a chance to prepare." Victoria sounded depressed.

"Hey, Vic." Lillian patted her arm. "Don't let it get you down. I think you'll make more money when Jeff starts letting you design gardens. How's the course going anyway?"

"It's going okay. I have a little trouble with the computer assignments, but Joe helps, so I'm getting them done. I wish I was more computer savvy."

"That will come," Jane said. "You'll be surprised how fast you pick it up."

"That's easy for you to say, you've always worked on a computer," Victoria said. Her friend Jane was a very successful businesswoman. She had worked all her life at developing her career in computer technology. She'd never married. There had been a few relationships, but they hadn't lasted. It was always surprising to Victoria that they were such good friends. Their lives had been so different.

"Well, I can also help you if Joe gets on your nerves too much."

"No, he's okay. It just wasn't a very good morning. But anyway, the teacher of this course is more irritating than Joe. She talks in this high-pitched voice and kind of sings what she says. She's really caught up in color. We're doing garden designs and she says, 'These flowers are a pale azure with just a hint of plum.'" Victoria sang the words going high and low. "Now tell me, what color is that?"

They all laughed. It was fun being with the girls. It was surprising that she had these two good friends and that they were friends with each other. That was nice. Lillian was so much younger than they were. But it really made no difference. Victoria smiled.

"Now, that's better," Jane said. "Money problems can get you down, but they can't keep you down."

"How come Jeff's giving you all these courses? He's never offered one to me." Lillian sounded like a spoiled child.

"You're studying psychology. He knows this job is just a way to get you through school. You'll probably never work in a nursery again," Victoria soothed. "He just thinks I'm some old lady who needs a lift. He's not wrong about that," she sighed.

"If you're old, what am I?" Jane said.

"No, that's not it. He has a thing for you," Lillian said. "I see the way he looks at you." She turned to Jane. "You should've seen the terror on Jeff's face when she fell into the compost bin." She laughed. "Then it turned to delight when her butt stayed in sight over the edge and he got to go rescue her."

"Actually, this new job of yours sounds interesting, Tori, falling into compost bins and being rescued by men. What does Jeff look like?" Jane asked Lillian.

"He's beautiful," she replied.

"As beautiful as Joe?"

"Well, it's kind of a toss up there. They're both pretty sexy." Lillian blushed.

"So you've noticed how she seems to attract beautiful men. I'm not sure what it is about her." Jane eyed Victoria appraisingly. "She isn't bad looking, but neither are we." She nudged Lillian with her elbow. "I don't know about you, but I don't have a bunch of beautiful men following me around."

"No, I don't either," Lillian agreed. "I think it's the way she gets so excited about every little thing—like this stupid job. How many people would just quit a high-paying job like the one she had and go to work for a nursery? I mean you're digging in dirt all day, lifting heavy things, spreading manure. I do it because it was the only job I could find, and now that I'm used to it, I don't want to change. But Victoria acts like it's a glamorous new career."

"Yeah, I bet that's it. Well, I'm hopeless then," Jane said. "I'm not going to quit my high-paying job and go dig in the dirt."

"Stop it, you two. Jeff doesn't have a thing for me. He has become a really good friend, though," Victoria sighed. "I hope he doesn't have a thing for me, because then I'd have to stop being friends with him and he's been so supportive and encouraging. It's not that Joe hasn't been supportive, but he's just putting up with me." She sounded sad.

"Are things still not going well with Joe?" Jane asked, concerned. Victoria had talked to Jane about the problems she'd been having. How she felt dead inside. "You know you've been married to him for a long time. Maybe it's time to take a break. Be on your own for a while."

"He's been worried about me doing that. Truth is, I hadn't even thought about it until he asked me not to leave him. He said he could see that I was building up to that and said he would make me want to stay," Victoria said.

"Has he made you want to stay?" Jane asked.

"No, but I don't really want to go, either. I guess I'm still confused. Anyway, he brought me a dog."

Victoria smiled. "That was nice. Ethel makes me happy."

Lunch arrived and they all fell silent for a while. The food was good. They commented on that. Then Jane put down her fork and said, "I've got an idea. Lets all go on a girls-only weekend. I'm going to Savannah in mid July for a seminar. It lasts a week, but will be over by the weekend. Why don't you two meet me down there on Friday, and we can spend the weekend in Savannah? There are lots of things to do down there."

"Sorry, count me out. That's summer midterms. I'll be studying," Lillian said.

"I don't know about driving all the way down there by myself," Victoria said. "I've never traveled alone."

"You're kidding." Jane laughed. "You've led such a sheltered life. Well, it's time you had a little adventure. Let's do it. If it works out, we'll plan another trip when you can come, Lillian."

"Okay." Victoria was starting to feel excited. "I'll go, if it's all right with Joe."

"You don't have to ask his permission, Vic," Lillian said. "He's your husband, not your keeper."

"No, but I have to consider him." She paused, thoughtful. "He did say, not too long ago, that he thought it was good for us to spend a little time apart."

"That's right. Maybe a little distance will make you more interested in that sexy body of his," Jane said.

"You really think Joe is sexy?" She addressed the question to both of them. "I guess I'm just so used to him I don't notice anymore. Well, okay. I'll tell him I'm going. Remind me to get that weekend off, Lillian."

"Good, let's have a glass of wine to celebrate," Jane said.

"Not me." Lillian put her money on the table. "Here's my part of lunch. I've got studying to do. See you guys next time." She hurried out of the café.

"She's a nerd." Jane laughed and watched her go. "Well, want some wine?"

"You know I don't drink."

"It's time for you to start that, too." Jane flagged the waitress and ordered two glasses of white Zinfandel. "That's a light wine. It won't knock you out. You'll be able to drive home."

"To Savannah," Jane clinked the glasses together and took a sip. Victoria sipped her wine. It was nice. She really never drank wine unless they were out for a special occasion, something like an anniversary or a birthday. She liked it. Joe drank scotch sometimes. He kept a bottle of it in his office and some brandy, but he didn't drink wine with dinner.

On the ride home, she realized that she did have a nice buzz going. "Since I don't drink much I guess it affects me pretty fast," she said aloud. "I'm going to plant when I get home. Remember?" She laughed at herself. "I love conversations with you, Victoria. They're so much fun."

When she got home she started right away in the garden. There wasn't as much to do as she'd thought there was. The soil had already been prepared, so all she had to do was put the seedlings in. She put in petunias of different colors, red, blue, and pink.

Then in another bed, she put in purslane of orange, pink, and yellow. She had started all of them from seed in the growing booths that Joe had built for her in the basement.

The place was looking pretty good. She had worked all spring. The weeds she didn't like had been replaced by a variety of different flowers, some of them perennials, some annuals. The weeds she liked had been trimmed and cultivated. She always liked to stay as close to the natural flora as possible. She had wild day lilies, and ginger. There were rose of Sharon trees with blooms of every color. She even had some dwarf wild iris she had found in the woods in the back yard. She'd replaced the weeds that they had mowed down to pass for grass for years and put in dwarf Mondo grass. It was coming in beautifully. She would put in bulbs of crocus and daffodils in the fall.

She sighed with satisfaction at her work. It had been a good thing to do. She felt hopeful for the first time in years.

She was still feeling a bit of a buzz from the glass of wine she'd had with Jane at lunch and thought it would be nice to have another one. Remembering the bottle of wine that a friend of Joe's had given him at Christmas, she said, "I think I'll open that baby up."

"What baby is that, Victoria?" She cringed at the sound of Dolores Crisp's voice, and turned slowly.

"I was talking to myself, again, Dolores. How do you like my garden?"

"Oh, dear, you've been drinking." Could she

smell it on her breath? Victoria wondered. It was only one glass of wine almost an hour ago.

"Yes, I had a glass of wine over lunch with a friend." Victoria turned back to her work and started gathering her tools. "As if it's any of your business," she murmured.

"Have you been drinking long?" She turned back to Dolores with surprise. The woman was actually scowling at her.

"Oh, I only drink a little in the morning. I don't really get started until about lunchtime. In the evening I usually just sock back a pint or two of whisky." She turned and walked to the house. Looking over her shoulder, she laughed at the startled expression on Dolores's face. "She's got a lot of nerve." She slammed the door.

She looked in the small refrigerator they kept in the garage for soft drinks, and found the wine, chardonnay. "I don't know what that is, but I'm about to find out." It was a struggle to open it, since she hadn't ever used a corkscrew before. The thing had arms that went up in the air and a screw in the middle of a round thing the shape of the bottle top. That was pretty self-explanatory. She propped it on top of the bottle and started to screw the thing down. Sure enough, the arms came up. When she lowered them they pulled the cork out.

"Smart, really smart." She laughed.

Taking a glass off the shelf, she poured herself some and went into the living room. Noticing the photo albums on the table next to her chair, she looked through them while she sipped her wine. She started with photos of the kids growing up. They really were cute little girls, such an interesting combination of features from Joe and her. Ellen had Joe's dark hair and eyes, but the features of her face were more like Victoria's, except the square jaw. That was Joe's. Her hair, though dark like Joe's, was straight like Victoria's. Patricia had the blond hair, curly like Joe's. It was a little darker than Victoria's, a little more gold than platinum. But her eyes were the color of Joe's. She also had the square jaw, and his dimples. Patricia and Joe had dimples in their cheeks. She and Ellen didn't. "I envy them those dimples."

It was that jaw that had first attracted her to Joe. It was just so firm. The muscles in his neck seemed to be toned just to hold up that beautiful jaw. She'd thought he was beautiful then.

"I need another glass of wine," she said, as she tried to take a sip and found the glass empty. Feeling just a little bit wobbly, she walked to the kitchen, poured another glass, and went back to the living room. She picked up the album of her wedding pictures and started flipping through.

There it was again, that beautiful jaw. In fact, the whole face was beautiful. He'd been a very attractive young man. Apparently, some people thought he was an attractive middle-aged man. She flipped to a picture of their honeymoon. They'd gone to Jamaica. Joe stood on the beach in his swimming trunks. He was tall, thin, almost to the point of skinny, but his shoulders were broad, his stomach was flat, and his legs were muscled and nicely shaped.

"He has a cute butt, too." She turned the page to a picture of him standing with his back to her, facing the ocean.

"What does his body look like now?" she wondered. "I haven't even looked in so long I don't know."

She finished her wine just as she heard Joe's car pull in the driveway. "Good, he's home." She got up and swayed, sat back down hard, and giggled. "Uh oh, I'm drunk."

Joe came in the kitchen door from the garage. "Victoria, where are you?"

"I'm in the living room."

"I just had the strangest conversation with Dolores Crisp. She waved me to a stop when I pulled into the street." He walked into the room and stopped.

"Joe," Victoria said seriously. "Take off your clothes."

"My God! You *are* drunk! She asked me how long you'd had a drinking problem and I assured her that you didn't. You don't drink, Victoria." He picked up the glass. "How much have you had?"

"I don't know. I can't remember. But seriously, Joe, take off your clothes. I want to look at you naked." She rose and walked over to him. She was pleased that she didn't stagger. "See, I can walk, I must not be too drunk." She started to pull his shirt-tail out of his pants.

"Victoria." Joe stopped her. "What happened? Why are you drinking?"

"Because I think it's about time for me to have some adventures." She smiled and started tugging at his shirt again. "Jane thinks so too. We're going to Savannah next month. Now take off your clothes."

"No, Victoria, I'm not going to do that right now.

Not that I wouldn't love to take advantage of you in your present state." Joe smiled at her. She looked up into his face. His mouth was smiling, but his eyes were concerned.

"I'm okay, Joe, really." She became distracted with his jaw. "It's still there," she said. "That beautiful jaw. You know the girls both have that jaw."

"Honey, maybe you should lie down." Joe put his arm around her waist and started walking toward the steps.

"Not without you," she said. "But first I want to see you naked. I need to look at something."

Joe laughed. "I don't think this is the time."

"Yes it is. This will be one of my adventures, meaningless sex." She was weaving a little now.

"Our sex isn't meaningless, Victoria." Joe was struggling to keep her from falling now. Finally he picked her up and carried her into the bedroom.

"It could be if we wanted it to." She smiled and putting her arms around his neck, started nibbling his ear.

"You want to have sex, but you don't want to make love?" He looked at her curiously as he put her down on the bed.

"Right." she said. "I want to fuck." Joe jumped like she had hit him.

"What's the matter? You've heard that word before."

"Yes, and I've heard it from you lately too, but I've never heard you say that before."

"Well that's what I want to do, but first, I want you to take off your clothes so I can get a good look at you. See if you're really as sexy as everyone seems to think." She was slurring her words now. She could hear it herself and the room was beginning to spin. "But right now, I don't feel too good."

"Victoria, are you about to vomit?" Joe pulled the trashcan from next to the nightstand just in time. Victoria dropped her head and vomited into the can. When she was finished, Joe took the can into the bathroom and rinsed it. Victoria fell back on the bed and started to cry.

"Don't cry, sweetheart. You don't drink very much. That's why you can't hold it very well. You'll feel better in a while. Take a nap." Joe pulled off her shoes and pants, and tucked her into the bed. "We'll talk tomorrow. Getting sick was probably the best thing. Maybe you won't have too much of a hangover."

"What will you eat for dinner?" She sniffled.

"I'll find something." He laughed. "Right now, I don't have much appetite."

Victoria sat in the shade of a dogwood tree in her front yard. It was a warm summer day. The weather hadn't really gotten hot yet, but it was very warm. Luckily there was a breeze. It wasn't cool, but the movement of the air helped keep the humidity bearable. That was good considering that Victoria wasn't feeling her best.

Getting up that morning was painful. Joe had suggested that she stay home and rest, but she was not going to let a hangover stop her from going to work. Apparently, she'd looked pale, because Jeff sent her home early in the afternoon. He had come upon her trapped by the wheelbarrow when she'd slid under it going down a hill, landing on her butt with the handles on either side of her waist. It was full of potting soil, so it was too heavy to lift.

He'd looked serious as he pulled it off her. Making a few comments about women drivers under his breath, he asked, "Are you okay, Vic?"

"Yes, but I think you're right about going home," she sighed. "I'm not well today." Puking hadn't kept her from having a hangover as Joe had predicted. She felt terrible. She felt even worse when she thought of the way she'd attacked Joe the night before. "What got into me?" she said. "About half a bottle of wine, that's what."

Now she was sitting in a folding chair in the front yard with her sketchpad drawing plans of her garden. The problem with that was that you were supposed to draw the plans before you planted the garden. She just wasn't sure how to start. She needed a plot of land to work with that hadn't been planted, so she could go through the whole process of planning and organizing a garden.

Joe came out of the front door with a stool in his hand. He came over to where she was sitting and set the stool down in front of her. He sat down and looked into her face. "I don't want to dwell on the negative, Victoria, but what happened last night? You never drink."

"I wish I could tell you. I was feeling so powerful after lunch. Jane got me all excited about this trip to Savannah. She insisted that we have a glass of wine to celebrate." She paused and took a deep breath.

"One glass wouldn't have hurt. Why didn't you stop there?" Joe prodded.

"I don't know. It was a mistake, Joe. Don't read more into it than there is." She really didn't want to talk about it.

"Okay." He patted her knee. "It just puzzled me, that's all. Honey, tell me about these plans for Savannah."

"Jane has a seminar down there next month. She asked me to join her for the weekend. She's flying down with her company. I'll drive down and meet her on Friday, and we'll drive back together on Sunday."

"You'll drive down alone?" He looked surprised and a little concerned.

"Joe, I'm not a child." She tried to huff, but couldn't put much energy into it.

"No, but you haven't had much experience traveling alone. Couldn't Lillian go with you or something?" His brows creased in worry.

"Lillian has midterms." Victoria continued to sketch as she talked, trying to look confident. "Anyway, it's time I got some experience traveling alone. You went to the beach by yourself not long ago. You said it was good for you and we should do more of that."

"That's true. Well, I wasn't trying to talk you out of it. I just wish someone was going with you." He stopped talking and reached down to pat the little dog that had just stretched out at his feet. "Hello, Ethel," he said. "Where did you come from? Do you think she should be in the front yard off leash?" he asked.

"She's so good. She does whatever I tell her. I only let her come out here when she's with me. I think I'll put in an invisible fence out here, though. I wouldn't want any accidents." Victoria continued to draw.

"What are you drawing?" Joe asked. He reached for the sketchpad and Victoria turned it around to show him.

"Victoria, that's really good."

"You're surprised?"

"Well, yeah, I am. I've known you for a long time and I didn't know you could draw." She'd drawn her garden with Ethel in it.

"You've even captured Ethel, expression and all. I'm really impressed." He touched her shoulder.

The praise was feeling good now. Victoria smiled. "I'm glad I took those courses. I didn't realize how much I enjoy drawing. I'm a little worried about the course I'm taking now, though. I'm having a hard time figuring out how to sketch a design for a garden that hasn't been put in yet. I need a yard that isn't landscaped, but mine is all filled up."

"Ours," he corrected.

"Ours." She laughed.

"I've got an idea. One of the contractors that I'm working with on this job in Villa Rica is building a house. Maybe he would let you use his yard. I went out there with him the last time I was there. It's completely stripped immediately around the house. They left an apple tree, that's all. It's not completely flat, though. It might work." He raised his brows in question.

"That would be great, but what if he doesn't like my plans? Or maybe he has a landscaper." She sounded unsure.

"He doesn't have to use your plans. You already know how to plant a garden. It would just be an exercise. You don't even have to show them to him if you don't want to." Joe paused. "Want me to call him?"

"I guess so," she said hesitantly. "Yes, call him, Joe. I've got to get started somewhere."

"If he's agreeable, we could drive up together on your next day off. It would be nice to do something together. It's been a long time since we've gone anywhere. We could pack a picnic and I could bring some work along so I won't bother you while you work." He sounded excited and the excitement was catching.

Victoria could feel the muscles in her legs working. She thought she could almost feel the individual muscles working together to form the movements. "That's dumb," she said. She was on one of her favorite routes to run on and she was really enjoying it. The summer was well underway, but the mornings were still cool. It was about 6:00 a.m. This was her "before work run."

The birds were singing and the air felt fresh and damp. She was almost home. It was time to slow to a walk so that she could cool down before she reached the house. It was nice after a run when her heart was pumping and she felt all tingly. "I guess that's the endorphins everyone's always talking about."

She went into the kitchen and smelled fresh coffee. It was really a nice morning. Morning had become her favorite time of day. After pouring a glass of water, she sat down at the table. Joe came in and kissed her on the top of her head.

"Yuck, I'm sweaty, Joe, that must have tasted terrible."

"Just a little salty is all." He laughed. "Did you have a nice run?"

"Yeah, you know I'm really enjoying running these days. When I first started, I didn't think I'd ever get in shape. Remember, I said I felt like I was carrying lead."

"So you got the lead out." They both laughed.

"Well, there's still some lead. It's funny. Some days are better than others, and I don't really know the difference. What makes me run better one day than another?"

"Who knows? I'm sure it's the same for everyone. I'm proud of you for continuing."

"So am I."

They shared a cup of coffee and chatted, then went their separate ways.

At work, Victoria told Jeff about the empty yard that she was going to design. "That is if the owner doesn't mind. Joe said he'd call him today and ask."

"I doubt he'll mind. Why would he? He doesn't have to use your plan if he doesn't want to."

"I probably won't even show it to him."

"Why not? Who knows, maybe he'll like it."

Victoria thought about it for a minute. "Well, when I finish it, I'll decide whether I should show it to anyone."

"That won't work." Jeff picked up Ethel and rocked her back in his arms. He tickled her belly. "You never give yourself credit for what you do. You'd better let me decide."

"You sure have changed your tune about Ethel. In fact, I thought I overheard you talking to her the other day." She laughed.

Jeff put the dog down. "Me? No way. I don't talk to dogs." He smiled. "So will you let me see your plans?"

"I guess I could show them to you. But you have to wait until they're finished."

"Come in here and look at these plans I'm working on. I'd like to hear what you think." Jeff had been consulting her more and more. He actually did use some of her ideas. It was really fun.

A few minutes later Lillian popped her head in the door. "You two have your heads so close together that if you look up too fast, you'll bump. Big project?"

"Yes. One of the biggest I've done." Jeff sounded a little tense. "I really want to do a good job. It would be great to get some more like this."

"Well, don't stress. Vic, can you help me in the storage room when you get a chance?"

"Sure, just give me a minute to finish up here."

As Victoria walked across the nursery toward the storage room, a customer stopped her. "Could you get someone to help me get that bag of vermiculite down off that shelf?" She pointed up to the highest shelf in the place.

"Sure, just let me get a ladder." She went in search of one of the big rolling ladders that they used to get to the top shelves. She pushed it to the shelf and climbed up. She reached as high as she could and couldn't quite reach it. She lacked only about an inch. Grabbing the metal post on the side of the shelf, she stepped on a box on the shelf below. Just as the ladder rolled away from her, she remembered Jeff's warning to always be sure to lock the wheels before stepping on the ladder. The floor of the nursery was on a slight slant so that water could run out of it. The ladder rolled all the way to the end of the aisle.

"Shit." Victoria hoped no one heard her swear. She looked down to tell the customer to go for help, but she had wandered off.

Before she had a chance to think of what to do, Jeff came out of his office. He spotted her hanging from the top shelf and ran over to her. The look on his face was sheer panic. Victoria started to laugh. Looking around for the ladder, he spotted it way down the aisle.

"Jeff, I can hold on, just go and get the ladder." It was already too late though. He was climbing up the shelves. When he reached her, he grabbed her around the waist and pulled her close to him. She had her back up against his chest. Her legs and arms were dangling, one hand clutching the bag of vermiculite. He climbed back down, holding her like a sack of beans.

When they reached the bottom, he set her down and turned her around. He was visibly upset. His hands were shaking and he was out of breath. "You scared me to death."

"I'm sorry, Jeff. I was okay. I would have been able to climb down. You shouldn't get so worried about me. You'll have a stroke or something." His breathing was slowing down and his hands had stopped shaking where they held her shoulders.

"Victoria, we need to talk. Come to my office for a minute."

She looked around hoping to find the customer she was helping. Maybe that would distract him, but she was nowhere in sight. Jeff had her by the elbow and was propelling her to the office. His tension was making her nervous. She'd had a number of accidents. "I suppose they were pretty much due to my carelessness, that and clumsiness."

"Damn right that was due to carelessness," Jeff huffed.

She hadn't realized she'd said it out loud. "I was talking to myself."

Jeff pushed open the door to his office and pulled her in. He seated her in a chair and began to pace. He ran his hand through his hair. She couldn't help but watch the way the silky waves of brown hair fell right back in place. Not like Joe's hair. His stays mussed when he runs his hands through it. She panicked for a minute until she realized that she hadn't said that out loud.

"Vic, I really enjoy working with you."

"I enjoy working with you, too, Jeff." Victoria looked at him and widened her eyes in question.

"But...I'm starting to feel like you're a liability."

Victoria widened her eyes even more, this time in concern.

"Don't look at me like that, Vic. It won't work."

"Are you firing me? Oh, please, Jeff, don't fire me. I love this job." She jumped to her feet and hurried over to him. She looked up into his eyes imploringly.

He turned around and walked to the other end of the room. He ran both hands through his hair this time, one at a time. It still fell back into place. He turned back around, a little more composed. "Victoria..."

He must be really mad. He never calls me Victoria. She widened her eyes again.

"Since you came to work here I have happened across you *numerous* times in some sort of *perilous* bind."

"You're being dramatic."

"I am not being dramatic."

"You're exaggerating."

"I am not exaggerating." His voice was starting to get louder. "Vic..."

"You're firing me. I can't believe it." Victoria sounded hysterical. Her voice shook. She was fighting tears. Now she started to pace. She ran her hands through her hair, knowing it would probably not fall back in place.

Jeff stopped her by putting his hands on her shoulders from behind. "I'm not firing you. I wouldn't do that without giving you a chance to change."

"Change?" Victoria turned around and looked up at him.

"I'm sending you to a workplace safety seminar. I've been thinking about this for a while, but what just happened out there convinced me. Otherwise, it's just not safe for you to work here." He finished and dropped his hands.

"A workplace safety seminar, how long is it?"

"Three days. There's a group putting one on here in Atlanta in two weeks. I think I can still get you in." He went back to his desk and started rifling through papers. "I know that notice is here somewhere."

"What a waste of time. I'll be more careful. I promise."

"Vic, I just feel like you're thinking like a young person. You don't realize that you're not invincible. I think this will put things into perspective for you." Still looking down at the papers on his desk, he didn't see the expression on her face change.

"Put what things into perspective for me?"

"Like what could happen to a person your age if

she fell from twenty feet up onto a concrete floor." He was still rifling through papers.

"A person my age?"

Jeff stopped what he was doing and looked up at her. The eyes that had been so wide and beseeching were now quite narrow.

"Vic, I'm just concerned about you." He shuffled his feet nervously.

"You think I'm old."

"I didn't say that." Jeff was looking nervously around the room now. "I just meant...at our age, we have to be a little more careful."

"I'm a lot older than you. If you think you need to be more careful, you must think I should live in a padded room."

"Okay, I've handled this badly." Jeff was looking at the floor now. "I just think this seminar will be beneficial for you."

"Well, you'd better get me signed up for one soon. Otherwise, I might not live to see it." Victoria turned and walked out of the room with her chin held high and her hands fisted at her side.

"Shit," Jeff said out loud.

"I went to see Mom today," Victoria said to Joe. They were at dinner in The Place Around The Corner, their regular restaurant. They didn't go out much, but when they did, it was usually this place. It was easy and the food was good, didn't cost too much, either. Not exciting, of course.

"How's she doing? I need to go with you some-time soon. I haven't seen her lately."

"It's hard for me. She's gotten so feeble. You probably should go. She really likes you, and I'm afraid she might not be around much longer." Her eyes clouded a little.

"Really, Victoria?" Joe sat back and looked at her. "I didn't realize things had gotten so bad." He seemed surprised. Her mother had been aging fast for a while now. Apparently, he hadn't noticed or he'd been pretending not to.

Joe's parents had died when he was a child. An aunt and uncle, who were much younger than his parents, raised him. In fact, they weren't much older than Joe. His aunt, his mother's sister, was only eighteen when she inherited him. He was five years old. She'd married at twenty-two. Her husband was only twenty-three. They had been a happy fam-ily, but a young one. They'd raised Joe and their own children who were in their forties now, but they were still very active people.

Victoria had come along late. Her parents hadn't planned to have children. They were both professionals and a child really didn't fit in. They'd loved her, but she wasn't their main focus.

"Joe, she's ninety three years old. It's hard for you to relate, with Johnny and Sue still traveling the world the way they do. I keep expecting a call from the home telling me of some disaster."

"Has she seen a doctor? Maybe something could be done," Joe said, looking at his plate.

"I don't think they've found a cure for old age," Victoria snapped. She looked at Joe. He really wasn't paying much attention. He just didn't understand. As good as he was, there were some things that she couldn't get support on. There are a lot of things that he does support me on, she reminded herself. She would have to handle this on her own. It was hard, though.

She walked into work the next day preoccupied with her mother. She'd left the home feeling very concerned, hadn't gotten any encouragement from Joe. She went directly to her locker, unloaded her belongings, went into the potting room and started to work on potted arrangements.

Maybe it was time to have her mother moved to the convalescent care part of the home. "I'm just not sure that assisted living is enough any more."

"Talking to yourself again, Vic?" Jeff came into the room.

"I like talking to myself. I wouldn't want to miss out just because I have to hold both sides of the conversation." She didn't look up from her work. Tears were threatening and she wanted to keep them to herself.

"What's up? You looked upset when you walked past my office. Is something wrong?"

"It's my mom." She brushed away a tear. "You think I'm old. I was a late baby, so she's really old. I just don't know how to take care of her." Why had she said anything about that? If Joe didn't understand, and he had known her mother for thirty-three years, then why did she think that Jeff would?

"I don't think you're old," Jeff said. "Where does your mom live?" he asked.

"She lives in an elderly community. They have assisted living, but they also have convalescent care. Right now she's in assisted living, but I saw her yesterday and I'm concerned. If anything happened, I'm not sure she could get the help she would need."

"How does she feel about going to convalescent care?"

"I don't know. I haven't brought it up." Victoria looked at Jeff. He seemed really interested.

"Is your mother still lucid or is she confused?"

"No, she understands what's going on, but she falls asleep in the middle of conversations, and she doesn't hear very well. She refuses to wear a hearing aid. I'm worried."

"Does she wear an alarm that goes off if she falls or has a disaster in the kitchen or bathroom?"

"Yes, I got her one of those a long time ago, but what if she takes it off to go to bed and then has to go to the bathroom or something and..." Victoria started to cry. The tears just wouldn't stop. She put her hands to her face and sobbed. She hadn't realized how tense she was.

She felt strong hands on her shoulders. Jeff turned her around and held her to his chest. She cried for a few minutes. His shirt was saturated with tears when she got hold of herself again.

"I'm sorry." She hiccupped. "I didn't realize how upset I was about this."

"I know how you feel. I've watched both of my parents grow old and die. I was a late baby too. It's so hard to switch roles. Some part of you still sees them as the person you can go to for answers, but now when you go to them, you realize that if anyone needs answers, they'll have to come from you." He paused. He was still holding her. Her sobs had subsided, but he still stroked her hair. "The scary thing is that these questions are new and you're not at all sure you can find the answers."

Victoria lifted her head and looked into Jeff's eyes. "I don't know what to do. I want to take care of her, but she's such an independent person. I don't want to intrude. Besides, she gets mad when I do anything."

"Talk to her. Tell her about your concerns. Find out what her feelings are. Then think about what action you should take." Jeff set her away from him by her shoulders and looked into her eyes. "You'll do the right thing, I'm sure."

"Jeff, you've become such a good friend. I appreciate that. I haven't always had a lot of friends. Joe's great, but some things he just can't relate to."

Jeff put his hand under her chin and lifted it so that they were looking at each other. "You know

I wanted it to be more than friendship." He paused and searched her eyes. "When you first came, I sensed that things weren't good in your marriage. I thought maybe I had a chance. But now I think things are better between you and Joe." He looked at her for confirmation. "I guess I'll have to settle for friendship."

Victoria stepped back, wanting to put some distance between them. She thought maybe Jeff was going to kiss her and was afraid of what her reaction would be.

"Really, Jeff, you were attracted to me?"

"You sound so surprised. Why?"

"Well, after all, I'm not young and pretty any more." She looked down at her feet.

"You're not young, but you're definitely pretty." Jeff smiled. "But that's not what attracted me to you. It was the way you spoke up to me for the job that attracted me at first. Insisting that you were strong enough, even showing me your muscle." Jeff laughed. "Then when you came to work you were so determined to do a good job. It's hard to find people with that determination any more." Jeff stepped forward and took hold of her wrist when she tried to step back again. "I think you're great, Vic. If I can't explore a romantic connection with you, I'll be happy with being a friend."

"I think that's the nicest thing anybody's ever said to me."

"Don't cry again. My shirt is just starting to dry out from the last time." Jeff leaned toward her and kissed her check.

"Victoria?" She jumped at the sound of Joe's voice.

"Joe?" She definitely sounded guilty. "What are you doing here? Is something wrong?"

"If there is, I didn't know about it." Joe had his arms folded across his chest in a defensive posture. "I have some news for you and wanted to give it to you right away. I was out anyway and thought I'd drop by. I'm glad I did. Could I see you alone?"

She glanced at Jeff who had let go of her wrist and stepped away from her. "I'll just be in my office if you need me, Vic." He left the room. Joe walked over to where she stood and looked closely at her.

"You've been crying. What's wrong?"

"I was just upset about Mom. Jeff was talking to me about it. He was a late baby, too. His parents have both died. He understands what I'm going through." She was talking fast and sounded defensive. She took a deep breath and tried to calm down.

"And he was comforting you?"

"That's right."

"Comforting you includes kissing you?"

"It was a friendly kiss on the cheek," she said. There was a warm feeling growing in her chest. "Joe, are you jealous?" she said, sounding surprised and a little bit excited.

"Damn right I'm jealous!" Joe said it so sharply that Victoria jumped.

A slow smile started at her mouth and spread to her eyes, eventually engaging her entire face. "That's great!" she said.

"What do you mean, that's great?" Joe scowled. "I'm going to stop at the office on my way out and extend a warning to that man—Stay away from my wife!"

"Okay," she said, and then laughed. "As long as you don't hit him or anything."

"I'm not a violent man, but I will hit him if I ever catch him kissing you again."

Victoria giggled a little then straightened her face when she saw the stormy expression on his.

"What's gotten into you, Victoria? I don't think this is funny."

"I'm sorry, I just can't believe frumpy little me could inspire jealously in anyone. It's kind of invigorating." She turned and started working on the pots again. "So what's the good news? Why did you drop by?"

Joe didn't respond for a moment. "Well, I talked to Brad and he said that it would be fine for you to use his yard to design a garden. The house is finished, but he's taking his family on vacation for two weeks so they won't move in right away. He said he'd like to look at the plans when you're finished. They don't have a landscaper yet." He leaned on the counter she was working on and folded his arms. "However, I'm not sure I want you working here anymore, after what I just saw."

"Joe, that's dumb, besides it isn't up to you where I work." She smiled wickedly. Then looking at Joe, she stopped. What was that look in his eyes? Was it fear? "You're not really concerned about my relationship with Jeff, are you?"

"Yes, I am." His eyes searched her face. "And I wish you weren't so happy about it."

"Joe, he's become a very dear friend. I won't give

that up for anything in the world, but I'm married to you."

"You told me you didn't love me anymore." He sounded hurt.

She hadn't thought of his feelings at all when she'd said that. "Selfish Bitch."

"What?"

"Nothing, I was talking to myself. Joe, I didn't say I didn't love you. I said I couldn't feel it. I said I couldn't feel love for the girls, either. But I must love them. I'm their mother." She turned back to her work.

"Can you feel it now, Victoria?" Joe said so quietly that she wasn't sure she'd heard it.

She thought about it for a minute. "I don't know." They were both silent for a few minutes.

"When are you off again?" Joe asked.

"Thursday."

"We'll go up together. I'll take some work to do and you bring your art supplies. We'll make a day of it."

"Sounds like fun. I want to bring Ethel. Is that okay?"

"Of course." Joe started to leave then turned back. Victoria heard him approach her from behind. He took her by the elbow and turned her to face him. He lowered his mouth to hers and kissed her. Gently at first, then increasing the pressure and flicking her lips with his tongue. He slowly took her bottom lip between his teeth, tugging slightly and releasing. He looked at her for a second then brushed her lips with his once more, turned and left the room.

She was a little bit breathless as she walked to

the door to watch him go. He went across the shop to Jeff's office, knocked and went inside.

She turned back into the room, flattened herself against the wall beside the door and pressed her hand to her chest. Her heart was beating fast. "Oh, my God, this is fun." Feeling wicked, she smiled and went back to her work.

That afternoon she went by her mother's apartment on the way home. She knocked. As usual she had to unlock the door and go in.

"Mom," she called. There was no answer. The television was not on and she suddenly had an uneasy feeling. She went into the living room. It was empty. Feeling panicky, she went into the bedroom. The door was open, so she didn't knock. The bedroom was empty, too. Becoming more concerned, she looked at the closed bathroom door. Cautiously, she knocked on the door. "Mom, are you in there?" No answer. She slowly opened the door. The room was empty. "Oh, shit!" She sat down on the toilet and let out her breath. "I've been holding my breath the whole time. I can't believe I didn't faint. I've got to get a hold of myself."

She heard the front door open and close. "Tori!" her mother's voice called.

Victoria's legs were too shaky to stand on so she called out. "I'm in here."

Her mother came around the corner into the room looking anxious. Finding Victoria sitting on the toilet, she said, "What's wrong, honey, are you sick?" She put her hand on Victoria's forehead to feel for a fever.

Victoria started to laugh, maybe just a little hysterically. "I'm okay, Mom. I was worried about you. When I didn't find you here, I guess I panicked."

Her mother smoothed Victoria's hair away from her face and looked into her eyes. "Why, honey, did you forget that I play Bingo on Tuesday afternoons?"

"I did." Victoria was just a little too shaken to say much more.

"Well, this brings up something I've been meaning to talk to you about." Her mother kissed her on the top of the head, and said, "Let's not talk in the bathroom, though. Let's go out into the living room." She turned and walked away. Victoria took a deep breath and got up. Still feeling a little shaky, she went into the living room.

"Can I get you a glass of wine?" her mom called from the kitchen.

"No thanks."

She came out of the kitchen with a glass of wine. "I'll have one. Would you like some water or ice tea?"

"No thanks."

Her mother settled into the chair and sipped her wine for a minute. Victoria noticed that she was wearing her hearing aid.

"Tori, I love you." She turned her attention to her daughter and just looked at her.

"I love you too, Mom."

"Honey, you need to back off."

"What?" The statement startled Victoria. "What have I done? Does it bother you when I come to visit you? What do I do wrong?"

"You look at me like you think I'm going to die any minute. You look sad all the time. You won't let me do anything myself. I can't even tend my own roses." She took another sip of wine.

"Mom, don't drink so fast. It'll make you sick."

Her mother turned her head and gave her a cold stare.

"I'm sorry I said that." Victoria looked at her hands. "Tell me what to do, Mama." She was surprised. She hadn't called her "Mama" since she was about six years old.

"Honey." Her mother reached over and patted her clasped hands. "Let me live out my life. I know what you're going through. Remember I had parents, too. I was older when you were born, so you probably don't remember them, but I did have parents. I had to do what you're doing now with me. That's why I've had such a hard time talking to you about it. I understand. I haven't wanted to hurt you, but I realized the last time you came to see me that I haven't been very nice to you lately, so I have to tell you how I'm feeling. I want us to be close."

"What have I done wrong?"

"If I said you'd done anything wrong, it would mean that loving me is wrong. I would never say or feel that. But, I'm okay, Tori, I'm old. Nobody knows how much longer I'll live. I could go tomorrow, or I could be here for another ten years. At this point I can still take care of myself. If I need your help, I'll tell you." She squeezed her daughter's hands and looked into her eyes, then turned back and took another sip of wine. "And another thing, I've been drinking wine for a lot of years and at ninety three years old, if I want to get drunk, I will." She laughed.

"Oh, Mom, I love you so much. What if you need help and can't get it?" Victoria was crying now.

"Then I won't get it. That's still my decision to make. If I get where I can't make decisions for myself, then you'll have to make them. But, I can do it for myself now." She rocked back in the chair for a minute. They were both silent. "I want you to know that I'm happy. I've had a wonderful life. I had a wonderful partner. I had a wonderful career. When I look at you, I feel like I've made a wonderful contribution to the future. Not to mention my two beautiful granddaughters. But, I've earned time for myself. And that's what I'm having now."

"You don't want me to come to see you anymore?" Victoria asked, crying openly now.

"Of course I do. I just want you to stop hanging over me. Let me enjoy the status I've earned in this life. When the end comes, I'll be ready. But until then, I'm happy to be right where I am." She pulled her legs up in the rocking chair and let gravity make it rock.

"What about your roses?" Victoria's voice sounded small.

"When I need help with them, I'll tell you. I like weeds, at least some of them. I pull the ones I don't like."

Victoria laughed. "I love you, Mom."

"I love you too, honey. Now, it's time for you to go. I'm sure Joe is hungry and it's time for Jeopardy."

Victoria watched the landscape out of the car window. She and Joe were on their way to Villa Rica, to start work on her garden plans. She hadn't packed a picnic, but Joe had said not to worry. He said there were plenty of places to eat in Villa Rica. She was excited about it. She brought along all of her pencils and a thick sketchpad and a folding chair that she could move around easily. They had started early. It was nearly midsummer, but the air was still cool and crisp at that time of day.

"We're almost there," Joe said. "The turnoff is right along here somewhere. It's a new subdivision, but Brad's house is the first one on his street, so there isn't much going on around it. We'll have lots of peace and quiet."

"Good. I guess I'll have to learn to work with activity around, but for the first job it'll be nice to have no distractions." She looked out the window again and was silent for a minute. "I hope I can do this. Nothing has meant so much to me in a long time."

"I think you'll do well." They didn't talk for a few minutes. "Victoria, I hope you don't mind, but I took that sketch you did of the yard with Ethel in it to the framers. I want to hang it in my office. After I took it, I felt like maybe I should have asked you.

I wouldn't have gone into your notebook to get it or anything, but you left it on the kitchen counter." Joe kept his eyes on the road the whole time he talked. He sounded uncomfortable.

She hadn't even thought of that picture since she'd finished it. He wanted to hang it on his office wall. That was nice. "That's fine, Joe, I'm glad you like it that much." She felt warm inside. Maybe she did have some talent.

"You know what else I've been thinking? You should have an office, too. Well, I guess it would be more of a studio. We don't have a lot of spare money, but if we did most of the work ourselves, we could turn the guest room into a studio for you. That little desk you have in there isn't really sufficient."

"Really, Joe? I've been wishing I had a studio. I wanted to leave the girls' rooms the way they are so they would know that any time they need to come home they're welcome."

"Well, that's what I thought, too. But, unless we have a guest and both girls are home at the same time—and that's highly unlikely—we don't need a guest room." He was silent for a minute. "We could put a futon in there or something, just in case."

They traveled in silence the rest of the way. They had turned off the highway onto a back road. It wound around a little. The landscape was beautiful. Victoria was getting ideas about landscaping to blend with the natural lay of the land.

Joe pulled off the road to a two-story house with a short driveway and small front yard. "This is it," he said. Victoria's heart fell. There was no yard at all. It was on a pie shaped lot in a cul-de-sac. The front yard was no bigger that a few feet. It was Georgia red clay and weeds. It needed landscaping, but it wouldn't take much to do it.

Joe said, "This part will be easy. It's the back yard that will challenge you." He got out of the car and signaled her to follow. She followed him around the house to the back yard.

"Oh," she said on a breath. "It's beautiful." The pie shape continued. It became wider at the back. The terrain was rolling. It slanted down from the back of the house. There was a slight hill to the right of the property. Then it gradually tapered down to a wooded area with a small pathway through the woods that opened to a pond. Only the beginning of the pond could be seen from where she stood. The ground around the house was torn up from construction, but where the forest started, everything was completely natural.

"I hope I can do it justice," she whispered.

"I'm sure you will." Joe put his arm around her shoulder and kissed her on the head. "Let's get your stuff." He went back to the car and started unloading.

She sat under a tree, sketching her ideas. The sun was hot, but in the shade she was okay. She had spent the first hour walking around the property and trying to learn the yard. She wanted to know which parts of it were high and would be drier, which parts would tend to collect water, where the sun hit in the morning, and estimated where it would hit in the afternoon. She had to know these things before she could choose which plants would be right.

Ethel had run around at her heels the whole

time, chasing bugs and sniffing the air occasionally, but she'd responded to all of Victoria's commands. She was such a smart little dog. Victoria looked down at her now, sleeping at her feet. She was so cute, such a good companion. She had finally sat down and begun to draw. There were several pages of ideas. The work was so much fun that the time passed without notice. Joe had set up a card table and was working on some plans next to her, but she was hardly aware of him.

Her stomach growled and she looked at her watch. It was 1:15. "Joe, I'm hungry. Where should we go to eat?"

"Not a problem," he said, getting up from his work. He disappeared around the house. She continued to work, trying to wind it up so she could pack things up and head out with him. Just as she had gotten to a stopping point, Joe came back around the house with a picnic basket in his hand. She recognized it as one that they had used when the kids were young. It had been a wedding gift from his aunt and uncle, and had been well used over the years. It contained plastic plates and utensils, a picnic blanket tablecloth, and a cooling compartment so you could keep food cold.

"Did you pack lunch?" she said, surprised.

"Actually, I had it catered," Joe said. He put the basket down on the ground under the tree and opened it. He looked around at her and said, "I know we can't afford it, but I thought this was a special occasion." He turned back to his work.

"What's the occasion?"

"We're doing something together for the first

time in years. Okay, its work, but we're both enjoying it." He stopped and looked at her. "At least I am. Are you?"

"I am."

Joe spread the cloth and took out the plates, napkins and utensils. He looked inside the cooler and said, "Let's see. We have sandwiches, turkey and swiss, your favorite. There's potato salad, carrot salad, your favorite, cole slaw, my favorite." He paused and flashed her a sly grin. "And for dessert, there are brownies, our favorite. And what is this?" Acting surprised, he reached into the basket. "Champagne." He turned to her smiling broadly.

"Joe, you planned all of this?"

"Oh yes, I did. I wanted us to have a nice day together. Can I see your sketches?" He was taking the foil off of the champagne.

"I'm not ready to show them to anyone yet," she said. "Joe, after my last experience, I'm not sure about champagne."

"You won't drink too much this time. I'm here, and I'll distract you. One glass won't hurt you. It won't taste bad to you, either. You didn't vomit champagne. You vomited chardonnay.

"Don't remind me."

"You know I didn't take advantage of you that night. I hope you appreciate that."

She laughed. "I'm not sure. Maybe if you had I wouldn't have been so sick."

Joe extended his hand to her. She took it and he pulled her up from the chair she had been sitting in all morning and motioned her to sit on the blanket. They both sat down cross-legged. He pulled the food out and they served themselves. They were silent while they ate. Both of them were hungry. They hadn't eaten much that morning and had both been lost in their work until after lunchtime. After they slowed down a little, Joe poured two glasses of champagne and handed one to her.

"To you, Victoria." He held his glass up. "My beautiful and talented wife."

"You're being very nice to me today, Joe."

"It's easy to be nice to you."

They sipped champagne for a few minutes. Joe had brought throw pillows and he stretched out and put his head on one of them. He folded his hands behind his head and looked at the sky through the tree. "I hope this works for you. If you don't want to show me your work, would you tell me how you feel about it? Is the property something you want to work with?"

"Oh, it's beautiful, Joe. Don't you think? I think I need to do something that blends with the natural flora, but something that you can maintain. I mean with a little bit of work you can keep it from becoming jungle, but it's still natural." She stretched out next to him with her head on her pillow and folded her hands over her stomach.

"That's what I was thinking. I usually try to do that with my buildings, too. I mean, it's different. I usually have to blend with the buildings around them, but I always like to make them look pleasant, but not out of place."

She looked sideways at him. She hadn't thought about what he did in years. How selfish could you be? "What are you working on now?" she asked, feeling guilty.

"Actually, it's a house. I haven't done a house in a long time." He yawned and smiled at her. "I always get a little sleepy after a good meal." He yawned again. "I got a call from a developer who's got some property in Buckhead. He bought up a couple of three acre lots and is going to divide them up and put houses on smaller lots. I've done work for him before, industrial, of course. Anyway, he wanted to see some house plans from me. They need to be upscale, but not too big for the lot. He wants tasteful. I thought it might be a nice change."

"You're really an artist, aren't you, Joe?"

"No. I would say I'm more of an engineer. My plans are practical first, then aesthetic."

"I don't know. I think you're an artist." She turned over onto her stomach and propped on her elbows to look at him.

He turned over on his side and put his hand behind her head. He pulled her close to him and kissed her. Ethel came running out of the woods and jumped between them. "Your timing sucks, Ethel," he said. He tossed her a half sandwich and she went to the edge of the blanket to munch.

"Where were we?" He reached for Victoria again. She pulled back a little, but he came after her. He gently pulled her closer. She was feeling a little shy. They hadn't actually had sex since the time he'd told her not to pretend. She was surprised how shy she felt. The champagne had loosened her up a little, and she could remember how much she had wanted him the night she got drunk on wine. Of course, they weren't going to have sex now. They were outside in broad daylight. They weren't at home in their bed. Maybe they would just make out a little, like when they were kids.

He was kissing her now. She let herself go with it. He stroked her cheek with his hand, and then curled his finger under her jaw. His mouth massaged her lips. He eased his hand down her neck to her shoulder and stroked her collarbone with his thumb. "You're so beautiful," he whispered.

She responded. It was different than when she was young and masculine attention had first started. Then it had made her feel powerful, but not really desirous. Now she didn't want it to stop. She kissed him back. Her arm went around his neck and he rolled over so that she was on her back. He put his leg over hers, lowered his hand to her breast and squeezed lightly. He continued to kiss her, moving to her cheek, her jaw, her neck. His hand went down to her waist and eased up under her shirt.

"Joe, maybe this is going too far." She sounded breathless even to herself. "We're not at home in bed."

"There's nobody here. We're completely alone." He didn't stop. He took her mouth again and kissed her until she couldn't think. Then his hands were both behind her, unfastening her bra. He did it so smoothly. Had he practiced? They hadn't had to do that for a long time. He stopped and sat up on his knees, straddling her. He pulled her top off and removed the bra.

"Joe, this is crazy, we're old people. We can't do this." She was laughing. They were acting like kids.

"We can do this." He lowered himself back down on top of her and kissed her again. Moving down to her breasts, he caressed them, lowered his mouth to one nipple, then the next. She gasped at the sensations that ran through her."

"Joe," she whispered. "What are loins?"

"What?" His words sounded muffled with her nipple in his mouth.

"In romance novels they always say that when someone is aroused they feel it in their loins. Where are they?" Her voice was husky.

"Here." He moved his hand down to her lower abdomen and spread across it. His thumb touched one side and his fingers touched the other. He moved his mouth down her belly to his hand.

"That's it. That's where I feel it."

He pulled her pants down over her bottom to her thighs.

"Joe, stop. I'll be completely naked if you don't." He still had all of his clothes on. Suddenly, she didn't care about propriety any more.

She grabbed hold of his shirt and pulled it out of his pants. Joe looked up at her face and smiled. He helped her pull the shirt off over his head then moved to the bottom of her feet, grabbed her pants legs and pulled.

"Now it's my turn," she said, and rolled him over on his back. Going to her knees, she unbuckled his belt and pants. He raised himself up on his heels and pulled his pants off over his feet. Then he rolled Victoria over on her back and kissed her again. They were both completely naked now. He moved down her body slowly, kissing her all the way. She wasn't quite sure what to do, but the sensations were making it hard to think.

Joe moved until his head was between her legs. He started to lick her, starting with the top of her and slowly moving to the most sensitive part. He inserted a finger into her and she gasped. "My God, that's good. Have we done this before?" He didn't respond. He continued to love her with his mouth. He moved up again in a minute and kissed her. She could taste herself on him. He stretched out on top of her and looked into her eyes.

"I love you, Victoria."

"Love me, Joe."

He eased inside of her then. It felt so good, stretching her, filling her. He started a rhythmic movement, stroking in and out. She could feel the tension mounting, wondered if he would make it until she was ready. Other times he hadn't, but she hadn't been so ready before. Yes, it was building.

"You feel like heaven," he whispered, and kissed her. She was lost. All she could do was feel. He continued to move and the feeling continued to mount, and then she climaxed. He did seconds later.

She was breathless, spent, relaxed. Her breath came rapidly. Joe was lying on top of her and it felt like heaven. His breathing was rapid, but slowing. She wrapped her arms around him and squeezed, kissed his cheek.

The weight of him felt lovely, like a warm shower or a heavy blanket. It would be nice to stay that way forever. Something wet touched her cheek and she turned her head to look at Ethel. The little dog was anxious about something.

"Joe, Ethel's worried about something. Is some-one here?" Suddenly she was horrified that they would get caught like this. Joe moved off of her and turned over. "I don't think so, but let's get dressed so we don't have to worry about it." He started to gather his clothes then stopped and looked at her. "I hope you enjoyed that as much as I did."

That was strange, he'd never been the one that was insecure, but he needed her reassurance. "It was heaven, Joe." She kissed him on the shoulder. He put his arms around her and held her tightly for a minute.

Ethel started to bark. "Oh, no! Someone is here and you and I are buck-naked." Victoria pushed away and started scrambling into her clothes.

"It's okay, Victoria, we're married and we're on private property."

"I know, but it's not our private property." She was pulling on her pants. Her blouse was buttoned wrong.

Joe laughed and started to dress. Ethel was get-ting frantic now. Joe stopped to listen with his pants on, and his shirt in his hand. There was the sound of something tramping through the bushes. Whatever it was, it was small.

"I don't know what it is, sweetheart, but it's not a person."

Victoria stopped and listened. "You're right. It's small and maybe hurt or handicapped." She started to walk toward the noise. "Joe!" she called. "It's a kit-ten and it is hurt."

Joe started in her direction, pulling his shirt on as he went. He looked where she pointed. There was a little striped kitten sitting back on its haunches staring at them. Its back right leg was stuck out at a strange angle and there was dried blood on it just above the knee.

"Its leg is injured," Victoria said. She reached down to pick up the kitten, but as her hand came close, it hissed and batted at her. "Joe, I think it's wild. What should we do?"

"Victoria, it's a kitten. How much damage can it do?" He reached down and scooped the little cat up. "Ahhh, shit!" he yelled, as he dropped the little creature back to the ground. "The little bastard bit me."

"Well, now you know how much damage it can do." She laughed.

"I'm not laughing, Victoria."

She ran back to the picnic area calling, "Watch where he goes."

"Damn right I'll watch where he goes, as far away from me as possible."

She picked up the empty picnic basket and ran back to where they had spotted the kitten. "Where is he?" Joe pointed to a bush. "You chase him out from under the bush toward me." At that moment, Ethel came running over from the blanket and started to bark at the kitten. Ethel was so small that when she darted into the bush, she was able to get almost to him. The little cat came running out and Victoria put the picnic basket down over him.

Everyone took a deep breath. The kitten was screeching inside the basket and Ethel was barking outside of it.

"Joe," Victoria said calmly. "Go and get me the table cloth." He didn't move. She looked up at him and saw him scowling at her and holding his finger. "We can't leave an injured kitten to die in the woods, can we?" she asked. He still didn't move. "Please, Joe? Let me catch him, then I'll see to your wound." He took a deep breath and went off for the cloth.

When he came back, Victoria took the cloth from him and slid it under the basket. The kitten had stopped screaming, it was whimpering pathetically now. She looked at Joe. His expression was softening. He looked back at her and went to the other side of the basket. Together they eased the blanket under the basket to trap the kitten inside. When they had it completely underneath, they turned the basket, holding the cloth to seal it and closed the lid with the kitten trapped inside.

Victoria looked at Joe, triumphantly. But he was still scowling. She looked at his finger and stopped smiling. "That kitten really got you." There was blood dripping from the finger. She took his hand and looked at it. The little cat had bitten right through the fingernail. "Ouch, that must really hurt." She looked up at him.

"It does, but what hurts worse is that it's my own stupid fault."

"Well, Joe, don't be hard on yourself. I was tempted to grab for him myself."

"Yes, but you didn't."

"No, I didn't." She turned so he couldn't see her smile, and picked up the basket. "Do you have a first aid kit in your car? You used to keep one."

"Yes, I do."

After cleaning the wound with the antiseptic pad in the first aid kit and applying a pressure bandage, she kissed it and then kissed his mouth. "You will let me take him to a vet to see what can be done for him, won't you?"

"We don't have to keep him, do we?" He was still frowning.

"Of course not, I'll find him a home."

"Right." He looked at her. "We've got a cat."

"Really, I'll find him a home, Joe, we can't leave him here."

He looked at the basket. The big frightened eyes peered out through the holes in the weave. "No we can't."

The two of them packed up their belongings together. Joe was calming down from his ordeal. The wound was nasty and it probably hurt, but he would be okay. Victoria watched him as he worked. She felt guilty, but she wasn't quite sure why.

"Joe, I had a really nice day. Thanks," she said, as they pulled out of the driveway.

"I had a nice day, too." He smiled.

"You're not really mad about the kitten, are you?" she asked.

"No. I wanted to help as much as you did. I just didn't expect him to bite me."

"He's afraid. He's probably wild and doesn't know that most humans are good. I don't even know if we'll be able to tame him, but if we can at least find out what's wrong with his leg, then he can go back to the wild."

The little cat was on the back seat in the picnic basket. Ethel was sitting in Victoria's lap, but she had her paws on the seat back and was keeping constant vigil on the cat.

"You'll tame him, and you'll name him, and he'll probably be with us for fifteen years." He sounded resigned.

"I'm sorry, Joe." She looked out the window.

"Don't be sorry. It's who you are."

"It's a part of me that you don't like."

Joe was silent for a while. He looked ahead at the highway. It was midafternoon. Victoria had wanted to leave right away so they could take the little cat to her vet in Atlanta.

"Actually, I like that part about you, too. The way you take in strays." He spoke as if from far away. "Sometimes I wish we didn't have to try to save the world, but I like animals too."

"I couldn't believe it when the vet brought him out to me and plopped him down in my lap. I was afraid at first, after what he did to Joe," Victoria said to Jane and Lillian. She smiled down at the kitten in her lap. "She said they'd been able to handle him ever since he woke up from the anesthesia."

"He sure seems to like you now. I can hear him purring all the way over here," Jane said, from across the patio table. She and Lillian were over for lunch. Victoria had served them cold cuts and potato salad on the patio.

"What's his name?" Lillian asked.

"Theodore," Victoria said, as she put the kitten down in the little padded bed at her side. His leg was bandaged stiffly. He stood up, crawled out of the bed and walked away holding the bandaged leg at an angle from his body and walking on his other three legs.

"Where do you come up with these names, Tori?" Jane asked, laughing.

"He just looks like a Theodore to me. I thought about Fred, to go with Ethel, but it just didn't fit." She picked up the bowl of sorbet that was melting fast in the hot air.

Lillian cocked her head to one side. "He looks

like a Theodore to me, too. I doubt I would've thought of it, though. What was wrong with his leg?"

"It's a broken femur, the bone above his knee. The vet said it wasn't hard to set, but he'll have to wear that splint for a while. He gets around okay with it, though." They all looked at the little cat's progress through the grass. Ethel walked up to him and licked him on the head. He rubbed up against her. "They've become fast friends. I was worried at first. She was defensive about Joe. It was so cute; all nine pounds of her trying to protect one hundred and eighty pounds of Joe from three pounds of kitten." They all laughed.

"I can't believe he bit him. He seems so gentle now," Lillian said.

"Well, he was hurt and frightened. That's what animals do when they're hurt and frightened."

"You've always been an animal person, Tori," Jane observed. "I've always liked your pets, but never wanted one of my own. That's one way I could tell that you were depressed. You didn't have any pets."

"I wasn't really depressed. I just had a hard time making the transition between being a young woman with children and an old woman who is of no importance to anyone."

"You really were depressed, weren't you?" Lillian looked at her. "I can't imagine you feeling like you were of no importance to anyone."

"Well, my children have moved all the way across the country to get away from me."

"I don't believe that's true. Kids just need their space. My parents live in Idaho. I still love them, but I just want some independence," Lillian said.

"She's right, Tori. Ellen and Patty just needed to become independent. It's not you they're running from. They're just living their own lives." Jane finished her sorbet and set down the bowl.

"I'm sure you're right." Victoria continued to eat her sorbet, wishing she hadn't even started the conversation.

She was relieved when Lillian changed the subject. "So, Jane, why do you call her Tori?"

"That's what her mother calls her."

"How long have you two known each other?"

"Forever, I lived next door to Tori when she was born. I was five years old and I loved to go over and play with her, even when she was in diapers. It was like having a live doll. I was her first and only babysitter." Jane smiled fondly at Victoria as she remembered.

"That's right," Victoria said. "I was an only child and so was Jane, so we decided that we'd adopt each other as sisters. I remember the day we made the decision. I even called her my big sister when I introduced her to people."

"That's funny, you always wanted to have a sister and I always wished I was an only child. I have six siblings, three older and three younger. Believe me, seven kids and two parents should never live under one roof. Nobody has any breathing room." She laughed. "That's one reason why I don't feel bad about living so far away from my parents. I don't think they've noticed I'm gone yet."

"I'm sure that's not true, Lillian," Victoria said.

"I'm only kidding." Changing the subject again

she said, "Are you two still planning to go down to Savannah next week?"

Victoria was startled. "Next week! Already?"

Jane looked at her warily. "You'd better not even try to weasel out of this," she said.

"No, I want to go, I'm just afraid to drive down by myself. The closer it gets, the more nervous I get."

"Tori, you're a big girl now. You can do it. And remember, you only have to drive alone one way. I'm coming back with you." She smiled. "I've arranged all sorts of great things to do. We're going parasailing, and I've got reservations at a great restaurant for Saturday night. We'll shop all morning."

"Parasailing?" Victoria's voice cracked. "Jane, I'm afraid of heights."

"You're afraid of everything. You'll get over it."

Joe came out of the kitchen door and walked over to the table. "Hello Jane, Lillian." He nodded at them both. He stood next to Victoria and put his hand on her shoulder. It was a sweet gesture and she blushed.

"Joe, you could have joined us for lunch," Jane said. "We don't bite."

"I had work to do." He sat down and picked up the pitcher of lemonade. He poured some into Victoria's empty glass and drank. "I had a late breakfast, so I wasn't hungry. I just wanted to come and say hello before you left."

"So, you don't mind Tori going to Savannah with me, do you?" Jane was obviously very comfortable with Joe. She had known him a long time. Lillian acted shy. He was older and so handsome.

"No, I don't mind," he said hesitantly. "I will

worry about her driving alone. I wish someone could go with her."

"Now don't be overly protective. She's a big girl." Jane looked over at her petite friend and laughed. "Well, okay, she's not a big girl, but she's a grown woman. She can handle it. I hadn't realized she was so sheltered."

"I guess you're right, but please do call me when you get there. Otherwise, I'll worry," Joe said to Victoria as he sipped his lemonade.

"Oh, I'll make sure she calls you right away. Do you want me to have her call you after we go parasailing, too?" Jane laughed.

"Parasailing?" Joe looked at Victoria. "You're afraid of heights. Why do you want to do a thing like that?"

She visibly bristled at his words. "I think it'll be fun." She hoped she sounded sure.

"Good for you, Tori," Jane said. "You can do anything you want, right?"

"Right," she said firmly, then, "I think," under her breath.

"We'll have a great time. You don't mind keeping the pets do you?" Jane looked back at Joe.

"I'm not crazy about keeping that cat." Joe looked in the direction of the little animals. He was scowling when he looked over there, but smiled when he saw the little kitten with the big splint all snuggled up to the fat puppy. "That dog of yours is a traitor, Victoria." He laughed. "She's gone over to the other side. You should have seen her, Jane, trying to protect me from him."

"That's what I heard."

"You're sure you can't go to Savannah next weekend." His question was directed at Lillian. She looked startled. Victoria was the only one who'd seen the awed look in her eyes while she was watching Joe's conversation with Jane. He is really a handsome man, she thought. Glancing down at his flat stomach, she wondered. Where did that paunch go? She'd noticed that he had one a couple of months ago. It was gone now.

"No." Lillian's voice squeaked a little. "I've got exams."

She's got a crush on him, Victoria thought. She was surprised to feel a little prickle of jealousy. How silly, but it was there just the same.

"Well, I guess I'll just have to trust you to take care of yourself." Joe turned to Victoria and kissed her lightly on the mouth. He stood up and said, "If you ladies will excuse me, I like to go for a jog about this time of day." He looked at his watch. "In fact, I'm a little late. The afternoon sun will be blazing if I don't get moving." He moved off in the direction of the house.

"I didn't know he was running, too." Jane followed him with her eyes.

"I didn't either." Victoria sounded distracted. She watched Joe as he walked toward the house. "He has a beautiful butt," she said. There was that ripple in her lower abdomen. Those loins of hers were acting up again.

"He does," Jane agreed, looking over at Victoria. "I guess things are better with you two."

"I guess."

The next day when she walked into the nursery, Jeff was standing in the door of his office. "Vic, come in here when you get settled, would you?"

"Sure," she said. He hadn't spent much time with her since the day Joe had stopped by. She had tried to find out what had transpired in the office, but neither of them was saying anything. She went to her locker and put her purse and lunch bag into it. She had left Ethel with Joe, hoping to ease the tension between Joe and Theodore. She went back to the office, knocked, and walked in. "Did you want to talk to me? I've been much more careful lately. I think that safety seminar was very helpful."

Jeff looked up from his plans and laughed. "You're not in any trouble, Vic. Come in and sit down. I want to hear about the drawings. Have you developed a landscape plan yet?"

"No." She sat down in the chair across the table from him. "I've drawn the yard the way it is now. I think I've got a pretty good feeling for it. I did everything you taught me, paced it out and looked for drainage, dry spots and wet. I think the sketch is pretty good." She smiled, remembering how her picture looked in the frame hanging in Joe's office.

"I'd like to see it." Jeff looked at her.

"Okay, I've got some ideas about landscaping. I haven't had a chance to sit down and draw them out yet, though. I plan to do that tonight." She smiled again, thinking about the room Joe was making into a studio for her. The two of them had cleared all the furniture out and painted it. They had found a drafting table online and ordered it. It would arrive in a week.

"What's made you so happy today? You keep smiling."

"I'm excited about my new studio. Joe and I are converting the guest room."

"Oh, really, that's great," he said. "Vic, I need to make reservations for the garden show in March. I get a better rate if I book them this far in advance. You are planning to go with me, aren't you?"

"Gosh, I haven't thought about that for a while." She looked down at her hands. She was concerned about how Joe would feel about it. She wished she knew what had gone on between them that day. "Give me a couple of days to make sure I don't have any family conflicts or anything, okay?" She looked up at him.

He smiled. He couldn't resist that under-the-brow look of hers. "Worried about how Joe will feel?"

"Well," she looked back down at her hands. "He seems to be concerned about my relationship with you." She could feel a smile tugging at the corners of her mouth.

"You're enjoying this, aren't you?" Jeff laughed and reached over to lift her chin. "I thought I saw a smile."

"Well, I have to admit, I haven't had any masculine attention in years. It's nice." She laughed and felt herself blush.

"It's not nice to play games with the men in your life, Vic." He was smiling, though. He didn't seem mad. "Did he tell you what I told him in my office that day?"

"No." She looked up at him, interested. "What?"

"I told him I could fall in love with you if I let myself, but I had enough conscience not to actively pursue another man's wife." He watched to see how that would affect her.

"No! You didn't tell him that!" She laughed. "Talk about playing games."

"I wasn't playing a game, Vic." He touched her cheek. "I could fall in love with you, but I won't let myself. So it's safe for you to come to the garden show with me." He turned back to his plans. "I want to make the reservations by the middle of next week. So make up your mind." Looking back at her he said, "I think this could be good for your career."

"Career, I've never thought of myself as having a career."

"Well, you do. It looks to me like you're interested enough."

When she got home that night, Joe was sitting in the living room looking at the family photo albums. There was a glass of wine sitting next to him. "Don't tell me you're drunk?" She laughed. She had never seen Joe drunk. He liked to have a drink once in a while, but it just didn't seem to affect him the way it did her.

"I've had half a glass of wine. I think I can handle it." They both laughed. "I'll be glad to take off my clothes, though, if you want me to." He got up and reached for her. Drawing her into his arms, he kissed her. She leaned into him and rested her head on his chest. He was so much taller than she, that he could rest his cheek against the top of her head.

"Maybe later," she said. "Right now I need to talk to you about something."

He leaned back and looked at her face. "Everything all right?" He searched her eyes.

"Oh yeah. Jeff just wants to make reservations for the garden show in D.C., in March. He gets a better price if he does it early. I just wanted to make sure you were comfortable with it."

Joe dropped his arms to his side and turned around. He picked up his wine glass and sipped. "Would it make any difference if I wasn't?" he asked.

"Probably not, Joe. Jeff said he thought it would be good for my career. I've never had a career before. I like the sound of it. I think if my plans are good he might consider using them in our display. Wouldn't that be great?"

"Yeah, it would be great. This trip would be great for him, too. He'd have you all to himself. You wouldn't be coming home to me every night."

"Oh Joe, that's dumb." She wasn't finding this fun anymore. Would he really try to interfere with this? It was so important to her. "I'm a fifty-four-year-old mother of two. I don't think I'm in danger of being seduced."

"He told me he was in love with you."

"He told you he could fall in love with me."

"The two of you have talked about this?" Joe looked up concerned.

"We're very good friends. I have to admit that it's

kind of nice knowing that I can still be attractive to someone, but we're just friends, very good friends."

"You're attractive to me."

"That doesn't count. You have to feel that way. Otherwise, why would you stay? You even liked me when I was pregnant."

He smiled. "You were beautiful when you were pregnant."

"Joe, your jealousy was fun at first, but give it up." She sat down in the chair across from him. "After all, I'm going away with Jane this weekend. You're not jealous of her."

He looked startled. "Jane's your sister!"

"No she isn't. How do you know I'm not a closet lesbian? We may have been having an ongoing affair all these years." She was getting into the ruse now. "Hell, I may have picked up Lillian because she's a pretty young thing." She laughed at his shocked expression.

"I'm not enjoying this, Victoria."

"That's because it's ridiculous." She leaned forward. "You've always trusted me before, Joe. Trust me now." She looked up at him from under her brows. His expression softened.

"That expression works every time." She laughed "It gets that same reaction from Jeff. I'll have to remember that." She got up and started toward the kitchen. "I'll get dinner started."

Joe followed her into the kitchen. He leaned on the counter while she pulled things out of the refrigerator. "Okay, I'll try not to be jealous. Of course, I trust you. It's him I don't trust."

"I trust him. He really is interested in my career.

He encourages me, and he even educates me. I really want to do this, Joe." She was cutting up onions now. She put them in a frying pan to sauté. "You know, you should get to know Jeff. You'd like him. He's got a great sense of humor. And he likes people."

"Maybe I will get to know him a little better." He sounded distant. She wondered what he was thinking.

"Oh, by the way, he's given me time off tomorrow to go to Villa Rica and look at the property again. I'll need directions from you. I'm going to work on my plans tonight and tomorrow morning. If I think they're any good, I'll show the sketches to Jeff tomorrow afternoon." She felt self-conscious. She could feel him watching her as she spoke.

"Will you show them to me first?" She looked up at him. He was studying her face.

She laughed. "Sure, I'll show them to you first."

Joe moved away and started setting the table. "I'll take you to Villa Rica."

"You don't have to do that. Can you spare the time?"

"I'll take the time."

Joe had gotten a call from a customer that morning and was unable to take her to Villa Rica. She was glad, really. She wanted to go by herself. He had given her directions, but it wasn't necessary.

She remembered the way. The morning was delightful. She spent it walking the terrain and sketching. She thought her plans were good. They needed work, of course, but she had time.

She started back at about 11:00 a.m. It would take her about an hour to get back. She slid a CD into the player, the *Nutcracker Suite*. There was a heady feeling about being all alone on the road. Maybe this trip to Savannah wouldn't be so bad. She really had been nervous about it, but this short drive had been nice. She felt empowered.

That evening after work, she pulled into the garage and ran through the house, looking for Joe. She found him in her studio assembling the drafting table. It must have arrived while she was gone.

"Joe," she called, and rushed into the room. "Jeff liked my plans. He said he wanted to use them for the garden show." She was beaming. "We'll miniaturize them, recreate Brad's yard in Villa Rica for the display. I'm so excited."

He looked up from his work and smiled at her. "That's great, sweetheart. I can't wait to see them." He got up and gave her a kiss on the cheek. "Your drafting table came. What do you think?"

"It's great. It came just in time." She ran her hand over the surface. "I'm so excited I can't sit still. Let's go out to dinner."

"Okay. We can't afford it, but I guess this a special occasion."

Victoria went into the bedroom to change her clothes. She was so happy about her new career. "Imagine that, little old me," she said out loud, realizing that she hadn't talked to herself for a while now. "Maybe you get over that when you have a life full of other people to talk to." She laughed at herself. "Or maybe not."

Victoria arrived in Savannah at four in the afternoon. The trip had gone smoothly. Once again, being on the road alone had felt empowering. She'd been so nervous that morning when she left that she'd held back tears until she was out of Joe's sight. Then she had actually cried. "What a baby!" she admonished herself out loud.

But then she put in a CD, dried her tears, and she was on her way. After that everything was great. She was a little bit nervous around Macon, where the road divided, but there was no problem knowing where to go. About an hour later, she had stopped for lunch. She took a few minutes to look through a gift shop and was on her way again. It was fun not having any deadlines or anyone to consider but herself.

The drive got a little long at the end. Feeling ready to have someone to talk to now, she pulled into the hotel and went to the front desk. Jane had left the key to the room with the clerk and a note. The note read:

I'll be in a meeting until 5:00, so go to the room and settle in. I'll be there right after the meeting.

Jane

The room was a typical motel room. There were two double beds and a desk. She put her bag on one of the stands. Jane's bag was on the other. Victoria took out the dress she had brought for dinner the next night and hung it up. It wasn't too badly wrinkled.

There was a small refrigerator in the hall going to the bathroom. She looked inside. There was a bottle of chardonnay. "Yuck!" There were a couple of cokes and some orange juice. She took out the orange juice and poured some into one of the bathroom cups. She pulled the book she was reading out of her suitcase and went out on the porch. The air always felt so nice at the ocean. It was moister, more humid, but a breeze always blew, so it didn't feel so hot.

Her mind drifted to her garden plans. She and Jeff had worked on them together. Jeff had made some suggestions, but for the most part, he liked her ideas. He had suggested a few changes to the plans themselves. After all, Jeff had been doing this for a long time. It was a family business, so probably all of his life.

Come to think of it, she really didn't know much about Jeff. She had spent so much time talking about herself she hadn't ever really asked him any questions. Some friend she was. Had he studied landscaping in school or had he just picked it up like she was doing? Had he ever been married? Did he have any children? Making a mental note to ask Jeff about himself, she went inside and got her garden plans from the bag she had packed them in.

She was lost in her work when Jane came in, and didn't hear the door open. She jumped when Jane spoke to her.

"I'm sorry; I didn't mean to startle you. I thought you heard me come in." Jane laughed. She was wearing a suit and looked so glamorous. Victoria felt dumpy beside her.

"That's okay. I was lost in my work."

Jane looked over her shoulder at the drawing. "That's great, Tori. I didn't know you could draw."

"That's what Joe said." She laughed. "Truth is I didn't know I could either. I've never tried before." She held the drawing out at arm's-length and looked at it critically. "You know it really isn't bad."

"Tori, it's good. You should frame it."

"Oh no, these are my garden plans. Oh!" she exclaimed. "I haven't told you the good news. Guess what?" Victoria's face was lit up like a Christmas tree.

"Don't tell me you're pregnant again." Jane looked horrified.

"Of course not, I'm post menopausal, remember?" Victoria laughed, and clutched her stomach. "Jane! Don't even suggest such a thing!"

They laughed heartily together. Jane said, "I just hadn't seen you so excited since you told me you were expecting Patricia. I guess I over reacted. So what's the good news?"

"Jeff is going to use my plans for our display in the garden show. He likes them that much. I'm going to the show in D.C. with him in March. I'm so excited. He called my job a career. Imagine that, Jane, me with a career."

"What's so surprising about that?" Jane went into the room. Victoria followed her in.

"Well, I'm just not the professional type."

"What's a professional type?" Jane was taking off her shoes and stockings.

"Well, someone like you, someone that wears a suit, and looks glamorous, and goes to meetings, and things like that." It sounded silly even to her.

"That's dumb, Tori." Jane looked at her closely. "I never realized you felt so inferior. I haven't done anything to make you feel that way, have I?"

"No, of course not. I just really never thought I could do anything but be a mom and a wife, and work at a grocery store as someone's flunky." She put her plans back in the bag and got out her cosmetic case. "I think I'll take a quick shower and brush my teeth."

"Okay, but don't take too long. There's a dinner tonight for the people that are still here from the seminar. I told them that you were my sister, so they included you in the invitation."

"Jane! I can't go to dinner with the people you work with. I wouldn't have anything to talk about. I don't even know anything about current events." Victoria's hands were shaking. The cosmetic case was rattling.

"Tori, you really don't get out enough." Jane reached out and took her hand. She gave it an encouraging squeeze. "I had no idea you were so timid."

"I'm just not used to being around professionals." Her voice sounded small.

"Tori, you make professional sound like some kind of monster. Don't worry about it. They're nice people and the food will be good."

"What should I wear?" She looked at the dress she'd brought. It suddenly looked so dowdy.

"It's casual. What you have on is fine."

They walked into the banquet room together. Victoria had never really paid attention to the difference in height between Jane and herself, but now she felt like a dwarf. Jane was 5'10" and she was 5'2". She walked over to the bar with Jane, feeling like a small child hiding behind her mother. Jane asked for two glasses of chardonnay. Victoria tapped her on the arm.

"What?" Jane looked at her.

"I can't drink chardonnay, remember?" she whispered. "It makes me throw up."

"That was just once, Tori, and you drank too much." She turned back to the bar and said, "Make that one glass of chardonnay, and one red wine spritzer."

"I don't know about wine, Jane," Victoria whispered again.

"This won't make you sick, I promise, and Tori, you don't have to whisper." They made their way over to a group of men. Actually, Victoria looked around and noticed that most of the people were men. There were a few women, but most of them seemed to be wives. Maybe here for the weekend, like she was.

Jane introduced her as her sister. She sipped her spritzer while they chatted about the seminar and talked about future work plans. The red wine spritzer was nice. She was sipping it slowly, just to be safe.

When it was time to be seated, they joined the group at a round table. She put her wine glass down and folded her napkin in her lap. The man next to her, she couldn't remember his name, said, "You and Jane don't look much alike."

She was startled when he spoke to her and jumped a little, but recovered nicely. "No, we don't. We're adopted." Victoria hated to lie, but it was almost the truth.

"I see," he said. "So what do you do?"

Oh gosh, he was trying to have a conversation with her. What would she do? She had nothing to say. Her mouth felt dry, so she took a sip of water. Then she had to swallow it and it didn't want to go down. The man was looking at her, waiting for an answer to his question.

"Tori, is a landscape designer, Mark," Jane said, from her other side.

"Gulp." The water went down loudly. She swung her head around to look at Jane, eyes wide.

Jane laughed and continued. "She was just showing me some plans that she made for an exhibit at the garden show in Washington, D.C., next spring. I was amazed at her artistic ability. I hadn't realized she was so good."

"Really, what an interesting line of work, have you been in it long?" Mark looked at her.

"Well, no, not very long." Luckily the waiter brought around the salad and everyone started to eat.

"You know," Mark said, after a minute. "I could

use some help on my garden. I like to do all of the work myself, but I've got one spot that I just don't know what to do with. Do you consult on that sort of thing?"

"Well, I guess so. I work for Landrum's in Atlanta. I'm pretty sure that would be something we do," she stuttered, and took another sip of wine.

"Could I have one of your business cards?"

"Business Cards?" Victoria gaped wide-eyed.

"You know, that's not a bad idea," one of the wives from across the table said. "I'd love to see your work. I need to change a large planter that I have at the entrance to the drive and I'm out of ideas. I'd like a card, too."

"Do you have any cards with you, Tori?" Jane asked.

"No, I didn't think I would need any tonight." She blushed at her lie.

"Well, she can give you her name and number," Jane said.

"Do you make terrariums?" someone asked from across the table.

She looked in the general direction of the voice and said, "Yes, I had a hard time learning how, but I've about mastered it now."

"I've had a problem with drainage in my terrarium. There's got to be a way to keep the water from pooling. How do you do that?"

Victoria answered his question and was surprised at how smart she sounded. By the end of the meal they were all chatting easily. They had moved on to different subjects, but she had been included in everything and was able to hold her own in the conversation.

The food was delicious and they left the room laughing. Everyone at the table had her name and the number to Landrum's. She doubted that she would ever hear from them. They were probably just being nice, but it felt good anyway.

When they got back to the room, Jane said, "You don't even have business cards, do you, Tori?"

"Nope," she said simply.

"Well, get some."

The next morning they ate at the breakfast buffet in the motel restaurant. The food was good. Then they hurried off to do some shopping on River Street. It had been a long time since Victoria had been to Savannah. She remembered it vaguely, but it was still quite an adventure.

"There used to be a kite shop along here somewhere," she said. "Joe used to love to go out on the beach and fly kites. He had the kind with two strings. He could make them do all kinds of stunts."

They found the store and Victoria bought Joe a new kite. He hadn't flown one in years. Atlanta wasn't a good place to fly kites, but maybe they'd take a trip to the beach and he could do it then.

They spent the morning in the shops and had lunch at a nice restaurant with a balcony on the second floor that looked out over the harbor. It was delightful. Jane had plans to see a museum down town and then they had reservations for parasailing at 3:30. The more she thought about it, the more nervous she got.

"Jane, I don't think I can go parasailing."

"How did I know that was what you were thinking about when I saw that worried expression on your face?" She laughed. "Listen, if you really don't want to go, you don't have to. You can just watch me. I'm going."

"You always were the adventurous one."

"How did I let you talk me into this?" Victoria shouted over the noise of the boat's motor.

"The same way you let me talk you into everything else." Jane laughed over her shoulder.

They were standing single file on a platform off the back of a boat, strapped into the harnesses of the parasail. Victoria had planned to say no, but they had watched a couple of people before them, and it did look like fun. The boat was gaining speed and the sail was lifting. Suddenly her feet lifted off the floor and she was airborne.

"Oh, my God!" she whispered, and shut her eyes. That made her stomach lurch, so she opened them again. The noise was gone. It was eerily quiet.

"Tori, do you have your eyes open?" Jane asked.

"Yes, I tried to close them, but it made me feel like throwing up."

"Don't throw up. You're too close behind me.

Look," Jane pointed to the water. "You can see the fish in the ocean."

"You're right. It's beautiful up here. Thanks for making me do this, Jane."

"I didn't make you do it, Tori. It was your decision. You're not as timid as you think you are."

"I guess you're right."

They watched the water in silence for a while.

"Jane, does it seem like we're getting lower?"

"Yes, they're dipping us."

"What?" Victoria sounded panicked.

"I read about this. They can control how high you go by the speed of the boat. They can actually dip you in the water by slowing down."

"I don't want to be dipped in the water. I can see jelly fish down there."

Suddenly they were only feet from the water. They hung there for a moment then dipped. Victoria rocked her legs up to keep her feet out of the water. Her bottom went in and water sprayed all over both of them. Squealing as the cold water hit, they dissolved into laughter.

The drive home was uneventful. They left at about 10:00 a.m. and drove until noon, stopped for lunch, and continued. It was nice to have someone to talk to this time. It was just too long a drive by herself. All in all, though, she felt good about the trip. She felt better about her independence now and they had really had a good time.

She couldn't wait to tell Joe about the business cards. Jeff probably already had business cards for himself. Maybe he would let her have some when she told him that people had asked for them.

"You know, I missed Joe."

"Did you? That's a good thing. You must be getting your feelings for him back." Jane yawned. The trip was almost over. They were almost home.

"Actually, I think I'm falling in love with him all over again," she sighed. "I was thinking a couple of months ago, when I was so depressed, that I would never experience falling in love again. But now, I am, and with my own husband."

"That's great, Tori. I'm proud of the way you've pulled yourself out of that rut you were in. You're a great kid."

"I'm hardly a kid."

Victoria dropped Jane at her condo. She lived in a high-rise over by Phipps Plaza. She got out of the car to help her with her bags. Jane hugged her. "Thanks for coming, Tori. I had a great time. Thank Joe for me, too, for keeping the pets."

When Victoria got home she went in the back door and called for Joe.

"I'm upstairs, Victoria," he called back. Something about his voice frightened her. Was something wrong? Had something happened to one of the animals? She ran up the stairs and stopped short inside the bedroom door. "What are you doing?" Joe was standing next to the bed. There was an open suitcase on the bed. He was packing, but it was her clothes that he was putting in the suitcase.

"Victoria, we've had some bad news." He turned

and put his hands on her shoulders. She suddenly felt chilled. All of her nerves were vibrating. She looked up at him, frightened.

"It's Patricia," he said. "Her roommate found her this morning at the bottom of the steps going to their apartment. She'd been badly beaten. She hasn't regained consciousness."

There was a crawling feeling on her scalp. It crept down her face and neck then moved to her shoulders. Her ears began to ring and there was blackness creeping around the outside of her vision. She was going to faint. She could feel it. Joe was holding her shoulders and saying something to her. She shook her head. She couldn't faint now. Patricia needed her.

"Sit down, Victoria." Joe was trying to move her over to the bed. "Are you all right? You got so pale. I thought you were about to faint."

"I did too. Joe, what happened to her?" She sat down on the bed. She could feel the tears pushing on the backs of her eyes then they were rolling down her cheeks.

"They're looking for the guy she was dating. The roommate said she had witnessed several temper tantrums that he had. She thinks that he beat her up and pushed her down the steps. She thinks he left her for dead." He was shaking as he talked. "He's disappeared, along with all of her money. Her bedroom was torn apart and everything of value was taken. There wasn't much, of course."

Looking at the suitcase, she said, "Why are you packing for me? Aren't you going out there with me?"

"I couldn't get a flight for both of us until tomorrow. I thought you'd want to go now, so I booked you on a flight that leaves in three hours. I'll follow in the morning."

"Yes, of course, you're right." She looked at the bag and noticed what was already in there, and then started packing the rest of what she would need. "Who did you talk to?"

"The police called me. I guess it was something that they had to do officially, and then the roommate called. I called the hospital, but since she's an adult, they couldn't tell me much. Jennifer, the roommate, said that both of Patricia's legs are broken, her right wrist is broken, and there's head trauma, obviously, otherwise she'd be conscious." Victoria could hear his voice crack. In the thirty-two years that they'd been married, she had only seen him cry a couple of times, but he was struggling with this. She went over and put her arms around him. He gathered her into his arms and put his cheek on her head. They wept together. She could feel his body shaking with his sobs, as she was sure hers was. They held each other for a few minutes then both went silently back to work.

"Will you have time to take Ethel and Theodore to a kennel tomorrow?" she asked, as Theodore limped into the room. She hadn't had time to greet them yet. She picked the kitten up and kissed him.

"I have to leave too early. My flight is at 8:00. I called Lillian and she said that she would house sit. She'll come over tomorrow between school and work to check on them. Then she'll come here after work and stay. I'll leave them in their crates. I told her if we ended up having to be there for a long period of time, she should take them to a kennel."

"Thank you for thinking of them. I guess Lillian can tell Jeff what happened. I'll call him from Sacramento." She closed the suitcase. "I guess we'd better go if I want to catch that flight."

Victoria went into the bathroom and washed her face. She came out and, picking up the kitten again, went downstairs to the kitchen. Joe had carried her bags down and gone out to the garage. She picked up the little dog and kissed her. Ethel wagged her tail and licked Victoria's face. She put her in her crate then did the same with Theodore.

Joe was in the driver's seat when she got to the car. She got into the passenger seat.

"I'll kill the bastard," Joe said. His knuckles were white where he gripped the steering wheel.

"We'll kill him together."

Twelve

Victoria looked at the landscape as she drove from San Francisco to Sacramento. It looked like a different planet than the eastern states. She had been out there a few times before to visit Patricia, and had made that observation every time. It was beautiful, of course, but different.

She was numb. There were no feelings. It must be some kind of inherent defense mechanism. She had told Joe that she thought she would go crazy on the flight. Instead she had slept the whole way. Waking up was a shock, though all the terror flooded back to her and she felt dizzy again. The steward had brought her a glass of water and she had drunk it down in one gulp. The expression on her face was blank when she looked at herself in the mirror in the small bathroom.

She noticed the change in landscape as she neared the hospital in Sacramento. It had become flat, kind of bare looking. She felt frightened. No one could have reached her for a long time now. What if...? No, she wouldn't think of that. She parked the car and went in. The woman at the information desk gave her the room number and she got into the elevator.

She stopped a nurse on the way out of the room. "I'm Patricia's mother. Can you tell me how she is?"

"She's conscious. She hasn't said much except to answer direct questions." She looked sympathetically at Victoria. "She's had a really bad time. She's sleeping now, but you can go in."

Victoria was torn between being hesitant to go into the room and wanting to rush in and scoop her child up in her arms. She went into the room peering cautiously around the corner. The breath was knocked out of her when she looked at her daughter. Her face was a mass of bruises. Her nose and lips were swollen, and one eye was black. There were bruises on her neck, small ones that looked like fingerprints.

"Oh, my God," Victoria whispered. She went to the other side of the bed and looked down at her youngest child. She looked so fragile and so vulnerable. Victoria swallowed the lump in her throat.

All the years seemed to disappear and there was her little girl again. She could see the baby that she'd been; all blond curls and blue eyes. She had dimples in her cheeks like Joe, and she was so tiny. Patricia had never even gotten as tall as her own five foot two. She was only a little over five feet tall.

Her right arm was folded over her belly. There was a cast on it about halfway to the elbow. She could see that the sheet was held higher than her legs. There must be casts under there, too.

"I love you, Patricia," Victoria whispered. She did love her. All the feelings that she'd been looking for came back with a force she hadn't expected.

She pulled up a chair and sat close to the bed. Picking up Patricia's hand, she pressed it against her lips, then her cheek. Tears rolled unchecked down her face. She sat there like that for what must have been hours.

"What are you doing to me, Mama?"

She was startled out of her daze by Patricia's voice. Victoria looked across at her daughter. Her head was turned in her direction and her eyes were large and confused.

"I'm loving you, baby." She touched her face gently, afraid she'd hurt her.

"Oh, Mama!" Patricia started to cry. Not the deep wracking sobs she had expected, but a weak, crooning. "I wish he'd killed me."

Victoria wanted to tell her never to say that. She wanted to tell her never to feel that way, but she knew she couldn't. Instead she said, "I know, baby."

"I can't do this, Mama. I can't get through this. I'll never be the same again."

Victoria slid her shoes off and gently crawled into the bed beside her. She gathered her daughter into her arms and stroked her hair. "No, you'll never be the same again."

She soothed and stroked her, until she fell back to sleep. That was the way Joe found them when he arrived late that afternoon. There was an untouched tray of lunch on the stand next to the bed. The nurse must have left it in case they woke up hungry. It was almost time for them to serve dinner.

Joe touched Victoria's hand where it rested on Patricia's shoulder. His wife opened her eyes. They warmed in recognition. Gently disentangling herself from her daughter, she got up and stood beside Joe. He put his arm around her shoulders and looked down at his child. Victoria could see the pain in his eyes as he looked at Patricia's face. She watched his jaw clench and the vessels swell on his temples.

Patricia opened her eyes and saw her father. Her face crumpled and she started to cry again. She raised her left hand to her face to cover it. "I'm so sorry, Dad. I'm so sorry." She was sobbing now.

"Patty, you don't have anything to be sorry about. You'll be all right, sweetheart. We'll take care of you now." He leaned over the bed, putting his hands on her cheeks. He kissed her forehead.

The door opened and someone came into the room. Victoria turned around to see who. It was a man in a white coat. He walked toward them with his hand outstretched. "I'm Dr. Smith," he said. "I've been handling Patricia's case since she arrived."

Victoria and Joe introduced themselves and shook his hand. Joe said, "Can you tell us about her injuries?"

"Not without Patricia's permission." He looked at her. "I would like to talk to you, Patricia. I can ask your parents to leave the room if you like."

"No, let them stay," she said. She sounded uninterested. The tears were dry and there was a blank look on her face. She stared past them all.

"All right, the head trauma seems to be minimal. Of course, I'll want to watch you closely for the next few days, but I don't think there will be any lasting affects. The right arm sustained a hairline fracture and will heal without any problem. The left leg was a little more seriously broken, but was easy to set. It should heal fine as well." He paused and looked around at her parents. They each acknowledged what he had said with a nod. "The right leg, however, is going to be a little more difficult." He looked back to Patricia.

"Go ahead," she said.

"The injury has involved the knee joint. There are some torn ligaments that will need surgery, and the patella—your kneecap—is broken into three pieces. You'll require a good bit of physical therapy. I'm not sure how extensive the damage to the joint is. We couldn't take you into surgery in the condition you were in when you arrived. That will have to wait until you're stabilized. The orthopedist that does the surgery will have to explore the injury further."

"She'll need a lot of care." He paused and looked at Victoria and Joe. "Is there someone who can stay with her?" he asked.

Victoria tensed. The girls had both been so adamant about living far away from them. What if she wouldn't let them take her home?

"I'll go with you to Atlanta, if that's all right." She looked at her parents.

They both said, "Of course it's all right."

"I might as well, there's nothing for me here." She lowered her head and stared at her hands. Again, she seemed to look past them to nothing. Her eyes were blank.

Victoria was both relieved and distressed, relieved because she hadn't put up a struggle about going home, distressed for the same reason. There seemed to be no energy left in her to struggle with.

The next day they went to the apartment. Joe called first to make sure that Jennifer would be there. She had said that she was supposed to be at work, but would take some time off to talk to them.

When they got there, she let them in and showed them to Patricia's room. Victoria couldn't help but gasp a little at the ransacked room. Joe put his arm around her shoulders and squeezed.

"I haven't done anything to it. I haven't even been able to come in here. I just couldn't bring myself to." Jennifer's voice shook.

"This must have been very hard for you, finding her like that," Victoria said.

"It was. I've had nightmares about it."

"I'm sorry."

"I know."

They were quiet for a minute. Then Jennifer said, "I knew he was bad news."

"The police told me you'd witnessed other struggles between them," Joe said. He continued to look at the mess.

"Yes, a number of them. He would hit her then it was like he got control. But I always had the feeling that he was just barely under control. I figured one day he wouldn't be able to stop." Jennifer was silent for a minute. "It's kind of a pattern with Patricia, though."

They both turned and looked at her then. "What do you mean?" Joe asked, puzzled.

"I don't know exactly how to say it." Pausing, she looked down at the rug. "Patricia always seems to go out with men who abuse her in some way. She seems to be attracted to losers." She looked up at them now. "This guy was the worst, but he certainly wasn't the first."

"Other men hit her?" Victoria asked, shocked.

"I'm not sure if anyone ever hit her before, but

there are a lot of different kinds of abuse." Jennifer turned and walked out of the room.

"How long have you known Patricia?" Joe asked, as they followed her into the living room.

"Three years. Would you like something to drink?" she asked.

They both shook their heads. The three of them sat down in the tidy little living room. "She's a year ahead of me in school. She was my "big sister" when I was a freshman. They assign someone to act as kind of a friend to the freshmen when they come in. She was mine. We became good friends right away. We've only lived together for about a year, though."

"And she's always had this tendency to go out with losers?" Victoria asked.

"Yes, I never could understand why. She could have dated anyone she wanted, with her blond hair and dimples."

"Yes, she's very pretty." Victoria looked at Jennifer. The girl was not unattractive, but perhaps a little plain. Maybe she envied Patricia a little.

"I just couldn't believe he would try to kill her. I had stayed the night with a friend who lives in Auburn, a town nearby. I didn't come home until about noon on Sunday. I felt kind of guilty. Maybe if I'd been here…"

"You'd both have been at the bottom of the steps," Joe said. "Don't feel bad. It's not your fault." Joe got up and walked across the room to look out the sliding glass door to the balcony.

Victoria said, "We'll be taking her home, Jennifer. She's going to need some surgery and some physical therapy."

"Oh, I'm sorry." She looked down at her hands in her lap. "But, it's probably a good thing to get her out of here, at least until they catch that asshole." She put her hand to her mouth and looked up at Victoria. "Oh, I'm sorry. I didn't mean to say that."

"That's okay. I feel the same way. Jennifer, she hasn't spoken to us about the man at all. You don't think she still loves him, do you?"

"I don't know. I really don't." She was quiet for a minute. "Knowing Patty, though, I wouldn't be surprised if she did."

Everyone was silent for a while. It was not an uncomfortable silence. They all had their own thoughts and feelings to sort out. Then Joe said, "Will you be able to find another roommate? We'll pay her rent until you do."

"That's nice. I appreciate it. I have a friend that I think I can move in with, but our lease isn't up until next month. Patricia and I had already planned to go our separate ways when the lease was up. But I could use help with the last month."

"How much is her part?" He looked at Victoria. "Do you have a check?"

"Yes, of course." She fumbled through her purse and found her checkbook.

They spent the afternoon at the hospital. Joe tried to draw Patricia into conversation by asking about school. She answered questions with one word if possible, sometimes making slightly longer explanations. It was clear that she was in considerable pain. She started asking for pain medication at least an hour before she could have any. Sometimes her eyes clouded, but she didn't talk about her injuries or the incident that had caused them.

Dr. Smith gave them the name of an orthopedic surgeon in Atlanta, but he wasn't ready to say that she could travel yet. He also suggested psychotherapy. They left, reluctantly, around dinnertime. Dr. Smith advised them to go, as he had the night before. He assured them that the pain medication she was on would help her sleep through the night and the nurses on duty would closely monitor her.

"This is all my fault." Joe had his head in his hands and he stared, unseeing, down at his plate. They were at the hotel restaurant. Victoria looked across the table at him. His shoulders were slumped forward. He looked defeated. "I didn't treat her right when she was growing up. I was always closer to Ellen." He looked up at her. His eyes were misty and they pleaded for understanding. "It wasn't that I loved her any less, really. I always loved her. Since the minute the doctor put her in my arms." He looked down at his arms, as if he could imagine her there. "It was just that Ellen and I had so much in common. She was kind of a tomboy, liked to play ball. Patricia was always so tiny and she seemed so fragile to me. I was afraid I'd hurt her."

"Joe, I've been feeling guilty all afternoon, too."

Victoria reached across the table and put her hand over his. "I keep thinking about how I said I didn't love her, or at least I said I couldn't feel it. How could I say that? Then when I saw her in the hospital, all the feelings came rushing back to me, and I thought, I'm being punished for being so selfish." She wiped the tears out of her eyes and went on. "But Joe, I don't think it matters who's to blame for this right now. This isn't happening to us, even though it feels like it is. It's happening to her and she needs us. So we've just got to put those feelings aside and do what ever we can to help her get through this."

They were silent for a moment. The waiter came and asked for their order. Joe looked confused, as if he'd forgotten he was in a restaurant. "We haven't decided yet," he said.

She looked at him again. He was still staring at his plate. "Why would she choose men who abuse her? I never abused her. Maybe I neglected her." He was almost pleading.

"You didn't do either one. You were a loving parent."

"I do love my children."

"We both love our children." She looked at the menu in front of her. She really didn't have any appetite. "Look, Joe, we both made mistakes raising the girls, but we can't go back and do it over again. Right now, we need to make sure we do this right."

They both looked at the menu and ordered something when the waiter came back. Neither knew what they'd ordered and neither one ate very much.

The next morning Victoria opened the door to Patricia's room. There was a tall, dark-haired woman standing with her back to her, holding Patricia's hand. She stopped, afraid she was interrupting something. "I'm sorry, I should have knocked." She started to back out of the room. The woman turned around. Victoria stopped and her mouth fell open. "Ellen!"

The girl rushed to her mother and wrapped her in a crushing embrace. Victoria's breath was momentarily taken away. Then Ellen held her away from her. "Mom, I had forgotten you were so small."

"I don't remember you being so tall." She was breathless. "Oh, honey, it's so good to see you. It hasn't been that long since we've seen each other, has it? You couldn't have grown."

"I think it's been a little over a year." She turned back to Patricia who was looking small and frightened. The sheet was pulled up to her chin. "I drove down as soon as Dad called me, but this was as soon as I could get here." She picked her sister's hand up again.

"Where's Dad?"

"He dropped me off and went to park the car."

"Ellen!" They both turned at the sound of Joe's voice. He hurried forward to embrace his daughter. He held her for a few minutes, rocking back and forth then stepped back a little and looked around. Walking to the other side of the bed, he took Patricia's other hand and said, "It's nice to see the whole family together in one room."

"It's too bad it had to be one of my disasters that brought us together," Patricia said. She sounded depressed.

"It doesn't matter why. I'm just glad to see you both." Joe looked like he didn't know what to say.

"Patty, what happened?" Ellen asked.

Victoria tensed. Ellen was so outspoken it worried her, but maybe that's what Patricia needed, someone to encourage her to talk about it. She waited, but there was no response.

"We're going to talk about this, Patty," Ellen said, with that commanding voice she used when she was determined to get her way.

"No, we're not," Patricia said quietly, but firmly.

"Patricia will talk about it when and if she gets ready to," Joe said. Both girls and Victoria looked up at him. He sounded so stern. "Do you want Mom and me to leave the room so that you can talk about this with Ellen?" he asked Patricia.

"No." She looked up at him, eyes pleading.

"Well then." He looked from Victoria to Ellen and then back to Patricia. "I was thinking you might like something to read or some puzzle books or something, Patty," he said. "Since we don't know how long you'll be here before we can take you home."

"No thanks, Dad. I don't think I could concentrate on them."

"I'd like to find something that would entertain you. Mom and I need to get your belongings packed up and shipped back to Atlanta. We won't be able to be here with you as much in the next few days." He looked concerned.

"I'll be okay. Don't worry. They watch me around the clock at this place. I won't kill myself or anything."

Victoria watched Joe's jaws clench and relax. He took a deep breath. "That wasn't what I was worried about. I just think it would be better if you didn't just sit here and brood."

"I like brooding."

Ellen had been watching the exchange. "I can stay with her, Dad, for a couple of days anyway. I have to be back to work on Monday." She looked at Patricia. "You don't mind if I stay with you, do you? I won't push you to talk about it."

"Suit yourself."

"Alex is here," Ellen said. Victoria and Joe exchanged a look.

"I don't want to see Alex," Patricia said.

"Patty, why not, Alex adores you. He'll be hurt if you won't see him."

"He'll understand."

"That was scary," Ellen said, as they left Patricia's room. She had taken her pain medication and fallen asleep. "She looks really bad. I'll kill that bastard." There was a young man standing at the end of the hall. Ellen waved at him, signaling him to join them. He was very tall. His hair was black and not very well-brushed; he wore thick glasses, but the features of his face were very pleasant. "This is Alex Burke, he drove me down here."

They both shook his hand. A rather uncomfortable silence followed.

"How's Shirley?" Alex said to Ellen.

"It's awful, Alex. She's a mass of bruises and casts." Tears shimmered in her eyes.

"I'll kill that bastard!" Alex muttered.

Victoria watched the exchange between them. "Who's Shirley?" she asked.

"That's what Alex calls Patty," Ellen responded. "He says she reminds him of Shirley Temple. He's an old movie buff." She looked at Alex fondly.

"Oh." Again there was an uncomfortable silence.

Finally, Joe said, "Would everyone like to go somewhere for lunch? I can drop you all back here afterward. I'll need to go to the hotel room and make a few calls, and then I can join you again."

"That sounds good," Ellen said. She linked arms with Alex, and they started down the hall.

They stopped at a restaurant around the corner from the hospital. There wasn't much conversation while they ate, but after they had finished dessert, Ellen said, "I know this isn't a good time, with all that's happened, but it's probably the only chance we'll have to see you face to face. Mom, Dad, we have something to tell you."

Joe and Victoria looked up at her, their faces apprehensive. "What is it?" Joe said.

Ellen took a deep breath. "Alex and I were married two weeks ago."

"Before we say any more," Alex said, taking Ellen's hand in his, "I want to assure you that I truly love your daughter. I'll never hurt her. I have wanted to make her my wife ever since I met her."

Victoria was puzzled. He sounded defensive, like he was making a case for himself. "Why didn't you tell us before, honey? We would have liked to be there, or at least to help with expenses."

"We were planning to tell you. We had even thought about asking you to come, but we kind of had to expedite things." She smiled and lowered her head, but not before Victoria noticed her blush.

"Why did you have to expedite things?" Joe asked warily.

"Because I'm pregnant, you're going to be grandparents." Ellen smiled radiantly.

She's really happy. Victoria thought. "No wonder you sounded like you were defending yourself," she said to Alex.

Joe was silent. He just stared. His mouth was slightly open and he had turned a little pale. "Are you all right, Joe?" Victoria put her hand on his arm.

She looked at Joe's blank face and suddenly everything seemed very funny. "Uh-Oh," she said out loud. Everyone looked at her and she giggled, and then straightened her face. It didn't work. In a minute her shoulders were rocking with suppressed laughter.

"Uh-oh." Joe snapped his mouth shut and looked at Ellen.

"Uh-oh," Ellen said.

"Uh-oh, what?" Alex looked very confused.

By now Victoria was clutching her sides and rocking back and forth with laughter. Joe had put his arm around her shoulders and was whispering something to her.

"Mom has a nervous laugh." Ellen looked at Alex. "It doesn't happen often, but sometimes if she's nervous, or confused, or just doesn't know how to feel about something, she starts to laugh." She looked over at her mother with concern.

"Some gene pool you waded into, huh Alex?" Victoria said, and erupted in a fresh peal of laughter. Suddenly, she pushed back her chair and said, "Excuse me, please." She got up and headed for the door. The three of them watched her walk out the door, still laughing, turn left, and walk quickly down the sidewalk.

Joe pulled out his wallet. He handed his credit card to Ellen, and said, "Take care of the bill. We'll be outside when you're finished." He got up and went after his wife.

"Victoria," he called, but she didn't stop. He had to run to catch up to her. Grabbing her by the shoulders, he turned her around. The tears were already forming in her eyes and she let him pull her into his arms. These episodes always ended with tears. She always felt somehow refreshed afterward, usually a little embarrassed, too. Joe held her until the sobs slowed.

"It's just one shock after another, isn't it?" he said into her hair.

She nodded and sniffled. "I'm so embarrassed. What a way to greet our new son-in-law." When she said it, she started to cry again.

"Are you upset about this?"

"No. I don't know how I feel about it."

"Me neither. I guess we'll just have to get to know him and see."

"Mom, Dad?" Ellen and Alex stood behind Joe.

Victoria turned to them and said, "Alex, I am so sorry. I guess the last few days have been a little too much for me."

"That's okay. I can think of a lot worse reactions

than laughter." He smiled. "I'm not worried about the gene pool." He put his arm around Ellen. "Are you worried about the gene pool?" he asked Victoria.

"Well, I don't know you yet." She smiled. "You're both really happy?" She looked from one of them to the other.

"Yes, we're very happy." They beamed and kissed each other lightly on the lips.

"Then I'm happy, too."

"I guess I'm happy, too." Joe didn't sound too certain. "So, Alex, what do you do for a living?" He took Alex by the arm and steered him toward the car. The young man looked over his shoulder nervously at Ellen and Victoria. They both smiled back at him.

Thirteen

"It was terrible. You know how I lose control when I have those laughing episodes." She was sitting across from Jane and Lillian at her kitchen table. They had been back for about a week. Patricia was in the den napping. Joe had set up a bed in the den downstairs because she couldn't climb stairs. In fact, she was still in a rented wheelchair.

"I can't believe that happened when Ellen made her announcement, the poor boy." Jane laughed. "Have you ever witnessed one of her laugh attacks?" she asked Lillian

"No, but I'd like to. It sounds like fun," Lillian said.

"It's not," Victoria said. "But, I have to admit, I always feel a lot better afterward. It sort of releases whatever was bottled up inside." She was quiet for a minute. "One good thing about it, though, was that it made Patricia smile." She looked toward the closed door to the den. "It's the only time I've seen her smile since this whole thing started."

"I thought you said it happened at a restaurant. How could Patricia have been there?" Lillian asked.

"Oh no, she wasn't. It was the next day. Ellen and I were at the hospital with her. Joe had gone to meet the moving company. Alex called on the phone. Patricia had refused to see him, I guess she was embarrassed or something. Apparently they're good friends." She was rambling. "Anyway, the phone rang and I picked it up. It was Alex. He asked me to give the phone to Patricia. I asked her if she wanted to talk to him and she nodded her head. They talked for a minute. I was watching her to see if she was getting upset. I didn't want her to get upset." She looked at her two friends for understanding. "Then, she smiled. It only lasted for a minute, but it made my heart, sort of flip-flop."

"So, why do you say your laughing fit made her smile?" Jane asked.

"I didn't want to be a nosey mother and ask her about her phone conversation. So I just sat there for a minute after she hung up and after a few minutes she said, 'Mom, Alex told me about your laughing fit. I didn't realize you still had those.'"

"I thought I would probably like Alex before," Jane said. "But now I'm certain. It sounds like the girls have stayed close."

"Yes, apparently they visit each other," Victoria said sadly. "I'm glad."

"Vic, don't look so sad. Things will get better." Lillian patted her arm.

Victoria looked at her two friends. "You two really came through. I hope you know how much I appreciate it. I can't believe you stayed with Ethel and Theodore the whole ten days," she said to Lillian.

"I didn't mind. It was kind of nice living in a house instead of an apartment."

"And Jane," Victoria reached across the table and took her friend's hand. "Thank you so much for telling my mother about this. I was so upset that first night when I realized I had left town without even telling her."

"I was glad to see your mom. I haven't seen her for a while."

"Jeff's been really good, too. To give me all that time off."

"What was he going to say, Vic?" Lillian laughed. "No, you can't go to your injured daughter?"

"No, but he could have made it more difficult. Anyway, I'm glad I'm back." She was quiet for a minute. "Have you seen my studio?"

"No, I haven't. Have you, Lillian?" Jane asked.

"Yes, I stayed here for ten days. I've pretty much explored everything." She laughed. "But let's go look. You should see it. Joe really did a great job on it."

"He didn't do it all by himself, you know," Victoria said. "I helped."

They all went upstairs to look.

"Are you sure you shouldn't be at home with Patricia?" Jeff asked. He had just come into the potting shed.

Victoria looked up from the terrarium she was working on. "No. Joe's there. The therapist advised that we not change our routine for her as long as someone is around to help her if she needs it. She said we shouldn't dote on her." She continued with her work.

"I guess that's hard," Jeff said. "I guess a parent

wants to do whatever they can to relieve their child's pain."

She turned around and leaned up against the counter. "Jeff, have you ever been married?"

He hesitated. The question seemed to surprise him. "Yes, when I was very young and not for very long," he said.

"Do you have any children?"

"No, I'm glad about that. I don't think I would have been a very good father." He looked down at the floor. "I wasn't a very good husband."

"I don't believe that! I know it's none of my business, but what happened to your marriage?" She turned around again and resumed her work.

"I worked too much. I love my work. Nothing ever interested me as much. I guess she just got tired of waiting for me to come home, so she found someone else."

"I'm sorry." She continued to work. "Do you ever get lonely?"

"Not really. I still love my work, and I have a lot of good friends." He walked over to the counter and leaned against it. "Why all the questions, you've never wondered about this before?"

"On my trip to Savannah I realized that I didn't know very much about you. Of course, you know every detail of my life. I'm a blabbermouth. I tell everyone everything. Can't shut up."

Jeff laughed. "I like that about you."

"Well, anyway, I thought that it was selfish of me to be that way, and I made a mental note to ask you about your life when I got back. But, of course—"

"I know. Other things came up." He reached

into the terrarium and rearranged one of the seedlings that she had put in.

She looked at it critically. It looked much better. "How do you do that? I thought it looked okay before, but it really looks better now."

"Practice." He laughed. "So now that you've asked, and you know that the reason I don't talk about my life is because I have no life, can we talk about yours?"

"Why do you want to talk about mine?" She turned to look at him again.

"Did Joe tell you that he and I had lunch when you were in Savannah?"

She widened her eyes in surprise. "No, I wonder why he didn't." She looked back down at the terrarium.

"Well, other things came up for him, too."

"That's true."

They were quiet for a minute while she worked. "Why did you bring that up?" she asked.

"Well, because I like him. He's a really nice guy. And, he's afraid that I'm moving in on you. I don't want to do that. At first, I did, but after getting to know him, I don't anymore." He hesitated after each sentence, obviously uncomfortable.

Victoria turned around and crossed her arms over her chest. "So, you're dumping me?" She laughed.

"That's right." Jeff laughed, too. "But I wanted you to know." He smiled down at her and kissed her forehead. "I still love you. You're not getting rid of me. I'm planning to make a great success of you." She turned back to her work.

"Thanks, Jeff. You've been a good friend."

They were quiet for a while. Victoria continued to work. Jeff stood and looked at her. "So back to what we were talking about," he said. "Does Patricia seem to be coming out of her depression at all?"

She sighed deeply. "No. I just don't know what to do. She's so hurt. We went to the orthopedist and had the consultation, and we got really pretty good news." She paused. "The injury to the knee isn't as bad as they thought at first. He'll still have to do surgery, but he was sure it would only take one surgery. He thinks that the recovery won't be so bad."

"Well, that's good news."

"Joe and I were so relieved, but Patricia just sat there staring at her hands."

"Has she said anything about the incident or the man who did this?"

"Not one thing."

"I'm sorry," Jeff said.

"We've asked her to go to see a therapist, but she refuses. We managed to get her to come with us to the counselor that we saw, but she just sat there. She didn't say anything." She looked up at him. Her eyes were cloudy. "I just feel so helpless."

"I don't have any ideas either. Like I said, I don't have much experience with relationships." Jeff was quiet again for a minute. "Have you showed her your sketches?"

Victoria looked at him, puzzled. "No. What good would that do?"

"Probably no good at all, but I was just thinking that if she thought about what you were doing a little, it might take her mind off what she's doing."

He laughed. "I guess it was a dumb idea." He moved toward the door. "I've got work to do, but if there's anything I can do to help, let me know." He stopped as he neared the door, and turned around. "Oh, I almost forgot to tell you, I've ordered you some business cards. I've gotten two calls from people who met you in Savannah. They want to make appointments with you. The messages are in my office. They told me that you didn't have your cards with you, but you gave them our number." He tapped her shoulder. "Way to go, Vic, drumming up business even when you're on vacation."

"Oh, that's right, I'd forgotten."

Jeff dug into his back pocket and pulled out a folded piece of paper. He handed it to Victoria. "These are the cards I ordered. If you don't like them we can change them next time we order."

Victoria unfolded it. It was an enlarged copy of a business card. Beneath the Landrum's Nursery logo and above the address and phone numbers was written, *Gardens by Victoria*. She looked up at him. "I love it. Thank you, Jeff. I hope I can live up to it."

"I know you will." He smiled and left the room.

That night when she got home, Joe's car wasn't in the garage. She hoped he had taken Patricia with him, wherever he'd gone. She went into the kitchen from the garage. The animals were in their crates. She let them out and cuddled each of them. Theodore was still in a splint, but he had learned to use it very well. He got around beautifully. She walked into the living room with them following after her. Patricia was sitting in her wheelchair staring out the window.

"Oh hi, honey," Victoria said. She was surprised to find her there. "Where's Dad?"

"He went to pick up dinner. He said he didn't want you to have to cook."

"That was nice of him." She was definitely surprised about that. He'd never had a problem with her having to cook before. That was one area where he was very old-fashioned. He thought the wife should cook.

"I think he just wanted to get away from me."

"I'm sure that's not true," Victoria said. "But I wish he hadn't left you alone."

"Mom, I'm a grown woman," Patricia said irritated.

"We're doting, aren't we?"

"Yes."

Victoria took a deep breath. "Well," she said. "Let me tell you my good news, then."

"Please do."

"I'm getting business cards. I went to Savannah the weekend before...well, last month with Aunt Jane, and some people there were interested in my work. They asked for business cards, but, of course, I didn't have any. I gave the number to the nursery and they called Jeff. He realized that I needed business cards, so he ordered me some."

Patricia was looking at her with a puzzled expression. "They were interested in what work?" she asked.

"Oh, I guess I haven't told you about it. The owner of the nursery where I work wants me to design a garden for the garden show in D.C. in the spring." Victoria smiled.

"You work in a nursery? I thought you worked at a grocery store."

"We've talked more than that, Patricia. Surely I told you that I changed jobs?"

"No, I'm pretty sure you didn't." She looked back out the window.

"Oh." Victoria paused to think about it. "Well, I started working at Landrum's nursery in about March, I think. Yes, it was March. Anyway, Jeff, the owner, sent me to a few courses on garden design, and I've been helping him with the landscaping. I really enjoy it." She put down her purse and lunch bag and sat in a chair next to the window. "I'm going to the garden show in March with him."

Patricia looked at her and the corners of her mouth turned up just a little. Her dimples didn't show, so it wasn't really a smile, but almost. "That's great, Mom. Sounds like your life is going great."

"It is." They were silent for a minute. Patricia looked back out the window. "Would you like to see my plans?" Victoria asked.

"Sure."

"I'll go get them." Victoria hurried up the stairs to her studio. She brought all of the plans, even the before sketches she had made of the property. Patricia looked at them politely, but she did seem impressed.

"They're good, Mom. I didn't know you could draw." It was the most animated she'd been since she'd been home.

"That's what everyone says." Victoria laughed. "Truth is, I didn't know I could draw either. Dad framed a picture I drew of the front yard. Would you like to see it?"

"Sure."

She went to Joe's office and took the picture off the wall. She felt a little foolish, like a child showing off. Patricia looked at the picture and almost smiled again. Jeff was right. This was working.

"That's really good, Mom. You've captured Ethel perfectly." She looked down at the little dog. Ethel was sitting at her feet with her tongue hanging out. It made her look like she was smiling. Patricia *did* smile this time. Her dimples showed, but the smile didn't reach her eyes.

"I'm back with dinner," Joe called from the kitchen.

"We're in the living room," Victoria called back to him.

Patricia handed her the picture and looked out the window. Victoria felt disappointed, but she had smiled for a minute. That was progress. "I'll take Ethel out," she said. "Then we'll go in for dinner."

"Okay."

"I'm frustrated," Joe said. They were both sitting up in bed. "I was hoping that this time we're spending together would bring us a little closer. I still feel responsible for Patricia's bad taste in men." He sounded sad. "But I can't get her to respond to anything."

"Jeff made a suggestion today," Victoria said.

"Speaking of Jeff, did I tell you that we had lunch while you were in Savannah?"

"No, but he did. He said he wasn't going to pursue me any more." She laughed.

"You're disappointed about that." Joe smiled at her. "You were enjoying the attention."

"Yes, I was. Now you'll have to give me even more attention." Joe leaned forward to kiss her and she smiled. "Anyway, Jeff said I should show Patricia my drawings. He said maybe if she thought about what I was doing, she wouldn't dwell so much on her problems."

"That's why you had the picture from my office when I came in."

"That's right, and you know, she actually did smile. Not just a flicker at the corners of her mouth, but enough to make her dimples show."

"Really?" Joe said. "I wish I'd seen that."

"I think Jeff was right. We have to stop trying to draw her out and just share ourselves with her. Let her get some distance from her problem. Hopefully, with some distance, she'll deal with it her way. Of course, if she asks for help, we'll give it to her."

"Maybe you're right." Joe was thoughtful. "You know, I really liked Jeff. I think you're right. Jeff and I could be friends. In fact, we decided to play racquetball together. I think I'll call him tomorrow and make a date to play. I haven't played in a long time. It'll be fun."

"That's right. You haven't played since you tried to teach me, and that was a disaster." They laughed.

The phone rang and Victoria jumped. "That

must be Ellen. She's the only one who calls at this time of night." She picked up the phone.

"Hi, Mom," Ellen said.

"Hi, honey. Is everything all right?"

"Yes, I just wanted to check on Patty. I'll try to call her tomorrow and talk to her, but I wanted to find out from you how things are."

"We went to the orthopedist and he's optimistic about her recovery. The surgery is scheduled for next Monday. She's still not talking much, although she did actually smile today. I was showing her my sketches."

"She smiled?" Ellen said. "That's great." She paused. "I didn't know you could draw."

"That's what everyone says." Victoria laughed. "I'm learning garden design. I've taken a few courses and I'm helping with the landscaping at work."

"I thought you worked at a grocery store."

"We've been out of touch for way too long, Ellen. We need to talk more."

"You're right."

"Well, I changed jobs in March. I work at Landrum's nursery now."

"Really, do you like it?"

"I love it. Honey, how are you? Are you feeling all right? You were still sick in the morning the last time I saw you. Has that passed?" Victoria could still remember the overwhelming nausea of pregnancy.

"Yes. One day I just woke up and realized I felt fine. Just like that, it was gone. Mom, I wanted to ask if you would come out when the baby comes, to help out. I don't know what it will involve."

"Of course, you couldn't keep me away." Victoria felt warm inside that Ellen had asked.

"Let me talk to Dad, okay? Alex just got home and we're going to some friend's house for dinner."

"Okay, bye honey, I love you." She wasn't just saying it this time. She could feel it. It felt good. She handed the phone to Joe.

She slid down in the bed and rolled over. Joe talked for a minute then hung up.

"She asked me to come to help out when the baby comes." A tear rolled across her nose and dropped onto the bed. "I can't believe I let us drift so far apart. I think it was all my fault."

Joe slid down in the bed and kissed her shoulder. "I think we all needed some distance for a while. It's the way families work."

Fourteen

Victoria stepped back off the ladder right into a clay pot. All of her weight was on that foot, so it wedged tightly into the pot. "Oh, shit," she said, turning around. She sat on the second rung of the ladder and contemplated her situation. Her foot was tightly wedged into the pot and her big toe hurt. "Ouch!"

"Interesting." Jeff stood in the doorway of the potting shed with his arms crossed. "Apparently the safety seminar didn't work."

"You would have to be standing there," she said defensively. "Will you help me get this thing off my foot? It hurts."

Jeff walked over and stooped in front of her. He reached into the pot and eased her heel up, releasing her toe. "You've probably broken that toe."

"Of course I haven't broken my toe." She moved her foot back and forth. The toe hurt like hell, but she wouldn't tell him that. "It's fine."

"You're sure?" He looked concerned.

"Jeff, I haven't had an accident since the seminar. This is the first time. Everyone makes an occasional mistake."

"I know. Don't worry, I won't fire you." He laughed. "But if the toe is injured, you have to take care of it. Even if it means admitting to me that you're in pain."

"I'm not in pain." She stood up and walked over to the counter, wincing as she went. It did hurt.

"Suit yourself. Vic, I wanted to have a look at your plans. Are they ready to show them to the customer?"

"Jeff, he's not a customer," she explained. "He's just a friend of Joe's. The understanding was that he's not under any obligation to use my plans."

"Even customers aren't under any obligation to use our plans, but they at least get to see them and make their own decision," Jeff said. "Vic, I know it's hard to put your work out there for criticism, but you have to do it."

"It's just that I've worked so hard on it. What if he doesn't like it?"

"It'll hurt, but you'll survive. Let me see them. I'll tell you if they need work. You know I'll tell the truth."

"That'll hurt too." She pouted, and looked at him under her brows.

"Don't look at me like that. I won't let you back out of this."

She sighed. "That look isn't working anymore." She went over to her locker and opened it up. "Okay, but be gentle."

Jeff took the plans and went to his office. Victoria followed him, trying not to limp. She watched as he unrolled them and put them on the table. He looked them over and tapped his cheek with his finger. He continued to study them for a while.

"Well?" Victoria asked.

He looked at her. "What's this?" He pointed to a spot on the paper.

"I plan to put a fountain there. Something simple, but I thought it would be something that the owner should decide. The other option is a planter."

"That's good. It's always a good idea to give the customer some decisions to make." He looked back down at the plans. "These are good. When do you meet with the owner again?"

"Well, I haven't actually met him. He was on vacation when I went to see the place. I guess he's back now. It's been a while. For all I know, he may have already hired someone."

"Can you find out from Joe? If he hasn't, I think he'd be interested in these." He rolled the plans back up. "I'll have a copy made for our files. It'll take a day or two."

The next morning, Victoria woke up early as usual to go for her morning run. She winced when she put her foot on the floor. "Ouch," she said out loud.

Joe rolled over and said, "What's wrong?"

"My toe hurts."

"I think Jeff's right. It's broken. You'd better not run."

"I refuse to lose my conditioning because of my big toe." She was emphatic. "I've worked hard to achieve this level of conditioning, and at my age, you lose it fast."

"You'll get it back, but don't do real damage to that toe, just because you're stubborn."

She got out of bed and went into her walk-in closet. She came out dressed in running clothes. "I'll stop if it hurts too much," she said in response to Joe's chastising look.

"Suit yourself," he said, and rolled back over in bed.

"Even walking hurts," she said, limping back into the bedroom half an hour later. She sat down on the bed, pulled off her shoe, and looked down at the offending toe. It was black and blue from the nail to about half way up her foot.

Joe looked down at it. "It's broken. You should go to the doctor."

"I'm not going to a doctor because of a toe. You can't do anything about a broken toe anyway."

"So you admit it's broken?"

"Maybe..." She pouted and looked at him over her shoulder.

He reached over to where she sat on the edge of the bed, put his arm around her waist, and pulled her back into the bed. He rolled on top of her and put his arms on either side of her head.

"I guess that look still works with you." She smiled. He kissed her lightly and rolled away. She got up and went into the bathroom to shower.

Joe came in behind her and pulled his razor out of the vanity drawer. "When you take Patricia for her follow up appointment this afternoon, you should ask the doctor to look at it."

"I'm not going to the doctor for a broken toe," she said firmly.

"Patricia's surgery was ten days ago," Joe continued. "When do you think they'll start physical therapy?"

"I imagine they'll want to start something right away. Dr. Fletcher said she would need to move the knee in order for it to heal properly. I think it will be very gradual, though." She talked from the shower.

"She's gotten through the surgery pretty well. She's very stoic," Joe said. "I feel bad for her. It's not like she can concentrate on that knee. Her other leg is broken, too, and her wrist."

"She's had a rough time," Victoria agreed. She got out of the shower and wrapped herself in a towel.

"You know, I just can't seem to reach her. I've tried telling her about my work, like you suggested. All I get is a distant look from her. Your work is new, I guess. I've been doing the same thing all her life. Of course, she's always been closer to you. I was hoping to change that."

"You have to keep at it, Joe. Don't give up, but don't push, either. She needs time, that's all. Tell her about something else." Her voice was muffled in the towel as she dried her hair. "Tell her about your trip to the beach or something like that."

"Okay. I'll try that." He studied his face in the mirror. "Maybe I'm just boring."

"You're not boring."

"Dad had to go to Macon, today," she said to Patricia on the way to the appointment. "I think he'll be there overnight. Would you like to do something tonight, maybe go to a movie?"

"No thanks." Patricia stared out the window.

"Honey, is there anything I can do to make you feel better."

"No."

"Okay." They rode in silence for a while.

"How does the knee feel?"

"It hurts, but it's not as bad as it was at first. I hope they don't make me do anything with it." Patricia looked down at her hands in her lap.

"I'm sure they will. Dr. Fletcher said it was important to start moving it right away. How's the other leg?"

"It doesn't hurt much anymore. And my wrist feels fine. I hope he takes the cast off today. It's already been six weeks."

"I hope so, too. It must be uncomfortable."

"It itches."

Victoria stopped at the entrance to the building and helped Patricia out of the car and into her wheelchair. She could stand on her left leg even with the cast, and hold her right leg up. Then she turned and sat down in the chair. They had the routine down. Victoria left her there for a minute while she parked the car.

Dr. Fletcher was optimistic about the knee. He removed the cast from her arm and left leg and X-rayed them. The healing was complete on the wrist. He gave her a removable plastic brace for her leg, and advised her to buy crutches or a walker to use while she was undergoing physical therapy.

"I want you out of that wheelchair," he said firmly. "You need to exercise these legs to get them well."

They left with a referral to a physical therapist and another follow-up appointment in two weeks.

"Do you want crutches or a walker?" Victoria asked. "We might as well stop at the medical supply store on the way home. I was also thinking of visiting Gramma on the way home. Would you mind?"

"I want crutches."

"What about Gramma?"

"I'd like to see Gramma."

"We had a nice visit with Mom," she told Joe, when he called that night. "She wore her hearing aid, so we were actually able to have a conversation."

"That's good. Did Patricia talk at all?"

"Yes, she chatted nicely. She told her about Ethel and Theodore. You know, she always was the animal lover. Ellen liked pets, but she never felt as strongly about them as Patricia." She stroked the floppy ears of the little dog in her lap.

"How's Theodore doing with his bandage off?"

"You'd never know anything had happened. He still carries his leg in the air sometimes, but I think that's just habit." She laughed as the playful kitten bounded out from behind a chair.

"Let me speak to Patty, I want to congratulate her on getting those casts off. I'll bet she's relieved."

"I guess she is, but she doesn't say much. I'll get her, she's in her room."

Patricia talked to Joe for a few minutes then

she called Victoria to come and get the phone. "He wants to talk to you again."

"I almost forgot," he said, when she took the phone back. "Brad called me on my cell phone today, he was wondering about the garden plans. His wife is getting tired of looking at the unfinished yard."

"Really, Jeff asked me about that the other day. He wants me to show Brad the plans. He thinks they're pretty good."

"They are good. I'm going up there on Friday. Can I take them with me?"

"I'd like to go along, let me check with Jeff. He's having them copied. They should be finished by then."

"That would be nice. I'd enjoy the company."

"I'm nervous. What if he doesn't like them?"

"You'll survive. But I think he'll like them."

"I guess it was just as well that Patricia didn't come. It's not such a nice drive with all this rain." It was pouring outside. The windshield wipers were on high speed. It was hard enough to see the other traffic, much less the scenery.

"It was nice of Jane to agree to check in on her this morning."

"Yes, it was." She looked thoughtful for a moment. "I hope Brad will have a few minutes to go over the plans with me. I think they need to be explained a little."

"He will. I asked him to put some time aside.

You'll be meeting with him and his wife. I'll have to drop you at their house, so I can go to my job site. That's the real reason I was coming up here."

"You're not staying with me?" She sounded frightened, even to herself.

Joe looked at her and smiled. "I don't know anything about gardening. This is your career, remember." He patted her knee. "You'll do fine."

They pulled into the driveway and stopped in the front of the house. "Stay put," Joe said. "I'll come around and get you with the umbrella." She waited while he came around the car.

"How will I show them anything in the yard with this rain?" She could feel her mouth going dry.

"You'll do fine, Victoria, really." Joe had his arm around her shoulders. He squeezed a little then let go and rang the doorbell.

"Joe, please don't leave." Before she could say any more the door opened.

"Come in out of the rain." The man standing in front of them was probably in his early thirties. He was extending his hand. "I'm Brad Pitman, and this is my wife, Sarah."

Victoria took the extended hand and shook it. She smiled at Sarah.

"This is my wife, Victoria," Joe said. "I can't stay. I've got to go to the site. I'll be back by noon," he said to Victoria.

"Are you sure you can't stay for some coffee?" Sarah asked.

"No thanks, I've got too much to get done this morning, and Victoria has to be back at work this afternoon."

"Well, maybe next time," Brad said.

"That would be nice." Joe left and suddenly Victoria's mouth was so dry, she didn't think she could open it.

"Would you like some coffee?" Sarah asked, leading the way into the kitchen.

"No thanks." Her mouth made a smacking sound when she opened it to talk. She hoped she was the only one that heard it. "Maybe just some water."

"Bring your plans over to the table where we can spread them out," Brad said.

She looked at the plans she was holding. She'd forgotten they were in her hands. "Oh, yes, the plans." She put them on the table. Sarah handed her a glass of ice water and she took a sip. Oh, no, she thought, now I have to swallow. She gulped loudly. I hope no one else heard that.

Sarah and Brad looked at the plans as Victoria spread them out on the table. "It's a really pretty drawing. You should frame it." Sarah smiled at Victoria. There were dimples in her cheeks, like Patricia's. Victoria smiled then realized they were both looking at her.

"Oh, thank you. I'm just learning. I really do enjoy it, though." She looked down at the plans and started explaining them. In a few minutes, she warmed up to the task. Brad and Sarah listened quietly, while she went through her plans.

"Can you do much of it now, or will you have to wait until spring?" Sarah asked.

"There's a lot that can be done now. Some of it will have to wait until spring."

Brad pointed at the window. "It's stopped raining outside. Maybe we could take a walk around. That way we can visualize it."

"I had planned on doing that, but with the rain, I didn't think we'd be able to. I'm glad it stopped."

They walked to the door. Victoria was beginning to feel relaxed. She was actually pretty good at this. She straightened her shoulders and walked out the door. They walked around the yard and she pointed out the areas for each plant.

She looked at the apple tree where she and Joe had spread the blanket, remembered what they'd done there, and felt a blush move up her face. "I would leave the apple tree, of course."

"We like it, too," Sarah said. "We wouldn't let them cut it down when they cleared the land."

Sarah and Brad stayed on the boards that were put down in the yard to walk on. The ground was wet and since there wasn't much growing, it was muddy. Victoria had on rubber gardening shoes, so she didn't mind the mud.

"Will Joe let you into the car with all of that mud on your shoes?" Sarah asked.

"No, but they're made of rubber. I can just hose them off."

"Well, Victoria," Sarah said. "It all sounds great. Can we keep the plans for a while before we make up our mind?"

"Of course, you'll have to call Jeff Landrum, the owner of the nursery, if you want a quote on it. I think he's already worked one out." She walked beside them up the slope toward the house. She was just about at the top when she hit a particularly slippery spot and fell face first into the mud. She grabbed for a hold on something, but there was nothing to grab. Sliding down the hill, she landed in a puddle at the bottom and sat up. I cannot cry, she told herself when she felt the tears fighting for release. So she smiled, real big.

"Victoria, are you all right?" Sarah called from the top of the hill.

"Embarrassed, that's all," she called back. If only the puddle was deeper, I could drown myself, she thought.

When Joe returned, he found her wearing a pair of Sarah's jeans and a T-shirt. They were much too big for her. Her hair was wet as if she'd taken a shower. She was sitting at the table drinking some tea with Sarah. Brad was in the laundry room off the kitchen. "Here are your clothes, Victoria," he said, coming into the kitchen with a plastic garbage bag. "I put them in a bag so they wouldn't get mud on Joe's car."

"What happened?" Joe looked at her. She had a very big smile on her face, too big.

"I just got a little muddy in the yard." She laughed. It sounded hysterical.

Sarah and Brad seemed to be studying their feet.

"Well, I guess we'd better go." She got up. "It was nice to have met you." She headed to the front door almost at a run. "I'll have Joe bring your clothes back to you the next time he comes up. Thanks again." She was out the door.

Joe hurried behind her and got into the drivers seat. "What happened?"

"Just get out of here." He was looking at her. She looked over at him. "Please!" She was still smiling.

"Okay, okay," he said, and started the car. He turned the car around and headed out of the driveway. They pulled onto the highway about the same time Victoria started to cry.

"What's wrong, honey? What happened?"

"Just leave me alone, Joe." She put her face down in her hands and sobbed.

By the time they got to the house, Joe had gotten the whole story out of her. When she finally looked at him, there was a smile tugging at the corners of his mouth. "Don't laugh at me. It's not funny."

"Of course it isn't. I wasn't laughing."

"You were smiling." She was still wiping at her tears. They pulled into the garage and got out of the car. Victoria stormed in the kitchen door with Joe right behind her. "Would you call Jeff and tell him that I had to change my clothes and I'll be there in about an hour." She ran up the stairs.

"What's wrong with Mom?" Patricia came out of the den in her wheelchair.

Joe picked up the phone and dialed. "She had a little accident this morning. I'll tell you about it in a minute." He gave Jeff the message and hung up.

"Shouldn't you be on crutches?" he asked. "Dr Fletcher said you needed to use your legs."

"I don't feel like it right now. Tell me about Mom's accident."

When Victoria came down the steps half an hour later, she stopped at the sound of laughter below. They're laughing at me, some support they are. She stopped again. Patricia was laughing. If it made her laugh, it was worth it. She stopped in the doorway of the kitchen where they were talking and leaned against the jam with her arms crossed. "You think this is funny, do you?" They both tried to straighten their faces, but failed.

"I'm sorry, Mom, but it just sounds so much like you." Patricia's smile reached her eyes.

"It is like me. I'm a klutz." She walked over to her daughter and kissed her on the head. "I've got to go to work. Although, when Jeff hears about this, I probably won't have a job anymore."

"I didn't tell him." Joe kissed her on the cheek. "Have a nice afternoon." He winked at Patricia. "Is there anything I can do for you before I start working?"

"No thanks, Dad. I'm fine."

"Victoria, can I see you for a minute?" Jeff called, as she came in the door.

"Shit!" She said under her breath. "I'll be there as soon as I put my stuff away," she called to him.

"I just had a long conversation with Mr. Pitman." He said when she came into the office.

"Oh, no." She frowned. "Jeff, I know you worry about safety, but it was just mud..."

"What are you talking about?" he interrupted. "Mr. Pitman called for a quote. I gave him one, and he accepted it. You've just sold your first job. Now what were you saying about mud?"

"Joe, he wants me to manage the job." Victoria sounded frantic. She was sounding that way a lot these days. It was better than sounding depressed, though. "I don't know how to manage a job."

"I'm sure Jeff will help you. He's teaching you."

"What if I mess it up?"

"You won't." Joe was helping her in the back yard. She was planting a Japanese magnolia, and it was a little too heavy for her to lift by herself.

"I don't know." She stood up and put her hands on the small of her back to stretch. "I just have this scary feeling that I'm in over my head. I have two appointments tomorrow with people I met in Savannah. They want me to consult with them on their gardens." She looked at him. "What do I know about consulting on something?"

"You're very creative and you have good ideas. If you can't think of anything, tell them that you'll have to draw up some plans and get back to them. With the pressure off, you'll be able to do it." Joe started to pick up the tree close to the root ball.

"Wait a minute." Victoria hurried over. "Let me help. We don't need any back injuries."

They were quiet while they carried the tree over to the hole they had dug. She had filled it with topsoil, fertilizer, and compost. They covered the root ball with more soil that she had prepared.

"Where's Patty?" Joe asked, looking toward the house.

"In her room. I tried to get her to come out and sit on the patio with me while I worked, but she didn't want to. I start to think we're making progress, like when she laughed at my accident the other day." They both smiled. "But then she just closes up again."

"Has she talked to you about the bastard?" Joe asked.

"No," Victoria said, shoveling soil around the base of the tree. "You?" She looked up at him.

"No. I feel like I should encourage her to, but I just don't know how." He leaned on the shovel. "I heard from the police in Sacramento. They've closed the file. There's no trace of the guy, and I guess there are more pressing issues. I just wish I could break a few of his bones, like he broke Patty's."

"I know. I do too." They looked at the job they had just finished. "It looks good. I can't wait until it blooms in the spring. I put in spring and winter bloomers all over this yard. I think it'll be nice."

"I'm sure it will." He put the shovel in the wheelbarrow and took Victoria's from her. "I wish she would see some of her old friends from high school. I'm sure some of them must still be around."

"It's hard, Joe, I know. But she'll get moving again when she's ready."

"I don't know. Remember how depressed you were for a while there. It took you a long time to come out of it, maybe years. I think you got depressed when you went through menopause, and it just never went away."

She was surprised. "I didn't realize you had noticed."

"Well, of course, I noticed." He was pushing the wheelbarrow toward the garden shed. Victoria followed him. "I just didn't know what to do about it, so I buried myself in my work and hoped it would go away." He stopped and looked at her. "I'm sorry I did that, Victoria. I should have tried to help you."

"It's not your fault, Joe. You probably wouldn't have gotten any further with me than we're getting with Patricia. People just don't pull out of depression until they're ready."

"But there must be something you can do to help them get ready."

"Well, if you think of something, let me know."

"Your next appointment is here, Ms. Vandor," Lillian said from the doorway of the potting shed.

"Very funny," Victoria answered. "I'll be right there." The first appointment had gone well, but it had just been advice about planting a terrarium. Jeff had insisted that she charge fifty dollars for an hour. She had felt too guilty, so had only charged thirty dollars. She could see his point, now. She'd spent an hour showing the customer how to plant a terrarium and suggesting good plants. Now she was behind on making the arrangements that they could sell in the shop for fifty dollars. Oh well, live and learn.

"They're in the classroom," Lillian said. "It's a couple and they have a folder with them. Wonder what that means."

"Me too." She washed her hands and dried them on a towel over the sink. "I guess I'll find out."

"Hello, Mr. Jasper, Mrs. Jasper. It's good to see you again." She shook their hands. "What's in the folder?"

"We brought pictures of the house," Mrs. Jasper said. Her husband smiled. "We thought you could get an idea of the other landscape and the style of the house so that you would better be able to design the planter."

"That's a wonderful idea," Victoria said. "But a planter shouldn't be too hard to design. It can't be too big."

"Oh no, dear," Mrs. Jasper said, putting the folder down on a table and opening it up. "My planter is very big." She pulled out a picture and put it on the table. Victoria felt her mouth fall open and closed it promptly. The house in the picture would be better described as a manor. It was three stories high at the entrance, which was covered by a portico. A circular drive ran under the portico. To each side of the entrance the building seemed to slope down and curve away into the distance. The driveway was at least a quarter of a mile long. There was a gate at the start of it. On one side of the drive there was a stand of trees. On the other side was the planter. It ran along the drive to the place where it became a circular driveway, maybe halfway to the house.

"Wow," Victoria said.

"It's two tenths of a mile long," Mr. Jasper said with a smile. It was the first thing he had said.

"Here's another angle." Mrs. Jasper pulled another picture out of the folder. "You see on this side there are steps every six feet for access." She pulled several other pictures out. In some of the pictures the planter had been landscaped, in some it was empty. "I wanted you to see what we've done with it before. I want something new, something different."

Victoria swallowed. Her mouth was dry again. "Well, can I study the pictures for a few days and draw up some plans?" Joe was right; she needed to get out from under the pressure. Right now her mind was blank.

"Of course," Mrs. Jasper said. "No one has come up with a plan in less than a month so far. I don't intend to do anything with it until spring. We put our Christmas decorations in it in the winter."

"That must be fun."

"Oh, it is. Now, we have our own garden staff, so you won't have to hire anyone. Of course, we always buy our plants from Landrum's." She smiled.

"That's good." Victoria felt tongue-tied.

"Well, we'll be going, dear. We'd like to hear from you before the month is up. Even though we won't plant until spring, we like to be involved in the planning process. Don't we, George?"

"Yes, we do." George extended his hand. Victoria shook it.

After they had gone, she sat down at the table and looked over the pictures. "I'm definitely in over my head."

"Talking to yourself again, Vic?" Jeff came into

the room and looked at the pictures spread out on the table. He laughed. "So you get the pleasure of landscaping the Jasper's planter this year?"

"You knew about this?"

"I didn't know they were coming here today. But I know about the planter. I've done my time on that planter." He didn't make it sound like much fun.

"Is it that bad?"

"No, it's not bad. It's just that the Jasper's like to be involved. The job demands patience." He laughed again and left the room.

"Wonder what he meant by that?" she said to herself.

Patricia and Joe were waiting for her in the kitchen when she got home that afternoon. "You two look like you're planning something," she said warily.

"We are," Joe said. "Can you leave now, or do you need to change."

"It depends on where we're going."

"We're going to the greyhound rescue shelter," Joe said. "I was telling Patricia about my trip to the beach last spring and I mentioned this friend I made while I was there. Remember, I told you about her. She has a shelter for retired racing dogs. She rehabilitates them and then finds them good homes." He stopped and looked at Patricia. "Patty said she'd like to go and see it."

"I hoped you'd come along," Patricia said. She didn't sound as excited about it as Joe did.

"Do you want one of these dogs?" Victoria asked her.

"I don't know." She looked down at her hands again. It was becoming a habit. Victoria's heart ached. Patricia looked so small, so wounded. "But I'd like to see them." She looked up. Were there tears in her eyes?

She looked at Joe. He seemed so excited. "She'd like to see them," he repeated, as though she hadn't heard him.

"Well, let's go then. Will it be open now?"

"I called Elizabeth. She said she'd meet us there."

They pulled up to the shelter. It was a big building with a large fenced area next to it. She assumed that was the area where they let the dogs out for exercise. There was a store in the front of the building. They got out of the car. Patricia was on her crutches. Joe had insisted that she bring them instead of the wheelchair.

Another car pulled up just as they were getting out. A very beautiful woman got out. She had fire-red hair that fell in curls around her face. She was tall, with long legs and a slim waist. She hurried toward them and put her arms around Joe. "It's so good to see you. I was afraid you'd never call, since it's been so long." She kissed Joe on the cheek.

Victoria felt a jolt. Starting at her chest, it ran through her limbs and her jaw clenched.

Joe hugged the woman back and then turned to where Victoria and Patricia stood. He must have read something in Victoria's face, because his eyes widened when he looked at her. Victoria smiled, sweetly.

"Elizabeth, this is my wife, Victoria, and my daughter Patricia."

Why is he smiling at her like that? Victoria thought. His dimples are showing. She smiled again.

"It's nice to meet you both. Come in and see the dogs." She turned in the direction of the building. Elizabeth and Joe walked side by side, chatting like old friends.

When they got inside, Patricia asked, "What made you decide to start rescuing greyhounds?" Victoria forgot her jealousy. Patricia actually sounded interested. Maybe this was a good idea.

"Well, I've always loved dogs. When I became aware of the plight of the greyhounds, I went to a racetrack and adopted a retired racer myself. When I discovered what a great friend he was, I decided to look into it."

"How do you manage to feed them? What about veterinary care?"

Joe and Victoria were speechless. It was the most their daughter had said since she'd been home.

"Well, I get donations from pet food companies. It's good advertising for them to be involved in this kind of thing. I have veterinary volunteers. The technicians can do a lot of the treatments that need to be done if a dog comes in sick or injured. The vet comes by once a week."

"What about the facility? It must cost a lot." Patricia looked around the room. They had walked through the storefront to a center room with Astro Turf on the floor. They were going toward the kennel.

"I *do* charge for my dogs. It pays the rent, and I can expect a better home if someone is willing to pay for the dog."

"That makes sense," Joe said.

Elizabeth unlatched the big door on the kennel and swung it open. All three of them stood staring for a minute. It was an awesome sight. There were greyhounds of every color in kennels along the walls and down the aisles. They were such beautiful creatures, so regal looking.

They walked down the first aisle. Elizabeth pointed out the different dogs. They all had names, of course, racing names. But they all had stories, too. She knew them all. She could tell you how old they were, how long they'd raced. What physical problems they'd had. Some had broken their legs. Some had scars from the starting gate. They all looked at the people with interest.

"I didn't realize that they came in so many colors," Patricia said.

"They come in every color you can imagine." Elizabeth laughed. "Most people think they're all gray."

"I guess I just never thought about it. You don't see a lot of them around." Patricia was going up the second aisle now. She was doing very well on her crutches. Victoria was watching her for any sign of pain or fatigue. She looked at Joe. He was watching her too.

They turned and started down the third aisle. "Patty, are you okay, honey. You're not overdoing it, are you?" Joe asked.

"I'm fine, Dad," she answered.

"What happened to your leg?" Elizabeth asked casually.

Victoria tensed and she heard Joe gasp beside her.

"I fell down the steps," Patricia said. She stopped in front of one of the last cages and just looked.

Elizabeth and Joe and Victoria had been looking at another dog a few cages back, but they caught up to her now and joined her. Patricia didn't say anything. She was just staring at the dog.

"This is Patch," Elizabeth said.

The dog was crouched in the corner of the cage. He was a dark gray color, almost blue, with a white patch on his right shoulder. He had his back turned to them as if he was trying to protect himself from something. His head was resting on his paws, but was turned back so that he could see them. His eyes were huge with a frightened look about them. He trembled as they stood there watching him.

"What happened to him?" Victoria asked.

"It's hard to tell. I would guess that he had a brutal trainer. You never know. Life isn't easy for them on the track. This dog is only about two years old. We've had him for two weeks. I can't seem to reach him," she sighed.

"What will happen to him if you can't reach him?" Joe asked.

"I don't know. I've never had to put one down. They can always be rehabilitated, but this dog, I don't know. He might just be too wounded." She turned and started back up the aisle.

"I want this dog," Patricia said.

"What?" Victoria looked at her.

"Honey, Elizabeth said she can't rehabilitate him," Joe said.

Elizabeth came back down the aisle toward them. "What did you say, Patricia?"

"I want this dog," she said louder and more firmly.

"She wants this dog," Victoria said to Joe. "How much do you charge for your dogs?" she said to Elizabeth.

"I can't let you have this dog," Elizabeth said gently. "It wouldn't be safe. Fear is a danger sign in dogs."

"I don't care. I want him. I need to have this dog." Patricia turned to Joe, her eyes pleading.

"Elizabeth." He looked at her. "I'll take full responsibility."

"We haven't even been able to get him out of the kennel. He's glued to the floor."

"I'll get him out," Joe said.

"This is not a good idea, Joe. He's never tried to snap at anyone, but as frightened as he is, you just don't know when he will."

"We'll put one of those muzzles on him until we're sure." He put his arm around her shoulder and turned her down the aisle away from Patricia and

Victoria. Victoria felt that stab of jealousy again, but swallowed it.

"Mom, he's just like me. We understand each other." She was staring at the dog again.

"I hope so. It's an awfully big dog."

Joe talked to Elizabeth for a few minutes then they came back down the aisle. "Patricia, Elizabeth has agreed to sell us the dog. You go to the car and I'll bring him."

"No, Dad, I want to stay with him."

"Honey, I can see the pain in your eyes. You've over done it."

"Please, Dad."

He sighed. "Okay. Victoria can you write Elizabeth a check for one hundred and fifty dollars?"

Elizabeth had gone into the kennel. She was talking quietly to the dog as she pulled the muzzle over his ears. Joe followed her into the kennel and picked up the dog. He carried him into the aisle and over to where Patricia was waiting. She put her hand on the dog's shoulder. His head hung over Joe's arm. She cupped his face in her hands and looked over the muzzle into his eyes. Victoria saw their eyes meet, a wounded girl and a wounded dog. Maybe they did understand each other. The little group walked out to the car like that.

Victoria wrote the check and got into the passenger seat.

"Let me know if you need any help," Elizabeth said, and leaned into Joe's window. "Don't wait so long to call again. Okay, Joe?"

"I'll be in touch. Thanks Elizabeth."

Victoria watched the back seat the whole way

home. The dog had his head on Patricia's lap, and she was stroking him. He was still cringing in fear, but the full weight of his head was resting on Patricia's thigh.

When they got home, Joe said, "Patty, please let me carry you in. I'm worried about that leg. I'll come right back out for the dog."

"Okay, Dad."

"Victoria, can you get some blankets together for him. I guess he'll sleep in Patty's room tonight."

"Okay, but with the muzzle, until we're sure."

"With the muzzle," Joe repeated.

"Okay," Patricia agreed.

Joe went around the car and picked up his daughter. She was so small it seemed no effort at all. Victoria followed them into the house. As they went toward the den where Patricia stayed, she put her arms around her father's neck and kissed him on the cheek. "Thank you, Dad," she said.

Victoria sniffed and wiped the tears from her eyes as she went to gather blankets for the dog.

"So let me make sure I'm clear on this," Victoria said, and sat up in bed. Joe was sitting on the side of the bed taking off his slippers. "You spent a week...in a cabin...at the beach...alone...next to the cabin... where that beautiful woman...was staying...alone."

"Sounds like you're clear on it." Joe leaned back on the pillows and stretched out. He put his hands behind his head and smiled at her.

"I don't suppose you noticed how pretty she is?"

"Of course I noticed. How does the saying go? I'm married, not dead." He laughed.

"Cute." She was quiet for a minute. "Did you do much together?"

"We had dinner a couple of times, walked on the beach a little."

"You walked on the beach with her?" Victoria gave him an angry look.

"Victoria, are you jealous?" He was smiling again.

"Of course I'm jealous. She's a tall, graceful redhead."

Joe rolled over on his side and put his hand across her waist. "Yes, she is, but I seem to be more attracted to short, clumsy, blondes." He pulled her down on the bed with him.

"I'm not clumsy," she said. "Did you kiss her?"

"Of course I didn't kiss her. Victoria, I'm a married man. We talked. I was feeling very insecure at that time. I needed a friend. I found one in Elizabeth. I haven't done anything I'm ashamed of." He studied her face for a minute. "It's not as much fun, when the shoe's on the other foot, is it?" He smiled. "Now that you're the one that's jealous, though, I can see why you enjoyed it so much."

Sixteen

"I can't believe I let you talk me into this," Victoria said to Jane. She was picking her way over rocks along the Chattahoochee River. It was Sunday. Jane had called her early that morning and suggested a picnic at the river.

"I'm a little surprised myself," Lillian said from behind her. "Aren't there snakes in these marshy areas of the river?"

"Oh, no, I hadn't thought of that," Victoria shrieked. "Jane, you know I'm afraid of snakes."

"You're afraid of everything, Tori," Jane said. "But it doesn't stop you." She stopped on a broad flat rock and took off her backpack. "This is the perfect spot for a picnic." By the time Victoria and Lillian had reached her, she had everything set up. "You were afraid to go parasailing, remember, but you went anyway."

"That's true. I'm glad I did, too. It was fun." Victoria took off her backpack and unzipped it. "She pulled out a pillow and sat on it."

"You brought a pillow?" Lillian laughed.

"I knew she'd make me sit on rocks and I have a boney butt."

Jane started pulling out food. "Now wasn't this worth the hike. Isn't it nice sitting here with the water rushing all around us?" She pulled out a bottle of wine and started to uncork it.

"Oh, no," Victoria said. "I'll drown trying to get back across if I drink that." She pulled a bottle of water out of her own backpack.

"Suit yourself. Would you like some, Lillian?" Jane offered a plastic wine glass to her.

"Maybe just one glass." Lillian took the glass and held it up for Jane to fill.

"Jane, you really shouldn't corrupt the young," Victoria scolded.

"She's a grown woman, and I have faith in her ability to make good decisions."

"Thanks, Jane." Lillian held her glass up in salute.

Jane started pulling out the food. There was a vegetable tray with ranch dressing, and a plastic container of cheese and whole-wheat crackers. She had grapes, and pears, with Brie. They all dug in. Everyone was silent for a few minutes while they ate.

"That was quite a hike," Lillian said. "How far would you say that was?"

"Actually, it was only about four miles."

"Oh, is *that* all?" Victoria laughed.

"You've been running for how long, Tori, ten months? This shouldn't be hard for you."

"Only about eight months," she said. "And besides, I haven't been able to run for a while since I broke my toe."

"You never told me how you broke that toe. What happened?" Jane asked.

"I'm not telling."

"Well, I'll tell you," Lillian said laughing. "She stepped off a ladder into a clay pot."

"Traitor," Victoria grumbled.

"Sorry, Vic, but it was funny. In fact, a lot of what you've done at the nursery has been funny." She looked back at Jane. "Did she tell you about falling into the compost bin?"

"Remind me." Jane leaned toward Lillian.

Lillian caught a glimpse of Victoria's stormy expression and said, "Another time." She continued to eat. "Anyway, Jeff made her go to a safety seminar. I don't think it did much good, though, because she broke her toe after that."

Jane looked over at her best friend. "Are we giving you a hard time, Tori? We're only teasing."

"Well, it wouldn't bother me if it wasn't all so true. I'm just so clumsy. There have been a couple of times I thought Jeff would fire me, for my own good." She looked worried.

"He won't fire you. He's crazy about you." Lillian looked back at Jane. "I think he's in love with her, but Joe has started hanging out with him, so I doubt he'll make a move."

"He's not in love with me," she sighed. "He is a good friend, though. I hate the thought of him being disgusted with me. But it seems like the harder I try to stay out of trouble, the more trouble I get into."

Jane looked closely at her friend. "This really bothers you, doesn't it, Tori?"

"I've never done anything that I enjoyed as much as this job," she said. "And Jeff has really encouraged me. I'm developing a career. I just hope I live through it."

"I think it's time I met this guy. Would he be bothered if I dropped by to see you at work one day?"

"What are you planning, Jane?" Victoria asked suspiciously.

"I'm not planning anything, Tori. What are you afraid of?"

"It's just so important to me, that's all."

"Well, then it's important to me, too." They were quiet for a while again. Jane passed the fruit and cheese. "Tell me about this dog, Tori. Whose idea was it to get Patricia a dog?"

"It happened in kind of a round about way." She paused to pop a grape in her mouth. She chewed and swallowed. "Joe was concerned because he couldn't seem to get close to Patricia. We've both had a hard time reaching her. She's just so depressed." She ate another grape. "Anyway, I suggested that he just tell her about himself. Not try to talk about her, but just talk about stuff. So he was telling her about his trip to the beach last spring."

"He went to the beach last spring without you?" Jane sounded surprised.

"Yes, we'd had, sort-of, a falling out."

"You had an argument, and he went to the beach?"

"That's right." She looked up at Jane. "Do you want to hear about the dog, or not?"

"Go ahead."

"Anyway, he met this woman when he was there." She frowned and was quiet for a minute. "She's really beautiful, tall and thin, red curly hair.

I can't believe he spent a week in a cabin next to hers."

"He spent a week in a cabin with a tall, beautiful redhead?" Jane demanded.

"Not in the cabin with her, in the cabin next to hers. They weren't staying together."

"Who are you trying to convince, Tori, me or you?"

"Both," she sighed. "I was so jealous when I met her. She ran up to him, and hugged him, and kissed his cheek. He smiled so big at her, it made his dimples show." Victoria realized she was angry, and stopped to look up.

"Tori, you don't think he's cheating on you, do you?" Jane sounded angry.

"No, of course I don't. He assures me it's innocent. He was in need of a friend and she was willing to listen. That's all." She looked down at the grape in her hand. "At least, that's what he says."

"Well, I hate to say it, Vic," Lillian cut in, "you really had it coming. You've been driving him crazy with jealousy over Jeff for months."

"That's different, Jeff is my boss. There's nothing going on between us." She looked up at her two friends. "Oh, well, I guess I did enjoy the attention. Anyway, he told Patricia about this friend. She has a facility where she rescues greyhounds, you know, the retired racing dogs. You should see them. I was in awe when she opened the door to the kennel. They're so beautiful."

"So, the three of you went over to look?"

"That's right. It was funny because when I got home from work, they were waiting for me. Joe had called and arranged to meet Elizabeth there. He seemed more excited about it than Patricia. I guess I know why now."

"Don't start that again. How did Patty pick out the dog?" Jane prompted.

"It was on the last row. She had been walking up and down the aisles of the kennel, using her crutches. Joe wouldn't let her take her wheelchair. I was noticing that she was limping more than usual. Joe and I were both concerned. Then she just stopped and stared into this kennel."

"It was like some kind of chemistry between them." Lillian's voice was dreamy.

"Well, yeah, I guess it was. This dog has been badly abused. He was crouched in a ball in the back of the kennel. His face was turned toward us, but it was down on the floor. He was so frightened that the whites of his eyes were showing."

"Oh, Tori, Patty could relate to him. That's awful," Jane said.

"I know, but it's working. She's been going to physical therapy for over a month now, but we couldn't get her to walk. She wanted to stay in her wheelchair. The therapist kept telling me that if she didn't use the leg, it would never get better. Dr. Fletcher told me to get rid of the chair, but I just couldn't take it away from her. It was like the security blanket she had when she was little." Victoria stopped for a minute and swallowed, struggling not to cry. She took a deep breath and continued. "Well, Joe had to pick the dog up and carry him out of the kennel, and that first morning, I tried to take him out of her room to go outside. I figured he had to pee and poop. But he wouldn't go."

"So what happened, surely you couldn't pick him up and carry him?" Jane prompted.

"No, I told Patricia that she would have to come with me, because he wouldn't leave her. She tried to come in her wheelchair, but he was so scared of the chair that he crouched on the floor and hid his face under the bed."

"Good for him. I guess that got her out of the chair." Jane laughed.

"It sure did, and she hasn't been back in it. She's using her crutches."

"Is it a nice dog?" Lillian asked.

"Seems to be. He won't let anyone except Patricia do much with him, but he loves Ethel and Theodore. Elizabeth said to watch him around small animals. She said that since these dogs are trained to chase rabbits, sometimes anything small isn't safe around them. We kept his muzzle on to introduce them, but they even play together, only when Patricia goes outside with him, though. He won't leave her."

"That's good."

"I was really happy for Joe. Patricia kissed him on the cheek and thanked him for it. It was really sweet." She dabbed at the tears on her cheek.

"Vic?" Jeff said. They were working together on a Thanksgiving display in the shop. "How are the plans for the Jasper's planter coming?"

"I've sketched a couple of ideas. It's really a challenge to do something different. I mean, there's only so much you can do with a planter."

"I know, that's why I was glad you were doing it this year." He walked around the display eyeing it critically. "Don't take too much time away from the Pitman's yard. How's that going?"

"I'm going up there on Wednesday, if that's okay with you?" She looked over at him.

"Sure."

"I think we've about finished what can be done this fall. It's getting late. We'll have to pick it back up in the spring."

"That's good. How does it look?"

"I was happy with it the last time I went up. Your crew does good work."

"Yeah, I trained all those boys myself. John graduates this year, though and will go on to better things. I guess I'll need to replace him. That's the only problem with hiring college students." He looked over to where Lillian was working at the cash register. "I'll really miss Lillian when she leaves."

"Gosh, I hadn't thought about that. We've become such good friends. You don't suppose she'll go back to Idaho, do you?" She looked at Jeff.

"Who knows?" The front door opened, bringing in a gust of cool fall air. Jeff turned around. "Wow!" he said. "Who's that? She's coming this way."

Victoria looked in the direction of the door. Jane was walking straight toward her. Jane always awed her. She was so beautiful, tall and slim, long, shapely legs moving beneath her knee-length skirt. Her snow-white hair swept up from her beautiful face in front, and fell to her shoulders in back. "That's my sister," she said with pride.

Jeff looked at Victoria. "I thought you were an only child?"

"We adopted each other."

Jane was smiling. "Tori, I was driving by and decided this would be a good time to drop in and see what you do."

Victoria smiled. "Jane, this is my employer, Jeff," she said. "Jeff, my sister, Jane."

Jeff extended his hand then noticed the potting soil on it. "Nice to meet you," he said, wiping his hand on his jeans.

"Hey Jane," Lillian joined them. "Came by to check him out, huh?" She nodded at Jeff and smiled.

"Check me out?" Jeff questioned. "Why?" He looked over at Victoria. She blushed.

"We have lunch together a couple of times a month," Jane explained. "They talk about you, and they talk about this place." She looked around. "I just wanted to be able to visualize it." She paused. "So who will show me around?"

"I'll show you around," Jeff said, before anyone else had time to speak. "You keep working on the display," he said to Victoria. Taking Jane's arm, he guided her away from the little group.

"That's interesting," Lillian said, as they watched the two of them move away. "He seems smitten."

"He does," Victoria was surprised to feel a pang of jealousy.

"Are you jealous?" Lillian looked at her.

"Of course I'm not." She started back to her

work. "If I was jealous of Jane, I'd have killed myself by now. Everyone falls in love with her."

"Why do you suppose she never got married?"

"She never wanted to." She watched Jane and Jeff disappear into the potting shed. He was telling her something, but she couldn't hear what. A customer came up to her and asked a question. A line had formed at the checkout counter, so Lillian went back over there.

"Let's go to lunch," Jane said from behind her.

Victoria jumped. "You startled me." She laughed.

"You were concentrating on what you were doing. I see why you love this job. It seems like a fun place to work," Jane said. "And Jeff is very handsome and charming."

"Of course, now that he's seen you, he won't pay attention to me any more." She pouted.

"Tori, you can't have all the men." Jane laughed. "Jeff said I could take you to lunch if I didn't keep you too long. Let's go." She went toward the door.

"Wait," Victoria called after her. "I have to get my purse. I'll meet you out front."

When she got out to the car, Jeff was standing beside the driver's side window talking to Jane. He smiled when Victoria came over to the car. He walked around to the passenger side door and opened it for her. "What a gentleman," she teased. She got into the car and opened the window.

Jeff leaned in and said, "Don't be gone too long, Vic. I need to talk to you about something." He looked over at Jane. "I guess I'll see you Sunday."

"Sounds good." Jane smiled.

"Sunday?" Victoria questioned, as they pulled out of the lot.

"We're going cycling." Jane looked at her. "Do you mind?"

"No." She looked out the window for a minute then said, "He's even younger than me, you know."

"So?"

"Jeff, during lunch Jane asked me if I would draw up some plans for the lobby of her office building. They fired their other plant people because they weren't doing a good job. Do we do that kind of thing?" Victoria asked.

"I never have gotten into that part of the market. I prefer outdoor gardening, myself." He was up on a ladder reaching down for the stack of plastic pots that she was holding. "But if it interests you, then go for it. There's really a lot of money in it. If you get much corporate work, though, you'll need a whole different staff. You'll have to train people on how to keep plants alive and looking good."

"I could do that. Will you help me figure out how to price it?" She handed him another stack.

"Sure." They worked quietly for a while. "That reminds me, Vic, I'm going to hire someone part-time, to help you out. With all the contract work you've been doing, we're not getting the in-house stuff finished."

"I've been worrying about that. I thought I'd try to put in more hours, but with having to take Patricia to physical therapy and doctor appointments and all, I really don't have any more time."

"Don't worry about that. I think we can justify a part-time person." He came down from the ladder. "How's Patricia doing, anyway?"

"Better, I think. That dog helps a lot. At least he got her out of the wheelchair. She works with him a lot, so she's not brooding so much. But sometimes I look at her and she just seems so sad. She won't talk to us about what happened. That's okay. We don't have to know all of her secrets, but I just can't help but believe that she'll never get over this if she doesn't talk about it to someone."

"She still won't see a therapist?"

"We suggested it again. She refuses to go. We can't make her go. She is a grown woman after all."

"That's true. Gosh, Vic, I'm sorry. This is hard on you. It's hard on Joe, too. When we played racquetball last week, he told me how guilty he feels."

"I know. He blames himself for the whole thing." She worked in silence for a while.

"I heard from the garden show committee," Jeff said after a minute. They were in the potting shed putting away supplies. "Each year they select a number of people from different parts of the country to talk about the past year's growing season. Kind of give everyone an idea of what the weather was like, what plants did well, which ones didn't, that kind of thing. This year we were chosen. I want you to do it. I think it'll be good experience for you." He hung the ladder on the peg on the wall and left the room.

Victoria stood still for a moment with her mouth

open. Then she closed it and ran after him. "No Jeff, I'm afraid to speak in public. I can't do it."

"Sure you can." He continued across the showroom and into his office.

"You don't understand." She had to run to keep up with him. "I couldn't even participate in class when I was in school. I'm really shy."

He studied her face for a moment. "You really are scared to do this."

"Yes." She sighed in relief. He'd seen her point. She was off the hook.

"Well, that won't do. You have to get over that. This is the perfect opportunity for you to start." He looked at his computer screen.

"No, Jeff," she cried. "I'll probably die, or something, if you make me do it."

"You won't die." He continued to work. "I'll help you with the speech. I'll draw up an outline that you can fill in with your own words. You can practice it on me. You'll do fine. You'll see." He was dismissing her and her fears.

"You are just too pushy, sometimes. You've pushed me into doing everything I've done in the past six months. It's time for you to stop. I'm putting my foot down. I won't do it." She spoke very firmly.

He stopped what he was doing and looked at her. She crossed her arms and looked him in the eyes. After a minute, she was uncomfortable, so she lifted her chin. He smiled slowly at her.

"Okay. I guess it's your decision."

"Yes, it is."

"What if I say please? I really want you to do this."

"Why?"

"Because I'm proud to have you to represent my nursery, and because I know you can do this well, and because it will be a good experience for you."

She sat down in a chair and put her face in her hands. "I can't, Jeff. You just don't understand how scared I am."

"Jane says you're afraid of everything, but you do it all anyway."

"Jane talks too much," she mumbled into her hands. Taking a deep breath, she looked up at him. "I'll think about it."

"What did you say?"

She looked up at him and stuck out her tongue. "I'll think about it, but don't get your hopes up."

"All right, it's entirely your decision."

Seventeen

Something was bothering her. It was a terrible noise, a ringing sound.

"Victoria, the phone's ringing." Joe was shaking her shoulder. "Answer it." He reached over her. "Here, I'll get it." She'd been so sound asleep that she hadn't realized what it was. Now Joe had the cord stretched across her face. "Hello," he said into the receiver.

Victoria sat up in bed and waited. She looked at the clock. It was 2:00 a.m.

"All right, we'll be there as soon as we can get there." He reached across her and hung up the phone.

"What is it?" Her heart was pounding. It couldn't be good.

"It's your mother. They're taking her to the emergency room. We need to meet them there." Joe got out of bed.

"What happened? What's wrong with her?" she asked.

"I don't know. The ambulance driver just said that they were going to North Side Hospital ER and that we should meet them there." He was putting on a pair of jeans. "Come on, Victoria, we need to go."

She jumped out of bed and ran into her closet. She grabbed the jeans and sweatshirt she had worn the day before, and pulled them on, pulled on a pair of socks and sneakers and turned to run down the steps. "Should we tell Patricia?"

"No, let her sleep, we'll leave her a note so she'll know where we've gone if she wakes up, but I hate to worry her until we know more." They hurried into the kitchen. Joe wrote a quick note on the dry erase board and they hurried out to the car.

"I'm scared to death," Victoria said.

"I know." Joe patted her hand. "I am too."

The hospital wasn't far from their house, so it only took a couple of minutes. They hurried up to the desk. "We were told that Amanda Bailey was being brought here from the assisted living complex. Has she arrived?"

"I'll have to check, sir. You can be seated. I'll be right back." The girl went through a door behind the desk.

Joe and Victoria looked at each other. Joe put his arm around her shoulders and guided her to a row of chairs. They sat down. Neither one of them said anything. There was nothing to say. They didn't know what had happened. They didn't know what they were facing. There was nothing to do but wait and hope that they could deal with whatever it was.

"I should have gone to see her yesterday. I thought about it on my way home from work, but I was so tired." Victoria finally broke the silence.

"This isn't your fault, Victoria," Joe said, and took her hand.

"I know, but I wish I had gone to see her."

They were silent again. It seemed like hours before the attendant came back.

"Mr. and Mrs. Vandor," she called to them. "You can come back." She motioned for them to follow her. She took them to an office and told them to be seated. "The doctor will be in shortly," she said, and left them there.

"This isn't good. Why aren't we in an exam room with her?" Victoria stood and started to pace. "It must be bad news or she wouldn't have put us in the doctor's office."

"There's nothing we can do, but wait, Victoria. Come and sit down."

"I don't want to sit down. Let me pace."

"Okay." Silence again.

The door opened and the doctor came in. He held out his hand to them. "I'm Dr. Henry," he said.

"I remember you," Victoria said. "You treated me when I had a car accident last spring."

"Of course, that's right. I trust your recovery was complete."

"Yes. Dr. Henry, how is my mother?"

He sighed. "I'm afraid there was nothing we could do. She died just minutes after she arrived. It was a ruptured aneurism. I'm very sorry."

Suddenly the lights in the room were so bright that they hurt her eyes. The voices and sounds from the hall were too loud. She could feel an indescribable current of some kind run through her body. Her ears were ringing and she couldn't remember how to breathe. "No," she whispered.

"Victoria," Joe was holding her by the shoulders. "Honey, sit down. You don't look well."

"I didn't say goodbye," she whispered.

"Mrs. Vandor, can I get you a sedative," Dr. Henry suggested. "You're shaking."

"That's a good idea," Joe said, easing her into a chair.

"No, I don't want a drug." Victoria stood up again. "I need to see her. I can see her, can't I?"

"Of course, I'll take you to her." Dr. Henry led them to an exam room. "Take all the time you need." He left them outside the door.

Victoria looked up at Joe. He looked at her with concern. "Do you want to be alone or should I come in with you?"

"You come with me." She turned and pushed the door open. Her mother lay on the bed. Victoria could see the familiar outline of her body under a sheet that was drawn over her face. Victoria walked slowly over to the bed. She pulled the sheet down to reveal her face. Her beautiful face, the face that had looked at her with love, and pride, and anger, and worry, and all the feelings that had shown on mother's face; the face she loved to see when she got home after school, or when she was afraid at night. Tears were rolling down her cheeks. "I can't live without her, Joe," she said. She looked up at him. His face was streaked with tears too.

"You'll have to, Victoria, we both will." He drew her into his arms and she wrapped her arms around his waist. They cried together for a few minutes and then held on to each other. Victoria pulled the sheet back up and whispered, "I love you, Mom."

"I don't know what to do now, Joe." They were on their way home from the hospital. "Do I have to decide something about the body, or make some kind of arrangements? My father died when I was only fifteen years old. My mother made all the arrangements then."

"I don't know either, but I guess we'll find out."

"I think she wanted to be cremated. I don't think we'll have a viewing. I've never felt right about that."

"Whatever you think."

"I just can't believe she's gone. I knew she would die someday, but I don't think I ever really believed it would happen." She looked out the window at the night sky. "I guess that's stupid, isn't it?"

"No, I don't think I believed it would really happen either."

"Vic," Jeff said, two days later when she walked into work. "It's perfectly understandable for you to take some time off right now."

"It's better for me to keep working," she answered. "Otherwise, I just cry."

"It's understandable for you to cry, too." He pulled her against his chest and held her. He smelled nice like soap, and soil, and man.

"I should be ashamed of myself," she said.

"Why?"

"Nothing, I didn't mean to say that out loud," she said, not wanting to admit that she was enjoying the way he smelled. She let him hold her for a minute then pushed away when she felt tears collecting in her eyes again. "Don't be nice to me, Jeff. I don't want to cry again. It's giving me a headache."

"I know how much you loved your mother, Vic. It's hard to say goodbye for the last time. Allow yourself those feelings." He put his arm around her shoulders and walked with her back to the break-room where the lockers were.

"I know, but I need to get away from the grief for a little while." She put her purse and lunch bag in the locker. "What do you have for me to do around here? Have you heard anything from the Jaspers? They wanted to make an appointment to look over the plans with me."

"Yes, they called. I told them that I'd have you call them." He tilted her face up and looked into her eyes. "You're sure you're all right?"

"I'm all right. I just don't know how I'll live without her. How do you live without your mother? I mean, it's the only person in the world who is always on your side."

"You have a lot of people on your side, Vic. How about me, I'm always on your side."

"That's true. Why is that, Jeff?" She looked up at him.

"I don't know. I guess I like you." He turned around and started toward the potting shed. "I've got pansies, and snapdragons in here that need to be repotted and put on display. The mums didn't come in yet. They're really late. I'll have to check on that order. Luckily, I have a fairly good supply in the greenhouse, but it won't be enough to get us through the holiday season."

It was mid-November and they were decorating for Thanksgiving. Immediately afterward would come the Christmas rush.

"I didn't realize this was such a busy season for you. I always thought it would be slow with the growing season over." She followed him into the shed and put on a fresh pair of gloves.

"The holiday's are busy for everyone." Jeff started to work. "I've got a high school kid coming for an interview this afternoon, for that part-time position. I thought you would like to meet him. Make sure you think he's someone you can work with. It'll be pretty much up to you to train him."

"I've trained people at the grocery before, I hope I can do it here."

"I'm sure you can."

"I hope he isn't coming too late, I need to leave about 4:30. Ellen and Alex are flying in this afternoon."

"Really, when is the memorial service? I'd like to come to it, if that's okay."

"It's Monday, at 2:00. You don't have to come, Jeff, you didn't know her."

"I'd like to be there with you and Joe. You wouldn't mind, would you?"

"Of course I wouldn't mind."

They worked in silence for a while. It was the first time she hadn't felt numb since her mother had died. She had gone through the last few days in a blur. There'd been the apartment to clear out. The complex wanted it ready as soon as possible. They had a long waiting list of people who wanted it. Imagine just waiting for someone to die. She'd had to make arrangements to have her mother's body cremated. They'd delivered the ashes to her, to hold on to until she could think more clearly about where they should be spread. Something meaningful would come to her. She was sure. "I keep thinking of something I want to tell her," she said, wiping at a tear.

"I remember that. It goes away after a while." Jeff touched her shoulder. "Someday you'll be able to think about her without pain."

They lapsed into silence again. The work was therapeutic. Victoria buried herself in it, using her hands to mix the soil and peat. She could feel the muscles in her hands and arms flexing and relaxing in rhythm with the movement. She dipped her arms deeply into the container of soil, scooping as much as she could hold and pulling it up. Her hands were in gloves, but she could feel the cool soft texture of the soil, the fluff and fiber of the moss on her arms above the gloves. Suddenly her legs began to ache with the need to stretch and flex. "Jeff, I want to run. Can I go home and change? I'll come back after lunch."

"Go ahead. You don't have to come back. Lillian's coming in. We can finish this."

"No. I'll be back." She hurried to her locker. The clock on the wall said 10:20 a.m. She could go home and run for an hour and still be back by noon or shortly after. "I can't believe how much I want to run," she said.

She passed Patricia on the way through the kitchen. She was drinking a cup of coffee. The dog was on the floor next to her. "Mom, are you all right?"

"Yes, I just need to run." She hurried through without slowing down.

Joe came out of his office. "Victoria," he called to her.

She didn't slow down. "I don't know when I've felt so driven," she said, loud enough for Joe to hear. He followed her up the stairs.

She was in her closet when he came into the room. In only seconds, she was on the way out the door, dressed for running.

"Do you want me to come along?" Joe asked.

"No. I want to go alone."

The sensations were incredible, the familiar ache of her calves when she first started to run. She loved the instant strain of her thighs that quickly gave way to the glorious feeling of a fully-engaged muscle. Her chest rose and fell with the speed of her run. Realizing that she was running too fast to maintain, she slowed to a more relaxed pace. That felt good. She didn't know how long she was lost in the fluid movements of her legs and the steady rhythm of her breathing. "I'll be all right, Mom," she said. The numbness had gone. In its place were a powerful sense of loss, and an equally powerful feeling of inner strength. Without conscious decision, Victoria turned toward home. When she arrived, she sat down on the front stoop for a minute. She wrapped her arms around her head and rested it on her knees.

"Mom," Patricia said. "What are you doing?'

She looked up. Her daughter stood in front of her. The greyhound stood slightly behind her, peering around her side. Smiling, she said, "Catching my breath. I had a good run." She panted a little, stood up and stretched her legs. Patricia leaned on one of her crutches. She had abandoned the other to hold the dog's leash. "When do you think you'll be able to give up that crutch?" Victoria asked.

"I don't know." Patricia looked at the ground. "I'm not in a hurry."

"I guess not." She started up the steps to the front door. "How's Patch?"

"He's doing better, but he's still afraid of everyone but me." She stroked the dog's head. Patricia had cried at the news of her grandmother's death. Other than that, she had shown very little emotion about anything else.

"I wish you could run," Victoria said, as she opened the door. "It works miracles." She went inside and up the stairs.

On the morning of the memorial service they all sat around the table in the kitchen eating breakfast. Ellen and Alex had arrived on Saturday evening. Ellen looked adorable with her round belly on her tall thin frame. She had her hair cut shorter than it had been before. It was straight like Victoria's, though it was a rich, deep-brown color like Joe's. She had cried, too, when she'd heard the news, but even in the face of this sad event, her happiness showed.

"Did we tell you that we're having a boy?" she asked.

"No." Joe looked up from his coffee. "That's great, a boy at last." He laughed. Patricia immediately looked down at her plate. Victoria looked at Joe. He'd noticed it too.

"How do you know?" Jane asked. She was over for breakfast. This was a family gathering, and she was part of this family.

"We had an ultrasound."

"I didn't know they could tell from that."

Alex said, "Yes, they can. The technology has become so advanced that they're usually right, too." Alex was as excited as Ellen. "Sometimes they make mistakes, though. So I still want to paint the nursery a neutral color."

"I don't." Ellen laughed. "I know it's a boy. Mothers know these things. Don't they, Mom?"

"I'm sure you do, but I didn't know anything. I'm not the one to decide what color to paint your nursery." She smiled. "Have you thought about names?"

"Well, we can't quite agree. So it's undecided. But he'll have a double last name. Vandor-Burke. It's just the first name we can't decide on."

"That's nice, honey, I like that," Victoria said.

"Where're you going, Shirley?" Alex asked, as Patricia rose from the table.

She collected her crutch and limped toward the door with the dog right behind her. "I'm taking Patch out back. He went out this morning, but I think he should go again, since I'll have to leave him alone for so long this afternoon."

"Do you want me to come with you?" Alex asked, hopefully.

"No. That's not necessary. He'd probably just be afraid of you." She left the kitchen and a few seconds later the back door shut.

"She's still so depressed." Ellen looked at her parents. "Isn't there something we can do?"

"Well, she won't see a therapist. She doesn't want to see any of her old friends. Anyone would be depressed if they stayed hidden in their own house all the time," Victoria said. "The dog really helped at first. He got her out of that wheelchair, at least. But now she seems to be using him as an excuse not to talk to people."

"I hate to see her like this," Alex said. "We were good friends. She's hardly said a word to me since I've been here."

"Don't feel bad, Alex, she doesn't talk to us either." Victoria started to clear the plates.

"Excuse me." Joe rose from the table and made his way through the room. Again, there was the sound of the back door closing.

Victoria watched out the kitchen window as Joe walked over to his daughter. He said something to her. She looked down at the dog and said something back. Joe took her hand and turned her to look at him. She wished she could hear what they were saying. Well, if they had wanted her to hear it, they'd have included her. She went back to clearing the table.

"So, Ellen," Jane said, "Do you think you'll move back to Atlanta?"

"Probably not, we're really happy in Seattle." She looked at her husband fondly.

He kissed her cheek. "Yes, we are, but you never know. I am subject to transfer with the company I work for."

"We'd love to have you a little closer. We all want

to know our grandchild while he's growing up." Jane laughed. "I am, after all, his Great Aunt Jane."

"Yes, you are. Did I tell you how close Mom and Jane are?" Ellen asked Alex.

"I think you may have mentioned it."

"I asked her why she apologized to me when she saw me at the hospital. Remember that first day, she said 'I'm so sorry, Dad.' I didn't understand it at the time and it's been bothering me ever since, but there never seemed to be a good time to ask." Joe was getting dressed for the service. It started at 2:00 and would probably last until about 5:00.

"What did she say?" Victoria was sitting on the bed. She'd been ready to go for a while.

"She said that she hated disappointing me again." He turned from the mirror and looked at her. His eyes were bright with pain. "I told you this was my fault."

"Did she explain it, Joe? What did she mean *disappoint you again*?"

"She didn't want to talk about it, but I pushed her. I had to know. She said that she knew I had wanted a boy when she was born. She said that not only was she a girl, but she was a runt who couldn't do anything." He turned back to the mirror to readjust his tie, and maybe to collect himself. "It's just like I told you, Victoria. She felt like she couldn't do anything right. Why didn't I realize she was feeling that way? I do love her, Victoria. I really do."

"I'm sure she knows that, Joe. I should have known that she felt that way, too. But I had no idea." Victoria looked distracted. "She was always such a quiet child."

"How will I make it up to her? How can I convince her that I love her, that I'm glad she's my daughter?" Joe's eyes were cloudy.

"I don't know. I don't know."

"Excuse me, Mrs. Vandor." Victoria was standing at the entrance of the room at the funeral home greeting people. She turned to find a young man at her side. He was average height, maybe a little stocky. He had brown hair and brown eyes, and a very pleasant face. Looking at him made her want to smile. "I'm Bobby Jessup, my mother works at the home where your mother lived. I was sorry to hear about her death."

"Thank you, did you know her?" she asked.

"No. I brought my mom here today. She doesn't drive, and, well, the truth is, I was hoping Patty might be here. I was in high school with her. We did a biology project together. I just thought it would be nice to see her again. Of course, this probably isn't the time." He was rambling.

"No. I think this is a good time. She is here." She looked around for Patricia. Spotting her across the room sitting in a chair against the wall alone, she said, "I'll take you over to her." They made their way through the crowd to Patricia. "Patricia, do you remember Bobby Jessup from high school?"

Patricia looked up at him. "Yes, we worked together on a project in Biology," she said without smiling. She looked back down at her hands.

"I was sorry to hear about your grandmother, Patty. I remember how close you were to her."

"Thanks."

Bobby looked at Victoria. She smiled apologetically. He looked back at Patricia and noticed the crutch beside her. He stepped back a little. "Do you mind if I sit with you for a minute? I brought my mother here and she seems to know a lot of people."

"If that's what you want to do."

He pulled up a chair and sat. "Your mom called you Patricia. Do you prefer that to Patty?"

"Yes," she said.

"I mean, we're not kids anymore. Of course, people still call me Bobby. I think I'd prefer Bob. I don't know about Robert, though. I'm not sure I like it."

"You don't like your name?" Patricia smiled briefly.

"I don't know. What do you think?"

"I think this is a silly conversation."

"Okay. Let's change the subject, then. What did you do after high school?"

Victoria moved away. She wanted to stay and listen, but that would be wrong.

"Thanks, Mom," she whispered.

"Hello, Vic," Jeff took her elbow. "Are you holding up okay?"

"Yes, I've been running every day. It helps a lot

with the stress. I know it's not good for my joints, but I'll stop going every day after things calm down."

"Whatever works. Who's the young man talking to Patricia?"

"Bobby Jessup, he went to high school with her. I hope he can get through to her."

"I do too. Ellen is radiant. She and her young man seem very happy." They looked across the room to where Ellen and Alex stood side by side, talking to an older couple. They seemed to move together as if invisible threads connected them.

"A match made in heaven," Jeff said.

"It certainly looks that way. It's hard to believe that Ellen is so settled. She was a wild teen and young adult."

"Was she really? You wouldn't know it to look at her now."

"If she put on a bathing suit, you would. She's covered with tattoos."

Jeff had stretched his arm across her shoulders and was leaning close to hear what she said.

"Unhand my wife, sir," Joe said, from behind them.

They both turned and smiled. "You get to enjoy her every day. I have to take what I can get," Jeff said.

"You probably see her as much as I do."

"Thanks, guys." Victoria laughed. "If you're trying to lift my spirits, it's working." The three of them had developed a solid friendship.

Jane joined them, and said, "This service is very nice, Tori. The wall of memories is a great idea." She pointed to where they had hung a collection of pictures of her mother at various stages of life, with various family members and friends. "I especially like the picture of her playing in the stream with the girls."

"The whole thing was Patricia's idea," Victoria said. "It was very therapeutic going through all those pictures. There wasn't time to get them framed professionally, so I bought frames and did it myself."

"Patty came up with that idea?" Joe sounded surprised.

"I thought you knew that," Victoria said. "She's very creative."

"No, I didn't know. Where is she? I think I'll go tell her how proud I am of her."

"She's over there talking to an old friend from high school." She pointed to where Patricia sat talking to Bobby.

"Do we know him?" Joe was frowning. "I hope he's a nice boy."

"He seemed very nice to me, Joe."

Joe left them and made his way across the room to Patricia. Victoria watched him go. "This whole thing with Patricia has really shaken Joe up," she said, and turned to Jane. "I'm concerned about him."

"I am too," Jeff said. "He really believes that it's his fault. I hope he doesn't become too possessive of Patricia. That won't help."

"No, it won't," Jane said.

They all watched as Joe stiffly shook Bobby's hand. He looked very intimidating, with his scowl. He stood a good six inches taller than the young man. Bobby returned the shake and began talking to him easily.

"He's a nice kid," Victoria said. "I hope he stays around and earns Joe's trust."

Eighteen

"Ellen said that she was sorry she didn't have much time to spend with me, said we'd get reacquainted when the baby comes," Victoria said to Jane and Lillian. They were riding Jane's tandem bicycle on the Silver Comet Trail. "Can you imagine? She hasn't wanted to talk to me for years, unless she wanted money, of course."

"Well, they say children come back around," Jane said. "How about you, Lillian? How do you feel about your mother?"

"I like to talk to her on the phone, but I'm glad we don't live in the same city. She's very critical. As far as she's concerned, I never do anything right." Lillian was riding beside them on her own bicycle.

"I don't remember being critical." Victoria thought about it for a while. "Well, I guess I did, kind of bitch at them. But they deserved it, especially Ellen. She was really a rotten kid."

"She probably had to break away from you in order to stop being rotten," Lillian said. "I mean, when you have someone to defy, you don't really think about what you do. You just do the opposite of what they want you to do." Everyone was quiet for a minute. "That sounded confusing, even to me."

They all laughed. "I think I know what you mean, though," Jane said.

"Actually, I thought it was pretty well said," Victoria agreed. "Anyway, it was nice having the whole family together. I sure do miss my mom, though."

"Of course, you never did anything right, as far as your mom was concerned either, Tori."

"That's true, but I think it was just her way of paying attention to me."

"You're so benevolent, Tori. That's what I love about you, one of the things, anyway."

"Why do you have a tandem bicycle, Jane?" Lillian changed the subject. "I thought you lived alone."

"She bought it so that she and I could ride together," Victoria said. "I never could learn to ride a bicycle."

"You're kidding?" Lillian laughed.

"No, she's not," Jane said. "That's how I first became an athlete. I ran along beside her bicycle so much trying to teach her, that I started to like exercise."

"But she never did learn?"

"Excuse me. Don't talk about me like I'm not here," Victoria interrupted. "No, I never could learn. Ellen and Joe used to flip a coin to decide who had to ride tandem with me, when we went to Callaway Gardens. Patricia was too small. She couldn't hold me up."

"What's wrong, no sense of balance?"

"I guess."

"Maybe that's why you get into so much trouble at the nursery. I don't think I've ever seen an employee that had so many accidents. Jeff worries about you, of course, he's crazy about you anyway."

"He is crazy about you, Tori," Jane said. "When he and I went cycling, you're all he talked about. I think you broke his heart."

"I don't think so," Victoria said. "Have you seen any more of him?"

"Why, are you jealous?"

"Believe it or not, yes." She laughed. "It surprised me when I realized it. I have to admit I was enjoying all of the attention."

"Well, he still gives you a lot of attention," Lillian said. "Have you seen him again, Jane?"

"We've had dinner a few times. He's really a very nice man, too young for me of course, but fun to be with."

They rode in silence for a while. It was beautiful out, one of those cool crisp winter days. The sun was warm, and as long as they kept moving, they weren't cold. When they stopped for lunch, though, they had to put their jackets on.

Jane rolled out a blanket and sat down on a grassy spot beside the road. She unpacked the basket and passed sandwiches and potato salad around. They ate in silence for a while.

"How's your project with the indoor gardening going, Vic?" Lillian asked.

"It's going really well. I have so much business it looks like we may have to hire another part-time person."

"How's it going with Jason?"

"Who's Jason?" Jane asked.

"He's the high school student Jeff hired to help Vic out. She's doing so much contract work that she can't get the in-house work done."

"That's great, Tori. Are you enjoying it?"

"Yes, it's fun. I like drawing the plans the most. Dealing with the people is a little bit stressful for someone as shy as me. I have to admit, I do miss the greenhouse work."

"You don't have as many accidents that way," Lillian pointed out.

"That's true."

"Have you given Jeff your answer about the speech he wants you to make?"

"You're making a speech, Tori? That's great." Jane was excited.

"I wish I felt that way. I'm scared to death."

"Tori, you're..."

"I know, I'm afraid of everything, but I do it anyway."

"Well, it's true."

"So you did tell Jeff that you'd do it?" Lillian asked again.

"Yes. He just wants me to so much. I can't understand why."

"Like I said, he's crazy about you."

"Well, I just hope I don't throw up or something."

Later that day, Victoria was in the front yard. Ethel and Theodore were with her. She was pulling the ivy off the trees. It was a never-ending battle. "I wish I could get rid of it all," she said out loud.

"All what, dear?" Dolores Crisp asked from behind her.

She turned around. "Hello Dolores, you always seem to catch me talking to myself."

"You talk to yourself a lot?" Dolores raised one brow.

"Yes, I do." Victoria turned back to what she was doing.

"My goodness, what an odd-looking little dog," Dolores said.

Victoria turned around to see Ethel sniffing her neighbor's leg. Dolores raised her foot as if to kick her. "Don't kick my dog," Victoria said firmly.

"Well, make it stop sniffing me," Dolores said. Just as Victoria called Ethel, Theodore bounced out from behind the tall monkey grass and latched onto the leg that was raised to kick the dog. "Ahhhg," Dolores yelled. "What is that?"

"It's Theodore. He's very protective of Ethel. You'd probably better go," she said, as she scooped up the cat. "If you don't threaten them, they won't hurt you." She turned back to her task and smiled a little to herself. She heard someone approach her a few minutes later and braced herself for another confrontation with her neighbor.

"Mrs. Vandor?"

She recognized Bobby Jessup's voice and turned around. "Hello, Bobby, it's nice to see you again." She felt genuinely pleased. He had such a pleasant face and friendly manner.

"I guess I'm taking a chance here." He shifted nervously from foot to foot. "I asked Patricia if she'd go to dinner with me and she said no. Said she wasn't comfortable going out to a restaurant. I haven't talked to her for a week, but I hoped she wouldn't mind if I came by to visit."

"I'm sorry, Bobby. She's had a hard time. I hope she didn't hurt your feelings."

"My feelings can take it. But, I would like to know what happened to her. She was shy in school, but she didn't seem so withdrawn then. I asked her what happened to her leg, but she just said she fell down some steps."

"I can't tell you any more. She'd have to be the one to do that. But I can invite you in, if you're still willing to take the chance."

"I'd like that."

She led him in the front door and looked around for Patricia. She knocked on the door of her room, but there was no answer. She went into the kitchen. Through the window she saw Patricia in the yard with Patch. She was leaning heavily on her crutch. "There she is. She's taken her dog out."

"Is that a greyhound? What a beautiful dog."

"Yes, he is. You can go out this door." She led him to the back door. "The dog has been badly abused, so approach him slowly. He's gentle, but very frightened."

She watched as Bobby crossed the yard toward Patricia. As he drew near to her, she looked up. Her expression was guarded. He said something to her and looked at the dog. She said something back and also looked at the dog. He held his hand out palm up, for Patch to sniff. The greyhound's eyes were huge and frightened, but he sniffed the extended hand. After a minute, Bobby stroked the side of the dog's face and then down his neck. "He knows something about dogs. Good," she said.

"What did you say, Victoria?" Joe asked from his office.

"Bobby Jessup is here to visit Patricia. He seems to have a way with dogs. Patch is actually letting him touch him. The dog is actually not hiding behind Patricia."

Joe came up behind her and looked out the window over her shoulder. "I guess that's good. He seems like an awfully nice kid. But I have to admit, I'm as anxious about young men as Patty is. I wish I could keep her from ever being hurt again."

She turned around and put her arms around him, burying her head in his chest, she inhaled the scent of him. "You're a wonderful man."

His arms closed around her. "I don't know about that, but I do love my girls. It was nice seeing Ellen again, too."

"Yes, it was."

They watched as Bobby walked slowly beside Patricia up to the patio. He arranged two chairs to look out toward the yard. Patch, of course, was right behind Patricia all the way. He held one of the chairs for her and then seated himself in the other. He proceeded to chat, occasionally gesturing with his hand. Patch shied away from his hand once so he put it down in his lap. Patricia looked interested in what he was talking about.

Ethel scratched at the door to go out. Joe opened it for her and the little cat followed her out. They joined Patch on the lawn in front of where Patricia and Bobby sat, and started to play. Ethel liked to weave in and out of Patch's legs. The playful kitten bounced along behind her, batting at her tail. Patch lowered his head and sniffed and nudged them playfully with his long nose, while Bobby and Patricia laughed at their antics.

"That's nice," Victoria said.

"Yes it is. I've got some work to finish. Then I'll help you with dinner." Joe went back into his office.

It was two o'clock in the morning. That was at least the fourth time Victoria had looked at the clock. It was becoming clear. She was not going to sleep. It wouldn't be so bad if she could just lie still and be comfortable, but she was restless. She hadn't found a comfortable position yet, even though she had tried every side, every way possible. It was a full moon. She never could sleep at full moon. "Maybe we just need heavier shades," she said, as she tried again for the right position.

"Maybe I should get up and read." She looked over at Joe. The moonlight was so bright she could see him clearly. He lay on his side, facing away from her. She looked at the way his broad shoulders tapered down to a narrow waist and hips. She could see the muscles of his legs through the sheet that was draped over him. His head was propped on a pillow. The dark and silver of his hair stood out against the white pillowcase. She smiled.

"Sex would be good right now," she said. Joe didn't move. "I'd love to have sex right now," she said a little louder. Still no reaction. "Oh, well, never mind." She rolled over on her side, facing away from him. He snored softly.

After a few minutes, she rolled back over and looked at him again. "He's so beautiful." He snored softly again.

She sighed and moved a little closer to him. Inching her body closer, she gently pressed her nose into his back and inhaled. He smelled so good, a fleshy smell, mixed with soap, and what else, maybe detergent or aftershave? "I'm not sure." He snored softly.

"He can sleep through anything."

She inched a little closer and put her hand on his hip. He squirmed a little, but didn't wake up. She ran her hand up his side and around to his chest. His nipples were soft, but came erect under her touch. The wiry hair of his chest felt good running through her fingers. She ran her thumb around his nipples and down his stomach. He took a deep breath and shuddered.

"Are you awake, Joe?" she asked softly, and was answered by another soft snore.

She ran her hand down his chest to his navel. The hair thickened there. It felt so soft on her hand. She reached lower to his sleeping genitals. They were soft and limp. She gently picked up his penis and stroked it, enjoying the feel of the soft flesh against her fingers. It slowly came to life, awakening in her hand and growing hard and heavy. She pulled back from him a little and rolled him onto his back. She looked at his face. His eyes were still closed.

Positioning herself on her knees beside him, she leaned down and took him into her mouth. He tasted sweet and salty at once. She ran her tongue along the underside of his penis and around his testicles. He gasped a little. Looking up at his face, she met his eyes. They locked with hers for a minute, and then she straddled him and slid down to cover him with her moist warmth. She was so ready. Riding him, she could feel the muscles in her thighs again, lifting her slowly and lowering, feeling every inch of every stroke, she could hear herself uttering soft cries of pleasure.

Joe pulled her nightgown off over her head and stroked her breasts. He put his hands on her bare hips and gently lifted her rolling them both over, never disengaging. He positioned himself on top and thrust deeply into her. She uttered a small cry of pleasure as he rose again and thrust, again, again. They rocked slowly, in rhythm to completion.

"I can feel your heart beating on my throat," she said into his neck. He pulled back to look at her. She wrapped her arms and legs around him and held him to her.

"You keep surprising me, Victoria." He kissed her lightly on the mouth.

"I couldn't sleep."

"Joe, let's buy a tandem bicycle," she said at dinner the next night. "I never get to ride unless I go with Jane."

"If we do, you'll never get to ride unless you go with me," he said, "or Jane."

"It would be something we could do together."

"I'd rather get two bikes, one for me and one for you. We could make it our new hobby."

"Joe, I can't ride a bike. I never have been able to."

"You've never given me a chance to teach you. I think I could. I taught both girls, and all three of my cousins. Give me a chance?"

"You'll just get frustrated with me. Everyone does." She looked down at her hands. Realizing that Patricia must have gotten that gesture from her, she looked up at his face.

"I won't." He paused in thought. "Listen, I'll know when to stop. If it becomes clear that you can't do it. I'll stop and we'll get a tandem. I do want to ride with you. I think it'll be a great way for us to spend time together."

"I don't know, Joe. I've been feeling so good about myself lately. I really don't need a failure. Plus, you know at my age, if I fall off a bike, I'll probably break something."

"You're not that old, and I won't let you fall. You're just a little thing." He leaned down to her face and said, "You know, lately, you've done a number of things that you've never done before." He smiled wickedly and kissed her on the cheek. "I'm thinking you can do anything you want."

"Well, I do want to ride a bike, but I just don't think I have much balance."

"I have some ideas about that, too."

"Just one more time, sweetheart," Joe said. "I know it's boring, but it'll help with your balance." He had set up a four-by-four board in the back yard. It was supported by cinder blocks, and he had made her walk back and forth on it. At first he had to hold her hand, but now she could do it by herself.

"You know, I used to take gymnastics when I was in high school. I never could do the balance beam, though. I was better at tumbling." She was almost enjoying this. Her balance actually was getting better.

"Didn't anybody work with you on it?"

"No, it was a really big class. There was only one teacher."

"Well, you're doing very well. There's nothing wrong with your balance. You just need practice."

He had also bought a balance exerciser. It was a board with a metal tube under it. She had to balance the two sides of the board on the tube. It was hard, but she was getting good at that, too. It was in the living room on carpet. Joe said the landing would be softer there if she fell. He wanted her to practice every day.

"What are you doing, Mrs. Vander?" Bobby asked, coming out of the back door.

"Hi, Bobby," she said. "I'm working on my balance. I think it's time to stop and get started on din-ner, though." She jumped off the board.

"Why are you working on your balance?" Bobby asked.

"Joe's going to try and teach me how to ride a bike."

"Oh." He looked a little puzzled.

"Would you like to have dinner with us, Bobby?" The young man had been over to see Patricia twice that week. She seemed to be glad to see him, but showed no sign of wanting to go out with him. Victoria was starting to worry that she'd never leave the house again.

"I'd like that, but only if Patricia's all right with it."

"I'll ask her. I won't tell her that I've already asked you. Thanks for thinking of that." She went inside. Joe picked up the board and took it to the garage. He and Bobby moved the blocks into the garage as well, and then came into the kitchen through the garage door.

Victoria came into the kitchen from the living room at the same time. She smiled. "Bobby, would you like to have dinner with us?"

He raised his brows in question.

Victoria smiled reassuringly.

"That would be nice. Can I help with anything?"

"Thanks, but no. I work better in the kitchen alone. You go join Patricia in the living room. It'll be about an hour."

They all sat down to dinner. They usually ate in the kitchen, but Victoria thought it would be a nice change to eat in the dining room. She'd been cooking a pot roast all afternoon. There were carrots and potatoes and salad. It was a nice meal.

"Bobby, what do you do?" Joe asked. He was a little uncomfortable with the boy. His paternal instincts were working overtime ever since they'd brought Patricia home.

"I'm in my first year of medical school at Emory. It's really hard work, but I'm enjoying it."

"That's great," Victoria said. "You know, Patricia majored in biology in college. I guess that biology project you two did in high school was just the beginning."

"That's right." Bobby looked at Patricia across the table. "Patricia, do you have any plans for your degree? What will you do now?"

Joe and Victoria tensed. How would she respond to questions about her future?

"I don't know." She looked at her plate and pushed her food around.

"You used to talk about going to vet school when we were kids. Do you still want to do that?" Bobby just kept talking.

"No, everyone thinks I'm too small to be a vet."

Joe put his fork down. "Who thinks you're too small to be a vet?" he demanded.

She looked up startled. "Someone I knew in California."

"Size doesn't have anything to do with it," Bobby continued. Victoria wondered if he felt the tension in the room. "Have you ever seen a picture of that vet at the Atlanta Zoo? She's this tiny little Asian woman.

She uses a step ladder to climb up and draw blood out of the Elephant's ear." He laughed.

"I've seen pictures of her," Victoria said. "She is small."

"Patty, you can do anything you want to do," Joe interrupted. "You did well in college. You graduated with honors. Have you really changed your mind about being a vet, or are you afraid to try?" Joe seemed to have forgotten that there was anyone else in the room.

"I don't want to talk about it, Dad." Patricia continued to look at her plate.

"Patricia, I'm sorry if I brought up a bad subject," Bobby said. "But I agree with your father, if you want to be a vet, you should."

The room was silent for a few minutes. "I think I'd have to take the boards." She spoke so softly that Victoria almost didn't hear what she said.

"You would, but that's not a problem. There are even study courses for those boards. I took mine in my senior year of college, but it's not too late. You can still take them," Bobby went on.

Patricia looked up at Bobby. She looked hopeful. Then she looked at her father. "Do you really think I could do it, Dad?"

"Of course I do, honey. You're as smart as a whip, and look at the way you deal with animals. You've got that poor abused dog eating out of your hand. I think it's just where you belong." Joe spoke with conviction.

She smiled a little. "I'll think about it." Looking

back down at her plate, she took a bite of pot roast, her first bite.

"Good." Joe looked at Bobby and smiled.

Nineteen

"You won't have leaky joints in the hose if you always prop the nozzle open when you turn off the water," Jeff said. He had found the nozzle closed and gathered all of the employees up to give them the same lecture. Victoria was glad he hadn't asked who left it closed. She was the guilty party. When he was finished, the employees dispersed to their various projects.

Victoria went out to the greenhouse. She needed to water the seeds she had just planted. It was only a week before Christmas and the weather had turned cold. She shivered as she crossed the yard to the greenhouse. Unwinding the hose from the wall caddy, she looked at the nozzle to see if it was open. It was. She pointed it away from her at the ground and turned on the faucet. Adjusting the flow of water, she moved up and down the rows soaking everything thoroughly. When she was done, she turned off the water and opened the nozzle all the way. Then she looped the hose back up on the caddy.

It was warm in the greenhouse. The water was already evaporating into the air making it humid. She looked up at the vent above the hose caddy. It was closed and really should be opened, just a little. She looked around and spotted a step stool she could use to get up to the vent.

The stool was just a little too short. She stretched as high as she could reach, but couldn't quite make the vent. "If only I had about four more inches," she said. Looking around she noticed the faucet on the wall. She put her foot on the handle of the faucet and pushed herself up. The handle turned under her foot and ice-cold water sprayed up at her from below. Looking down, she saw the open nozzle pointed up at her bottom. She tried to jump down, but misjudged the distance and tumbled onto the muddy floor, landing face down.

The water turned off and she looked up. Jeff stood above her, his arms crossed over his chest. "Why don't you ask for help when you need it? Are you all right?" He reached down to help her up. "You're soaking wet."

"Do you follow me around hoping I make a mistake? Why are you always there when something like this happens?" She was wiping at her face with dirty hands. It was only making her muddier; so she stopped.

"Because it's my shop, I'm always here, and something like this happens to you every day."

"Not every day." She started for the door.

"Where are you going? You can't go out there. It's 30 degrees. You'll catch pneumonia."

"I have to change. I'll just run home and come right back."

"No, you'll wait here while I go and get my truck. I'll bring it around to the door and you can come out and get in. I'll take you home to change."

"I really don't think that's necessary, Jeff."

"I'm doing it anyway." He walked out the door.

A few minutes later, Victoria heard the truck pull up. Jeff came back into the greenhouse. "Give it a minute to warm up." He was rubbing his arms. "The temperature has really dropped. Be fun to have a white Christmas, wouldn't it?" His smile was childishly enthusiastic.

She smiled back. "That would be nice. What do you do for Christmas, Jeff?" She felt a little bad. She hadn't thought about his parents being dead. She felt the familiar ache of her grief. This would be the first Christmas without her mother. Did Jeff spend Christmas alone?

"I go to my aunt's house. They have a big family. It's quite a celebration. Do you and Joe have big plans?"

"Jane always comes for dinner. It's the first time we've had one of the girls for a couple of years. It'll be nice to have Patricia here, and Bobby's joining us for Christmas dinner. His family celebrates Christmas Eve, so it won't interfere." She went to the door. "Let's go. I can't wait to get out of these wet clothes."

He followed her out to the truck and got into the driver's seat. He took a blanket out of the space behind the seat and tucked it around her.

"You don't have to do that," she protested, but she snuggled down into the blanket, grateful for the warmth.

"So Bobby's still trying. She hasn't discouraged him?"

"She's tried, but he just won't quit. I think we might be seeing some progress, too. He's been taking her to the park to walk. He won't let her take her crutch...says if she gets too tired, he'll carry her."

She looked out the window. "She is walking better, too. Not limping nearly as much."

"That's great, has she told him what happened to her yet?"

"I don't know. I don't think I can ask, and he hasn't said anything."

"I just can't help but feel that she'll never really get past it, if she doesn't talk to someone," Jeff said, as they pulled into the driveway. He stopped at the front walk.

"Yeah, I think you're probably right." They got out of the truck and walked to the front door. Victoria unlocked it and they went in.

"Is Joe in his office?" Jeff asked. "I'll go talk to him while you get dressed."

At the top of the stairs, Victoria stopped. She heard sounds coming from Patricia's old room. She went over to the door and knocked. Patricia opened the door. "You don't mind if I move back into my old room, do you?"

"Of course not, I'm glad you feel strong enough to use the steps." She stepped into the room and looked around. "Those sheets are clean, but they've been on the bed for years. Why don't we put fresh ones on?" Patch was sprawled on his bed in the corner. "Patch seems right at home."

"I'll change the sheets, Mom. You're getting my carpet wet. What happened to you?" She laughed.

Victoria looked down at her wet, muddy clothes. "I had a little accident. I have to change and go back to work. You know where the sheets are kept. If you need help, I'll help you after work tonight." She made

her way down the hall to her room feeling relieved.
Patricia was definitely making progress.

"I miss my mother," Victoria said on Christmas
morning. The grief had eased to the background as
life went on around her, but times like this brought
it back.

"I know you do," Joe said, pulling her into his
arms. "I miss her, too." They were lying in bed.

"Sometimes I miss her so much I ache all over,"
she said. "Will it ever get better?"

"I don't know, Victoria, I've really never lost anyone so close. I hope so."

"Well, I guess I'll go make coffee." She pulled
away and got up.

Victoria stopped in her tracks at the bottom of
the steps. She was on her way to the kitchen to make
coffee, but in the middle of the living room were three
bright new bicycles. She stopped and walked around
them. One was clearly bigger than the other two, it
was also a men's bike. The other two were women's
bikes, and smaller. "Joe," she called. "I told you not
to do that." He put his arms around her waist from
behind. She jumped, startled. She hadn't realized he
was right behind her. "What if I can't learn to ride?"

"You will." He kissed her neck from behind. "I
believe in you."

She continued to look them over. Running her
hand over the smooth metal, she smiled. "They sure
are pretty. I guess one of them is for Patricia. I wonder when she'll be able to ride it?"

"She's doing pretty well walking. Bobby's helped

her a lot. I wasn't sure I liked the idea of her having a boyfriend, but he's been good for her," Joe said.

"I don't think he's a boyfriend yet. I think he'd like to be, though."

"Well, what do you think about the bikes? Are they nice?" Joe asked.

"They're beautiful. I feel just like a kid." She laughed. "When can we start trying?"

"I think the weather will be nice enough today. I thought we'd wait until Bobby's here. That way you can ride back and forth between us." Joe had it all planned.

"No way, Joe, I'll be really embarrassed. We need to go out alone the first time, you know, to get an idea of how I'll do."

"Okay, we'll go after breakfast. Is Patty up yet?"

"I don't think so." Victoria went into the kitchen to make coffee. She was really excited about the new bike. "You know, Joe. I feel a little bad. I didn't get very much for you."

"Well, since I bought myself a bike, I think that's okay. Mine cost the most, of course." He was leaning on the counter beside her. "It's really a gift for the whole family, except for Ellen, of course. But I don't think she'll be riding a bike for a while."

"No, she won't. Our grandson is due at the end of January. How do you feel about it, Joe?" She looked up at him.

"I'm happy, I think. I have mixed feelings. It's not the perfect way to start a marriage."

"No, it isn't." She pulled out two mugs and put cream in both, measured a teaspoon of sugar for Joe, then waited for the coffee to finish brewing. "They seem happy about it. You know what, though?" She waited for a response from him.

"What? Is something worrying you?" He put his hand on her arm.

"Yes, I'm afraid. She's expecting me to come out there and help her with that baby. I haven't even held a baby since...I can't even remember." She poured the coffee into the mugs.

"Don't worry, it's like riding a bicycle, you don't forget how." He smiled at her.

She laughed. "I never knew how!"

"We'll do it together, just like we did with Ellen when she was born. Remember?" He laughed. "It took both of us to change a diaper."

They both laughed at the memory.

"Merry Christmas, Mom, Dad." Patricia came into the room. She had a smile on her face. Victoria noticed that it didn't quite reach her eyes.

"Merry Christmas, honey," Joe said, and kissed her cheek. "Did you see what's in the living room?"

"Surely one of those isn't for me?" she said, the smile turning to a frown. "I can barely walk. I can't ride a bike."

"You will be able to, if you want to," Joe said. He looked at her face for a minute. "But if you don't want it, I'll take it back and get you something you do want."

"That's okay, Dad. I don't mean to be ungrateful." She poured herself a cup of coffee and sat down at the table.

"Let's go out to the Christmas tree with our coffee," Victoria said. "I have a few things under there for you two." She led the way.

She pulled a gift out from under the tree and handed it to Patricia. "This one is for you." She waited for Patricia to open it.

"Mom, it's beautiful. It's such a good likeness." She turned it to show to Joe. It was a picture of Patch. He was standing in tall grass with Ethel and Theodore at his feet. He was looking down at them with interest. There were trees in the background. The picture was nicely framed. "You're really very good at this, Mom."

"Thank you, honey." She reached under the tree and pulled out another package. She handed it to Joe. "This one is for you."

He unwrapped it carefully. It was also a framed picture. He had unwrapped it face down, so he slowly turned it over. "Oh, Victoria." He looked up at her, his eyes wide.

"Let me see, Dad." Patricia reached for the picture. Before she could take it, he turned it to show her. "Oh," she whispered. It was a picture of her, sitting in the chair by the window, looking out at the back yard. Patch sat at her side, her hand rested on his shoulder. She was in profile and the likeness was perfect. She wasn't frowning, but not smiling either. She just looked lost.

No one said anything. Victoria began to feel concerned. "I didn't mean to upset any one."

"I'm not upset," Joe said. "I think it's beautiful. Are you upset, Patty?"

"I don't know. I look so lost in...I don't know. Is that really the way I look?" She got up and walked over to the window. Patch followed her and her hand fell to his shoulder, just like in the picture.

"I just saw you sitting there one day, and I couldn't get the picture out of my mind. When I went to my studio that night, this is just what happened. I think you're beautiful in it." Victoria was rambling. "I thought you'd like it, Joe. If it bothers you, we don't have to hang it."

"I think it's beautiful, too. I'll enjoy having a picture of my pretty little girl. Thank you." He kissed her.

"Yes, you're right, Dad. It is good. I'm sorry, Mom. I just hadn't realized how sad I'd become." She walked back over to where her parents sat. She bent and kissed them both. "I don't want to be sad anymore." She went to the tree and pulled out two packages. "Bob took me shopping, I'm afraid I didn't put much thought into these, but Merry Christmas."

Victoria pulled the paper off her gift. It was a nice gardening set, with a spade, trowel, and cultivator with matching handles, and matching gloves. "Thank you honey, it's beautiful."

For Joe there was a new racquet for racquetball and a box of balls. "That's great. I've been playing with Jeff and my racquet is just about worn out." Patricia had a pair of slippers from Victoria. Joe had the kite that she had bought for him in Savannah. Joe had wrapped up bicycle helmets for the three of them. The two dogs each had a rawhide chew, and Theodore got a catnip mouse.

Victoria went into the kitchen to prepare breakfast and Patricia went upstairs to get dressed. Joe came into the kitchen behind her. He stood behind her for a minute as she worked. "I feel bad," she said. "Maybe that picture will remind you of this difficult time." She had a lump in her throat.

"It's a beautiful picture. I'll always love it," he said. "You captured her so perfectly that she got a jolt of reality. Maybe, she didn't like what she saw." He put his hands on her shoulders and leaned close to her ear. "Victoria, you're right, this has been a difficult time, but it's been very valuable. I'm not sure I would have ever gotten this close to her otherwise, and I'm grateful for that closeness. That's what I'll remember when I look at that picture. Thank you." He kissed the back of her neck and said, "I'm going upstairs to get dressed. After breakfast, we'll get on those bikes."

Victoria was so excited. She was actually riding a bike by herself. Joe ran beside her a couple of steps. Then she took off to the end of the street. Her balance was good. She even thought to put on the brakes when she reached the cul-de-sac. She made a wide, shaky turn and started back up the road. When she got near Joe, she called out to him. "I did it, Joe." Unfortunately, when she turned her head to the left where he was standing, she turned the handlebars to the right, hit the curb, and went tumbling into a neighbor's yard.

When Joe reached her, she was laughing. "I can't believe I did it. Did you see that?"

"I sure did." Joe was grinning. "Did you hurt yourself when you fell?"

"No, the grass is dead, but it's still soft." She patted the ground next to her. She stood up and picked up her bike.

"I think until you get a little more practice, you should keep your eyes on where you're going."

"I think you're right." She got back on the bike. Joe helped her get started again. She rode around the cul-de-sac until she was getting more comfortable. Joe helped her learn to get herself started. He walked beside her ready to grab the back of the seat if she needed him to. Eventually she learned to start by herself. "I feel a little silly learning to ride a bike at fifty-five years of age."

"Better late than never." Joe laughed.

Bobby pulled up in his old Jeep Wrangler. They heard the muffler before they saw the car. He parked in front of the house and got out. "Looks to me like you know how to ride," he said, as Victoria pulled up to him and put her foot down.

"I can't believe it. You wouldn't believe how many times Jane tried to teach me." She was beaming.

"She never thought to work on your balance before she started, did she?" Joe asked.

"No. I guess not."

Patricia joined them. The limp was barely noticeable as she walked up the driveway. She stood beside Bobby and said, "I got a bike, too. I was thinking that maybe I should ask if I could use the stationary bike at physical therapy for a while. Slowly break my muscles in."

Everyone looked at her, but nobody said anything. That was the first time she had talked about wanting to do something. Bobby broke the silence. "That sounds like a great idea. You know what? My mom has an exercise bike in the basement. It's covered with dust of course, since she doesn't use it. I could bring it over and you could practice on it in between sessions."

"I'd like that. Thanks Bobby." She stood on tiptoes and kissed him on the cheek. His face promptly turned very red, and his smile stretched from ear to ear.

"Well, I need to start dinner." Victoria broke the awkward silence. "I'll just put my bike up. Joe, we'll have to put up some hooks in the garage to hang the bikes on. I don't want them to get damaged or stolen."

"That's a good idea." Joe followed her down the driveway leaving Patricia and Bobby at the top of the hill. They both looked back in time to see Bobby lean down and brush her lips with his.

"That's nice," Victoria said quietly.

"I guess so. I guess I'm a little jealous. I was enjoying having her to myself." Joe sounded sad.

"I understand." She touched his arm. "But we can't get in the way of her progress."

"No, of course we can't."

After they had put Victoria's bike in the garage, they went into the kitchen. Victoria had stuffed the turkey earlier, so all she had to do was put it in the oven. Once it was started, she put together a couple of snack trays and took them out to the living room. She had to put them up fairly high to keep them away from Patch. She just had to watch Theodore, though. He could get on the tables, no matter how high she put them.

After a few minutes, Bobby and Patricia came into the room with Jane right behind them. "Merry Christmas, Joe, Tori. Patricia tells me that you have actually done the impossible and taught Tori to ride a bike," she said to Joe.

"Apparently it wasn't impossible after all. Of course, we've been working on her balance for a couple of weeks." He smiled.

"I never even thought of that. What a great idea."

"You were just a kid yourself. I'm not surprised you didn't think of it. Honestly, I hadn't thought of it before. We always rode tandem when the kids were small."

"I guess I can get rid of that tandem now," Jane said.

"Oh don't, Jane," Victoria interrupted. "I like to ride tandem. We'll do both."

"Okay. I think I'd keep it anyway for sentimental reasons." They all laughed.

"Patricia," Bob said. "I have a gift for you. I have one for you, too." He looked at Joe and Victoria. He turned to Jane apologetically. "I didn't realize that you'd be here."

"I understand. I didn't bring anything for you either." Jane laughed as she started to pull gifts out of her bag. "Well, who goes first?"

"You go ahead." Bobby nodded to Jane. "Ladies first."

She had bought a daypack for Victoria. It had hidden compartments all over it and a place built into it for a water bottle. She had given Joe a bottle of Crown Royal Canadian whisky. For Patricia she had framed a picture that she had taken of her in the back yard with Patch. Patricia was leaning down with her arms around the dog's neck. Patch was rubbing the top of his head on her cheek.

"What a beautiful picture," she said. "Thank you, Aunt Jane." She kissed her on the cheek.

Then it was Bobby's turn. He handed small packages to both Joe and Victoria. Then stepped back and looked at them expectantly. They both pulled the paper off their gifts at the same time. He had given each of them a Walkman with headphones for running.

"Bobby, that's wonderful. How did you know that we both like to run?" Victoria asked.

"Patricia told me." Then he handed a package the size of a ring box to Patricia. She just looked at it. "Go ahead, open it," he prompted.

She pulled the paper off and popped the lid open. It was a pendant of white and gold polished pewter. The chain consisted of interwoven strands of white and gold, and the pendant was of a greyhound. It was white pewter with a gold patch on its shoulder. "It's Patch. Oh, Bob, thank you," she said. "Look, Mom."

"That's beautiful," Victoria said, relieved that it wasn't a ring. None of them were ready for that.

"Bobby?" Joe said. "I noticed that you always call Patty, Patricia. Didn't everyone call her Patty when she was in school?" he asked.

"Yes, they did, but she prefers Patricia," Bobby said.

"Is that right?" He looked at her.

"Yes, but you can call me Patty. You're my Dad. It doesn't bother me," Patricia assured him.

"No," he said. "I want to call you Patricia if you like it better." He paused. "After all, your name was my idea."

"It was?" Patricia looked at him.

"Yes, your mother wanted to name you Irene."

"Irene! Gross." She looked over at Victoria, horrified.

"I think it's a beautiful name," Victoria defended.

"I'm glad you thought of Patricia, Dad. I would hate to be named Irene."

"Well, actually, I thought of Patrick. I wanted a boy, you know," he teased. Patricia punched him playfully in the arm and grinned up at him. He grabbed her around the waist and kissed her cheek.

"Here, Bob, help me put this on." She handed him the pendant and turned around so he could clasp it behind her neck.

"How does it look?" she asked her Dad.

"It looks beautiful, honey. That's a nice gift, Bob," he said.

Victoria pulled gifts out from under the tree for Jane and Bobby. They were just sweet nothings, but brought smiles and thanks.

It was a wonderful day. The gifts were all perfect. The meal was good. Everyone went home feeling happy.

Twenty

"I want to buy a cemetery plot," Victoria said to the man behind the desk.

"That's what we sell here. Would you like to look at a few?" he asked.

"Yes, I chose your cemetery because you allow gardening. So many places don't these days," she said. "I need a plot that would be good for a rose garden."

"You want to put in a rose garden?" He looked puzzled. "Wouldn't you have to dig it up to be buried there?"

"Oh, it isn't for me. It's for my mother. She's already dead." Victoria felt the familiar lump in her throat. She brushed away a tear. "I'm sorry. I keep thinking I'll get used to it, but it always makes me cry."

"I understand." He handed her a tissue. "When did she die?"

"Two months ago." She sniffed and dabbed at her eyes with the tissue.

"And you haven't buried her yet?" The man was becoming agitated.

"No, I couldn't decide what to do. She's in a box, but I just think she should go somewhere more per- manent. I had thought about a rose garden in my own yard, but we might not always live there. If she's here, there's no chance of losing her." She looked up after drying her eyes and saw the shocked expression on the man's face. "I had her cremated."

"Oh." He snapped his mouth shut. "I was worried for a minute there." He laughed.

"So, I thought I would plant a rose garden. She loved roses and actually was better at growing them than I, but I think I can do it. When I get them growing well, I'll spread her ashes over the garden and put in a headstone."

"That's nice," he said. "I don't know anything about gardening, though. I'm not sure what you're looking for." He tapped the desk thoughtfully. "I've got an idea. We have a gardener that keeps the grounds. Maybe he could guide you to a good plot. Let's go see if we can find him."

They found the gardener at the back of the building and spent another hour riding around the cemetery in a golf cart looking at plots. They finally settled on one on the south side of a hill. There was full sun that was filtered through light foliage and the drainage was good.

"Thank you very much." She shook hands with the gardener and the salesman. "I won't be able to plant until after the last frost, but I'll start preparing the soil in about another month. I guess I'll see you then."

"I bought a cemetery plot for Mom yesterday," Victoria told Lillian and Jane. They were having lunch at the food court in the mall. They had spent the morning in the mall shopping.

"You bought a cemetery plot? I thought you had her cremated," Lillian said.

"I did, she's in a little box sitting on my mantle." She frowned. "I wanted to do something meaningful with her ashes, but I just couldn't figure out what. But, I've finally figured it out."

"What, Tori?" Jane asked.

"I'll plant a rose garden and scatter her ashes over that."

"That's perfect. Your mom loved her roses."

"Vic, I can help. I'm really good at roses. I can even grow them in pots on my balcony," Lillian said.

"Really, Lillian? That would be great. I'm not that good at roses. Mom was always more successful than me. But I'm determined to succeed this time."

"You will, Tori. You seem to be able to do anything you set your mind to these days." Jane leaned over and kissed her cheek. "Have I told you how impressed I am with you?"

"Thanks, Jane. That means a lot to me." She smiled. "I am doing things I've never done before, like riding a bike." She laughed. "Anyway, I thought it would be a good idea to plant the garden in a cemetery. That way, we'll always own it. I won't have to worry about a building being put on top of her or anything like that."

"I hope you thought about sunlight and drainage," Lillian said. "You can't just plant roses anywhere, you know."

"I did. The gardener of the cemetery showed me

284 / Marking Time

the best spots. He says he's good at roses, too. That'll be good. He can help me maintain it."

"You are so creative, Tori." They ate in silence for a minute. "How's Patty doing?" Jane asked. "She seemed to be feeling better when I saw her at Christmas."

"She is. She's making progress. Bobby's been taking her to physical therapy. They seem to be getting close. She's riding a stationary bike to build her muscles so she can ride the bike that Joe gave her for Christmas. I think we might need to buy her a car so she can be more independent."

"Can you afford that? Joe was giving you a hard time about money for a while there."

"We're doing better since I'm making commission on my contract work." She smiled. "That sounds so professional. I love it."

"You really have done well with your corporate business, Vic. Even Jeff says so," Lillian said.

"He does. He told me he'd never realized there was so much money in that part of the business," Jane said.

"So you're still seeing him?" Victoria asked.

"Yes, I'm enjoying him," Jane said. "He's so enthusiastic about everything. I haven't dated anyone like that for a while."

"You're dating?" Lillian asked.

"Yes, I think we are." Jane blushed.

"Are you sleeping with him?" Victoria asked.

"Vic!" Lillian cried. "You can't ask questions like that!"

"Yes, she can." Jane laughed. "Don't forget, we're

adoptive sisters." She turned to Victoria. "In answer to your question, yes, I am. Are you jealous?"

"Yes, but I'm glad, too. I worry about him being alone. He's such a great guy, he should have a partner."

"You don't worry about me being alone. I guess I'm not a great guy," Jane said.

"You don't need anyone. You've always been so self-sufficient."

"I don't know, lately I'm not satisfied with my life." Jane looked pensive.

"Really, Jane? I'm sorry, I should have noticed. I'm just so involved with my own things."

"Oh, I'm all right. I just need to do something different. I'll figure it out."

The phone was ringing when Victoria got home that afternoon. She rushed to answer it, wondering where Joe was. His car wasn't in the garage. He must have gone somewhere. She knew that Patricia was at physical therapy.

"Hello."

"Mama, I'm scared." Ellen sniffed. She was crying.

"Ellen, what's wrong?" She felt a tremor of fear.

"I'm in labor."

Victoria took a deep breath. "That's okay, honey, it's only a couple of days early. Everything will be fine."

"I'm afraid to have a baby." She was sobbing now.

"Of course you are. I remember being afraid." She laughed a little. "Everything will be all right, though. You're a big strong girl and you'll do fine."

"It's going to hurt. It already hurts."

"That's true, but when you hold that baby, you'll forget about the pain. I promise."

"But what about in the meantime?"

"Accept whatever they offer for pain."

"I'm going to." She had calmed down a little now. "I wish you were here."

"I do too. But I'll be there as soon as I can get there. Where are you now?"

"We're on the way to the hospital. Alex is driving like a crazy person."

"Tell him to slow down. You need to get there alive." Victoria said goodbye and hung up. She went upstairs to start packing. It would be a few days before she could go, but she might as well get started. There were things to tie up at work. She had to meet with the Jaspers, and she had to go over her speech with Jeff. She shivered at the thought. Time was running out.

She heard the garage door open and figured Joe was home. He came up the stairs. "What are you doing?" he asked

"Ellen just called. She's on her way to the hospital. I was just trying to figure out what to pack." She sat down on the bed. "I hope I can do this grandmother thing."

"You'll be a wonderful grandmother." Joe smiled at her. He sat down beside her and put his arm around her shoulders. "I'll make reservations. We'll go together this time. I wonder if Patty, I mean Patricia," he corrected, "will come."

"If Patricia will go where?" she said, as she came into the room.

"Out to Seattle to see your new nephew," Victoria said. "I just talked to Ellen, she's in labor. It's funny how you girls slip back to calling me Mama when you're upset about something." She laughed.

"What's she upset about?" Joe's brows pulled together.

"Pain." Victoria laughed.

"Ellen always was a big baby about pain," Patricia said.

"Well, she's in for a day of it now, and there isn't any way out." Victoria turned to Patricia. "So will you come with us out to Seattle? Bobby said he'd take care of Patch. You can trust him, can't you?"

"Yes, he's good with Patch, but I can't go, Mom, I just got a job. I start right away. I'll have to meet my nephew later when I've earned some vacation time." Patricia was smiling all the way to her eyes.

"You've got a job. Honey, that's wonderful. What is it?" Joe said.

"I'm going to be a vet technician at Riverview Animal hospital. I'm so excited. It'll give me a chance to see the business and decide if I can do it."

"We already know you can do it. The question is do you want to," Joe said.

"Patricia, I'm worried about that knee. I'm not sure you're ready for such a physical job," Victoria said.

"I talked to the physical therapist about it. She

said she could give me a plastic support to wear while I'm working. It'll prevent me from doing any damage to the joint until it's completely healed." She paused. "The only problem I'll have is transportation. I don't have a car. Is there any way we could buy a second-hand car or something? I could pay you back as soon as I start earning money."

"I had already been thinking about that." Victoria got up and gave her daughter a hug. "We'll get you a car, but it'll have to wait until we get back. In the meantime, you can use my truck. Dad can take me to work, can't you, Joe?"

"Of course, no problem." He gave Patricia a hug too. "I'm proud of you, sweetheart. You're doing great."

"Thanks, Dad, I told you I didn't want to be sad anymore."

"I'll be lonely at home all by myself all day." Joe pouted.

"Poor thing," Victoria teased. "Where did you go today?" she asked.

"I had lunch with Elizabeth," he said. "Oh, Patricia, she said she could use a hand with the dogs, if you were looking for something to do. Now that you have a job, you might not have time, but it would be good experience if you do have some time."

"Yes, it would, maybe on the weekends." She turned to leave the room. "I'm going to dinner with Bob, so I need to go take a shower. See ya."

"You had lunch with Elizabeth?" Victoria smiled. "You didn't tell me you were going."

"She called right after you left the house to meet the girls," he said. "We were going to play golf on

Saturday, but I guess I'll have to cancel. We'll probably be in Seattle by then, or on our way at least."

"You haven't played golf in years."

"No, I haven't had anyone to play with, but Elizabeth says she's pretty good." He looked at Victoria. "You don't have a problem with it, do you?"

"Of course, not, why should I?" She went into her walk-in closet to hide the look on her face. She knew the jealousy was showing.

"Good, because I'd hate to think you didn't trust me."

It was Sunday before they were able to fly out to Seattle. The baby had been born at 6 p.m., Seattle time, on Wednesday. They had gotten the call at 9:30. He was a healthy baby, eight pounds, six ounces, and twenty-two inches long. They named him Benjamin.

"I can't believe Alex passed out in the delivery room." Joe laughed.

"I know, Ellen said they had to carry him out on a stretcher. She said it distracted her so much she hardly noticed the pain." Victoria and Joe had flown to Seattle and rented a car at the airport. Victoria gasped a little when they pulled up to the house. "Oh, Joe, look at the house. It's beautiful. I didn't realize they were doing so well. They seem so young to have a house like this."

"They aren't that young, Victoria. Ellen will be thirty years old next year."

"I guess I have a hard time thinking of her as an

adult." She got out of the car. It was cold. She shivered and wrapped her coat around her. "I'm a little nervous. Of course you know that, since I've been telling you about it all the way out here."

"I am too," Joe said. "This grandparent thing is new to both of us." He rang the doorbell.

"Thank God you're here," Alex said when he opened the door. He looked agitated. "I don't know how much longer I could've held up."

"Is something wrong?" Victoria looked around. "Where's Ellen?"

"She's in the bedroom. I can't get her to stop crying. My mother has been helping out, but she only seems to make things worse." He ran his hand through his hair. He must have been doing a lot of that. It was sticking up at all angles.

"Show me the way," Victoria said, and followed him down the hall to the end. She knocked on the door and called, "Ellen, it's Mom. Can I come in?" The door swung open and she found herself wrapped in a bear hug. Ellen put her head on her mother's shoulder and sobbed.

"Oh, Mama, thank God you're here. I can't do this! I wanted to so much, but I just can't."

"Can't do what, honey?" Victoria gently pried Ellen's arms off of her and walked her over to a big easy chair that sat by a window. "Sit down."

"I can't be a mother. I didn't realize how hard it was. I took all the courses and read lots of books, but he's so fussy when I try to feed him. Maybe I don't have enough milk."

Victoria sat on the footstool and took Ellen's hands in her own. "It's probably your agitation coming through to him. Newborn babies are very tuned in to their mothers. They haven't really separated yet," she soothed. "It is hard at first. Couldn't Alex's mother help you?"

"She doesn't believe in breast feeding, says it's barbaric."

"Oh," Victoria said. "Well, we all have a right to our own opinion. Do you think it's barbaric?"

"No, I really wanted to do it. You always said it was such a pleasure. But I'm afraid he won't get enough to eat. I don't want to hurt him."

"If he doesn't get enough to eat, you'll know, because he won't gain the weight he should. Then you'll supplement." Victoria was a little surprised at how well she was handling this. She wanted to be angry with Alex's mother, but she would have to wait to meet her before she decided how to feel about her. "Where is he?" She looked around the room. On the other side of the bed was a bassinet. She got up and went over. He lay on his side. His fat cheek resting on the mattress, his lips folded in half. "He's beautiful."

"He is, isn't he?" Ellen had come over beside her. She smiled when she looked down at her baby. "I think he looks like Dad."

Victoria laughed. "It's hard to tell with his face all squished up like that."

"Don't wake him," Ellen whispered. "I don't think I could stand it right now."

"I think it's too late. He's awake." His small eyes had opened and he was looking at them. Then his little face screwed up and he started to wail. Victoria reached into the bed and picked him up. He felt perfect in her arms. She wasn't uncomfortable at all. She started to bounce a little, the way she had when her own babies were little, and he quieted.

"Thank God you're here, Mama." Ellen was back in the chair.

"I'm glad I'm here, too." Benjamin started to root at her breast. "I can't help you there, little guy," she said to her grandson. She looked at Ellen. Her face was covered with her hands and she was crying again.

"He won't nurse, Mama. What am I going to do?" she sobbed.

"Well, let's just see." She went over to the bed and pulled a pillow out from under the spread. "I used to like to put a pillow in my lap." She placed the pillow in Ellen's lap and put the baby on it. He started to wail again.

"See what I mean?" Ellen cried.

"Do you have on a nursing bra? Give him access," Victoria said.

Ellen opened her blouse and exposed her breast. Benjamin started to root around for it. Ellen pulled him closer to her body with her arm. Victoria could see her tense up. The baby latched on to the breast, but stopped and started to fuss again. "Maybe there isn't any milk," Ellen whimpered.

"You have to relax." Victoria walked around to the back of the chair and started to massage Ellen's shoulders. "I can see the tension in your shoulders. This really is scary. I remember. Dad and I were talking about it the other day. When you were born, it took both of us to change your diaper." She laughed.

They were silent for a minute while Victoria rubbed Ellen's shoulders and neck.

"He's starting to nurse," Ellen whispered. Victoria continued to rub Ellen's shoulders. She kissed her gently on the top of her head.

"What are you doing to me, Mama?"

"I'm loving you, baby." She remembered the same conversation with Patricia at the hospital. She was loving her, and her new grandson. It felt wonderful. "That's what you have to do, just relax and love him." She continued to rub Ellen's shoulders.

"I can feel the milk coming in now, oh Mama, thank you." She started to cry again, but this time it was a gentle sound, tears of relief.

"You just needed to relax, that's all." She kissed Ellen on the cheek and walked back around the chair. She sat on the stool again and watched the domestic scene. It was beautiful. "I'll paint this. I wonder if I can do it."

"I'm sure you can do it. Patricia says you're really good, but I don't know if I want my breast exposed for all eternity." Ellen sniffed and smiled.

"I'll put a blanket over your breast." They laughed together.

There was a knock at the door. "Can I come in?" It was Joe.

"You can come in if you're not squeamish about breast feeding," Ellen called. "From now on, no one is allowed in here who has a problem with breast feeding."

"I don't have a problem," Joe said, as he walked into the room. He came over and sat down next to Victoria on the stool. "He's beautiful, Ellen." He looked up at her face. "He looks like me."

Ellen laughed and wiped her eyes again. "That's what I think, too."

Alex came up behind them. "He seems to be nursing pretty well now," he said.

"He is." Ellen smiled up at him. "Mom says I just needed to relax." She switched breasts and smiled. They all sat quietly while Benjamin finished his meal. He stopped nursing and looked around at them all.

"It's nice to meet you, Ben," Joe said. Everyone laughed. "Can I hold him?" Joe looked at Ellen.

"Of course, but he needs to burp now," she said.

"That's okay. I might be able to remember how to do that." He smiled and picked up the baby. Victoria got up and put a cloth over Joe's shoulder. He patted the baby on the back until he burped. "Just like a drunken sailor," Joe said. Patting the baby's bottom, he said, "I think we need a diaper change." He walked over to a change table on the wall across from the bed. "Let's see if we can remember how to do this, Victoria."

She joined him at the table. He put the baby on his back and looked for a diaper. "Look at this, Victoria? They're store bought, they come in a bag." Everyone laughed again. He pulled one out and handed it to Victoria. She watched him pull the tabs off the dirty diaper and open it up. He screwed his face up a little, but didn't gag, while he pulled the soiled diaper out from under the baby. Folding it up, he handed it to Victoria. "Here, you take this."

"Thanks." She laughed. "What do you do with these?" she asked Alex.

"Put them in this can," he said, showing her the can next to the change table. "I'll take it out before we go to bed."

She dumped the diaper in the can, and looked back at Joe. He was looking at the tiny genitals of his grandson. "I never had a boy," he said. The tiny penis suddenly stood erect and let out a stream of urine. "Ahhhg," Joe jumped as it hit him in the face.

"Oh, Dad. I'm sorry," Ellen said. "I should have warned you."

Victoria dissolved into laughter as she stepped up to the change table, shielding herself with the diaper. "Like your father just said, we never had a boy."

Joe let Victoria take over and stepped back, wiping his face with his hand. "Alex, where are we staying?" he said.

"I'll show you to your room," Alex said, trying not to laugh. "Give me your keys. I'll get your bags."

Joe followed him out of the room. "I'd appreciate that," he said.

Twenty One

"She had worked herself into a terrible state, Joe," Victoria said, as they got ready for bed that night.

"A state?" Joe laughed. "That sounds like something your mother would say."

"Well, I am my mother's child," she said. "Alex asked me not to judge his mother too harshly, and I'm trying not to." She sat down on the bed.

"But...?" Joe asked. "Sounded like there was a *but* coming."

"Well, I just wish she hadn't criticized Ellen for wanting to nurse her own baby. I'll try not to decide how I feel about the woman before I meet her, but I do think she should have kept that opinion to herself."

"I agree, but we have to try to get along with Alex's family. He's a part of ours now," Joe said.

"You're right, of course. I'll try to be good. Maybe we should have them over for dinner while we're here. I'll cook something nice."

"That's a good idea. Come over here and snuggle up with me, Gramma." Joe reached for her and pulled her into his arms. She lay with her head on his chest, listening to his heartbeat.

"I want to be called Granny," she said.

Joe looked down at her. "Why?"

"I don't know. I just like the way it sounds."

"You don't look like a Granny. You're so young-looking."

"Thanks, Joe. That's a nice thing to say." She was quiet for a minute. "Did Patricia sound okay when you talked to her? I wanted to talk to her, but I was caught up in something with the baby. I'll call her tomorrow night."

"She was nervous about work tomorrow. It's actually her third day, but you know how a new job is. I hope it works out for her." Joe was protective of Patricia these days. They both were.

"I do, too." Victoria yawned. "It was really hard to leave her. I was surprised how hard. She's a grown woman. She can stay at home alone, but after all she's been through, my maternal instincts are working double time."

"I know what you mean." Joe yawned, too.

They lay quiet for a while. Then Joe started to snore softly. Victoria looked up at his face. His head had fallen sideways. Resting his cheek on his pillow made his lips fold in half. "You know," she said quietly. "Benjamin does look like you." He snored again. She kissed him on the cheek and rolled over. She was asleep in minutes.

"How many times were you up during the night?" Victoria asked Ellen, when she went into the kitchen the next morning. Ellen looked tired, she had circles under her eyes, and her hair hadn't been brushed.

"Twice." She yawned. "I don't think it's the getting up to feed him that makes me so tired. I just don't think I'm sleeping very well. I anticipate his cry."

"That's hard. Is there anything I can do? Maybe let him sleep in our room one night. I could come and get you for feedings."

"No, I think I just have to get used to it. I'll try not to take a nap today. Maybe that way I'll sleep better at night."

Victoria poured herself a cup of coffee and sat down at the table across from Ellen. "It's always hard adjusting to a new baby. After all the planning and dreaming, it's kind of a let down when reality sets in."

"That's an understatement." Ellen looked down into her coffee cup.

"It gets better."

"I hope so, because I'm not having much fun right now." She looked across the table at her mother. "I'm sorry I was such a bad kid. I wanted you to know that. I regret being so wild in my late teens."

"Don't regret it. I'm just glad you lived through it." She took a sip of coffee. "There's nothing like having a kid of your own to give you a different perspective on your parents. I don't blame anything on my parents anymore." She laughed. "Have you eaten anything?"

"No, I'm not very hungry." Ellen was definitely

depressed. She usually had a big appetite. Victoria had never had much post-partum depression herself. She had been sick during her pregnancies, so post-partum was a relief.

"Well, you need to eat. You're feeding two people, you know. Let's see, what have you got?" She opened the refrigerator and looked around.

"We haven't been to the grocery store in a while. There's probably not much there."

Ellen was right. There wasn't much at all. Victoria managed to find some bread for toast. She scrambled a couple of eggs, and mixed up some frozen concentrated orange juice. She gave Ellen the eggs, and sat down to share the toast and juice with her. There was a little bit of jam. They ate in silence.

"I hear the baby," Ellen said, and quickly left the room.

Victoria got up to clear the table. Ellen had eaten the eggs and toast. Her body was demanding food, even if she thought she wasn't hungry.

"Smells good in here." Joe came into the kitchen.

"Well, enjoy the smell, because there isn't any food. I just gave the last two eggs to Ellen. I'm having a hard time not being mad at Alex's mother," she said.

"Shhhh. Alex might hear you." Joe looked around.

"He's not here. He's gone to work." She put the pan down in the sink angrily. Then stopped and took a deep breath. "Why couldn't she have bought them some food? Does she expect Ellen to do it, just out of the hospital? Look at this." She opened the refrigerator. There was nothing in it, but a six-pack of beer and a jar of pickles. "I would have dropped everything and come right away, but Ellen said she'd have help."

"Mom, try not to be too hard on Meredith. She's a spoiled, pampered, rich person. She doesn't know how to help." Ellen came into the room carrying Benjamin.

"She's rich?" Victoria stretched her arms out for the baby. Ellen let her take him. "Come and see Granny," she said.

"Granny?" Ellen laughed.

"I like the way it sounds," Victoria said. "You like it too, don't you, Benjamin." She kissed his furry head. "He's quiet this morning. He must be feeling more relaxed."

"Yes, they're rich. Alex's family, I mean. I didn't realize it until we got married and moved here. They've got a huge house in one of the best parts of town. They're nice people, but they really don't know how the rest of us live."

"Well, if she couldn't help, she shouldn't have said she would. If they have money, couldn't they have hired someone to help?" Victoria was trying not to be mad, but she was losing the battle.

"Victoria, I know it's hard, but try to calm down. We need to get along with these people," Joe said. He turned to Ellen. "She's like a mother bear protecting her young." He laughed.

Ellen laughed too. "I know, Dad. Meredith was so excited about helping that I thought she'd come through. She really was happy about this baby. He's the first grandchild on Alex's side, too. But when I came home with him, and I didn't know anything about taking care of him, she panicked. She left here crying yesterday."

"Well, okay. I'll stop being mad at her. Let's just get things in order here. I think you and Dad should go to the grocery store together. You need to get out Ellen, move around a little. I'll stay with Benjamin."

"Oh, no, Mom, I couldn't leave him."

"Yes you can. I won't be pushy, if you really don't want to go, but I think it would be good for you."

"Your mom's right, honey. You have to get used to leaving him with other people or you'll go crazy. I know he's young, but we won't be gone long." Joe looked at her. "By the way, you look great. It's hard to believe you just had a baby." He put his arms around her and kissed her cheek.

"Thanks, Dad." She hugged him back. "Well, I guess if it won't take long. We should make a list. That way we can get in and out fast." She was looking brighter.

"I thought we should invite Alex's family over for dinner. I'd like to get to know them. Would that be all right with you, Ellen?" Victoria asked.

"That would be nice. I've bragged about what a good cook you are. I think we should prepare something southern, but not too southern." She laughed.

"No black eyed peas and hog jowls?" Joe laughed.

"Right, and no grits and collard greens." They were all laughing now.

"What do you think about country ham, cheese

potatoes, glazed carrots, a nice salad, and banana tarts for dessert?" Victoria said.

"That's perfect, Mom." They sat down at the table to make a list. Half an hour later, Ellen took a shower and got dressed, fed Benjamin once more, so he'd have a full stomach. And they were off. Victoria breathed a sigh of relief. It seemed like mothering was getting to be hard work again. "This sure is more fun than that teenage stuff, though," she said out loud and laughed.

When Alex got home that night, he opened the door to the smell of food cooking. "That sure smells good," he said, coming into the kitchen. He and Victoria both laughed when his stomach growled loudly. "Food has been kind of scarce around here lately."

"I noticed," she said, turning to the refrigerator to put away the butter.

"Whoa, look at that." Alex opened the door again to have a look. "I don't think there's ever been that much food in there. Thanks, Mom." He kissed her cheek. "Where's Ellen? Is she feeling any better?"

"I think she is. I made her go to the grocery store with her dad this morning. I think she needed to get out of the house." She started to set the table. "They're in the living room now."

"I hope you won't be too mad at my mother." Alex looked embarrassed. "She really wanted to help, but she just got scared. I love Ellen more than anything in the world, but when she's upset about something, she can be a little intimidating."

"That's true." Victoria thought about it for a minute. "I hadn't thought about it that way. Ellen hates not knowing what to do."

"And she really didn't know what to do, and I sure didn't know what to do, and Mother was even more lost than we were. I've never been so happy to see anyone in my life as I was to see you and Joe." He was running his hand through his hair again.

She reached up and smoothed it. He smiled. "My hair's been a mess ever since that baby was born."

"Go and join Ellen and Joe in the living room. I'll call you when dinner's ready. It won't be long."

"You learned how to ride a bike," Ellen said, "after all of those years of riding tandem? Remember how we used to fight over who had to ride with her, Dad?" They were gathered around the kitchen table for dinner. Benjamin was in the bassinet between Joe and Victoria. They were taking turns distracting him while Ellen ate.

"Yes, I remember." He laughed. "Lucky Patricia, she was always too small. She couldn't balance for both of them."

"How did you teach her, Dad?"

"I made her practice her balance on a beam in the back yard, and a balance board. I don't know why I didn't think of that before."

"Excuse me. I'm in the room. Don't talk about

me like I wasn't here," Victoria said. "Besides, what was so bad about riding with me?"

"Your balance was just so bad. It was a struggle, tiring. But we really didn't mind, honey," Joe soothed.

"Right," she said.

"Patty said that you were doing great in your job," Ellen said. "Tell me about it."

"How much do you talk to Patricia? I didn't realize you called so much," Victoria said.

"They're really close." Alex picked up Ellen's hand and kissed the back of it. "I envy them. I don't have any brothers or sisters."

"So tell me about your business, Mom." She smiled at Alex.

"Well, it's been really exciting. I started out just potting arrangements for sale in the nursery, but my employer liked my work, so he asked me to learn more about garden design. I took some courses, and started doing some of the designing." She took a bite and chewed thoughtfully for a minute.

"Her work wasn't all her employer liked," Joe said. "I was afraid she would run off with the guy for a while."

"You were not."

"You're kidding, right Dad?" Ellen laughed.

"No, I'm not. I walked in on them one day and he was kissing her."

Victoria punched his arm playfully. "Anyway, I drew up some garden plans for a friend of Dad's. It was sort of a project. I wasn't really planning on selling them, but they liked them. Jeff liked them too, so we're going to use them in the garden show in

Washington, D.C., in the spring. It's a real challenge, but I'm having a lot of fun with it."

"That's great, Mom. You always were good at gardening."

"Well, I always liked it. I have a big challenge ahead of me now. I'm planting a rose garden for Gramma," she said, reaching for her water.

"Explain that, Mom. Gramma's dead."

"I know, and I miss her so much it hurts." Victoria's eyes clouded a little, but then cleared. "I bought a cemetery plot. I had to look around to find a cemetery that would let me plant. Most of them don't want you to. Well, I found one and it's beautiful, but you know I never was as good at growing roses as Mom. Lillian, my friend from the nursery, is going to help me. She's good at growing roses. When I've got them growing well, I'll spread Mom's ashes over the garden and put in a headstone."

"I'd like to be there when you do that," Ellen said. "Spread the ashes. Okay?"

"That would be nice, honey. It'll be mid-April before I'll be ready."

"We could go back to Atlanta in mid-April, couldn't we, Alex?"

"I think that would be nice," he said.

"It must be hard to lose your mother," Ellen said. "Even though she was so old. That's one person that's always on your side." She smiled. "Unless, of course, you're fighting with your mother." They all laughed.

"I thought Friday night would be good, I mean to have your parents over for dinner, Alex," Victoria said. "That will give us time to get everything in order around here, then Dad and I leave on Sunday, so I'll have time to make some meals that I can freeze for you on Saturday."

"Can't you and Dad stay longer?" Ellen sounded nervous again.

"We'll stay if you want us to, but I suspect that by Sunday, you'll be ready for us to go," Joe said.

"Right now, I don't ever want you to leave."

"I don't either," Alex agreed.

"You'll be wanting your independence again. Believe me." Victoria laughed. "So is Friday night all right?"

"Yes, I think that's good. I've got a big week ahead of me at work. I really shouldn't socialize until the weekend," Alex said.

"Well, I think that was a very nice evening," Joe said on Saturday morning, as they all sat around the kitchen table.

"It was not," Victoria said. "It was a disaster."

"I wouldn't call it a disaster, Victoria. The food was excellent."

"That's right," Ellen said. "Meredith even commented on the banana cream tarts." Everyone laughed except Victoria. "I have to say, though, Mom, I was really surprised when you hit her in the face with her tart."

"Yeah," Joe said. "That was good aim. You threw it right at her mouth." There was more laughter.

"I didn't throw it at her. I tripped over the rug

and it flew off the plate." She looked around the room at all the smiling faces. "Do you think I could have hit her right in the mouth that way if I had aimed?" She shook her head. "My hand-to-eye coordination isn't that good."

"That's true," Joe said, looking at Ellen. She nodded.

"I really am sorry about the way my mother acted," Alex said. He was laughing, too, but obviously he felt embarrassed. "The way she was acting, I wouldn't have blamed you if you did aim it at her."

"I can't believe she wore her mink, and her diamonds," Ellen said. "She really isn't like that, Mom."

"No, she puts on airs when she's nervous, and after the way she ran out of here in tears an hour before you arrived, leaving us miserable and starving, I'm sure she was nervous," Alex said.

"Well, I hope we get a chance to patch up our relationship someday," Victoria said. "Alex, you believe I didn't really throw a pie at your mother, don't you?"

"Of course, I do."

"I suppose you two are ready for us to leave, aren't you?" Joe asked.

"Yes," they said together.

"Well, you don't have to be so enthusiastic." Joe laughed.

"I'm sorry, Dad, it's not that I haven't loved having you here, but..." Ellen said.

"It's okay, honey," Victoria said. "We know what it's like to have people in your house for a week. It's just time for you and Alex to find out what new normal is." She smiled.

"I really needed you when you got here, but I'm ready to try motherhood on my own now," Ellen said.

Victoria had been holding Benjamin on her lap. He was lying crosswise sleeping peacefully, but now he started to fuss. "I think you are," she said, handing the baby to his mother. "Besides that, I'm ready to go home. I miss my animals, and I've got a speech to write."

"You have a speech to write? You're giving a speech, Mom?"

"That's right," Joe said. "She's speaking to all the participants of the garden show in Washington, D.C., this year."

"Just the ones that stay for the awards, and dinner after the show is over. Jeff says most of the participants don't stay."

"That's not what he told me."

"Dad, stop playing on Mom's nerves. Tell me about the speech, Mom."

"Every year, the committee chooses a nursery from the different parts of the country to talk about the past growing season, and the obstacles they had to surmount, the plants that grew well, that kind of thing." She stopped and took a deep breath. "This year Landrum's was chosen, and Jeff wants me to do it."

"You've never been much of a public speaker, Mom. Are you sure it's what you want to do?"

"No, I'm sure it's what I don't want to do. But Jeff was just so determined."

"He said it was your decision. At least, that's what he told me," Joe said.

"He said I didn't have to do it if I didn't want to," she said. "I don't know why I said yes. I wish I hadn't now."

"I think it's great, Mom. I'm sure you'll do really well."

"Thanks, Ellen, I wish I felt that way."

Twenty Two

"So, Ellen was a wreck when you got there?" Jane said. She was sitting in a lounge chair watching Lillian and Victoria work on the rose garden.

"Oh, she had worked herself into a state," Victoria said.

"Tori, you sound just like your mother." Jane laughed.

"That's what Joe said. It's true though, she was sure the baby was going to starve to death. She was so upset that Benjamin went tense the minute she took him into her lap."

"And you stepped in and settled everything down." Jane laughed. "You're something else, Tori."

"Well, somebody had to. That mother of Alex's just had them both in a state." They all three laughed.

"Well, she did. I didn't like her much. I tried not to dislike her. Alex was so protective of her. I guess if I expect her to be open-minded about us, I need to be open-minded about her." She looked down at her work. Lillian had brought a tiller from the tool shed at the nursery, and tilled the soil. Now they were separating the weeds and grass from the topsoil. "But, really, she told Ellen breastfeeding was barbaric, then she left them with no food. Alex's stomach was growling so loud you could have heard it over here."

"I guess Alex could have gone to the store," Lillian said.

"I suppose so, but he was still working."

"You're protecting him, like he was one of yours," Jane said.

"Well, I really do like him. He calls me Mom. He calls his own mother, Mother. I'd probably really get along with his nanny." She studied the ground. "I hope they make it. It's not an easy way to start a marriage. Joe and I were married four years before we had kids."

"Do you really think that makes a difference?" Lillian asked.

"Yes, I do. It's not easy to live with another adult. It's even harder when you're married to them. They haven't even adjusted to each other. Now there's a baby, and babies put a strain on a relationship, even a well-established one." She looked around. "I need to mark the outside of the plot someway. Should I build a wall? What do you think?"

"Maybe just a small one," Jane said. "Red brick, I think."

"I can't lay brick." Victoria laughed.

"Hire someone," Lillian said. "You don't have to do everything yourself."

"I suppose I could do that. I wonder how much it would cost."

It was late afternoon when she got home. She had spent all of the morning working on the rose garden. There were plans rolling around in her head, and she was anxious to get to her studio to put them on paper. Joe was in the kitchen when she came in from the garage. "How'd it go with the garden?" he asked.

"Well, we got it tilled, and cleaned the soil. We can't plant for a while yet, but I have all sorts of ideas that I need to put on paper," she said, passing through the room.

The back door opened and Bobby came into the room. He was pale and his eyes looked angry.

"Are you all right, Bobby?" Victoria asked. "You don't look well, sit down." She guided him to a chair.

"I'll kill that bastard," he said.

"Patricia told you what happened," Joe said, more of a statement than a question.

"Yeah, she just did. No wonder she didn't want to talk about her accident." He was shaking. "I told her we should pursue it. Get an investigator if the police won't do anything, but she said no." He looked up at them. "Surely you can convince her."

"She just wants to put it behind her," Victoria said.

"He'll do this to someone else, if he isn't stopped." Bobby got up and started to pace.

"That's true. I hadn't thought about that," Joe said. "Maybe I'll contact the police in Sacramento again. See what they think."

"Where's Patricia?" Victoria asked. "Is she all right? What brought this up?"

"We were talking about moving in together." Patricia came through the back door and sat down. "I think I'm ready to have my own place. Bobby said he'd share rent with me. I just felt like he needed to know why I'm so neurotic if he's going to live with me."

"You're not neurotic, Patricia," Joe said.

Bobby looked down at his feet. He looked uncomfortable. "It would be a platonic relationship," he said, looking a little sad. "At least she wouldn't be living alone. I could take care of her."

"I think I need to learn to take care of myself."

"Patricia, I don't want you to leave," Joe said. "I have nothing against you, Bob, but I just don't think you two are ready for this."

"Dad, like Bob said, it would be a platonic arrangement." She looked at Bob. "For now, anyway. I don't make enough money at the Animal Hospital to live alone. It would work for both of us."

"I don't want you to leave," Joe repeated. Sitting down next to her, he took her small hand in his big one. "I've enjoyed getting close to you. I'll miss you."

"I appreciate that, Dad. I've enjoyed getting close to you, too. I didn't think you and I could be close, but I was wrong." She kissed him on the cheek. "But I can't stay here forever. I need to move on."

"I won't let anything happen to her, Mr. Vandor. We'll find a place close by, too. She can come and visit," Bobby said.

Victoria hadn't said anything. She couldn't think. The scene unfolding in front of her was touching, but she didn't seem to be a part of it. She sat down at the table and looked at her daughter and husband, then at Bob.

"Are you all right, Mom?" Patricia asked concerned.

"Yes, I think so."

"I think this is a good idea. We're going to do it. I hope you're all right with it," Patricia said firmly.

"I guess it's not up to me, is it?"

"No." She reached across the table and took her mother's hand. "But, I do appreciate all that you and Dad have done for me. You really came through when I needed you."

"The first time she left, I couldn't wait to see the back of her," Victoria said to Joe after dinner. They had eaten alone. Patricia and Bobby had gone out again. "This time I feel like crying."

"It's really out of our hands, isn't it?" Joe said. They were washing the dishes.

"You know, parents really have a tough deal. You never get to stop worrying, you're always on call if something bad happens, but you have no control. We make none of the decisions."

"You're right. Tough deal." Joe wiped his hands on a towel. "Nobody told us about that part of it before we had kids."

"That...or the teen years." Victoria took a deep breath. "I think I'd have done it anyway, even if I'd known."

"Yeah, you're probably right." Joe went into his office. "Well, I've got some work to finish up before bed."

Victoria finished wiping the counter and went upstairs to her studio. Ethel followed her up the stairs. Theodore stretched and yawned when they came into the studio. He jumped down from his place on the futon and rubbed against Victoria's leg.

"At least I can still make decisions for you two." Patch was with Patricia. He went everywhere with her.

"Does Patricia like working at the Animal Hospital?" Jeff asked. He was helping Victoria repot some seedlings in the greenhouse.

"She loves it. She comes home excited about it every day. You wouldn't believe all the things they let the technicians do, draw blood, place catheters. I don't even know what a catheter is."

"It's that thing they put in your vein when they give you fluids."

"Oh. Have you ever had fluids?" She looked at Jeff.

"Once. I got dehydrated working in the sun."

"You have to keep drinking water when you work in the sun," she scolded.

"Yes ma'am." He smiled.

"Anyway, she does like it, and she can take Patch with her. They don't mind, of course. So that's nice, too."

"Have she and Bobby found an apartment, yet?"

"No." Her brows drew together.

"What's wrong?" Jeff put his hand on her shoulder.

"I just don't know if I'll ever be able to stop worrying about her."

"You will. I think it'll just take time." They worked quietly for a while. Victoria was thinking about her garden. It was getting close to spring and she needed to make some plans.

"How's the speech coming, Vic?"

"I've finished writing it. All I need to do now is practice it."

"Practice it on me," Jeff said. "It's only two weeks until we go. Are you ready?"

"I guess. We've got the plants all ready for the display. I've never set up a display before. You'll have to direct me. Every garden I've ever planted was actually in the ground."

"It's not that hard. I've been doing this since I was a kid. We'll do fine."

"We packed the plants up yesterday and sent the truck up ahead of us. They should arrive just before we get there," Victoria told Joe on their way to the airport. "You know Jeff could have picked me up. We're on the same flight."

"I wanted to take you," Joe said. "I'm still not sure I'm happy about this."

"Joe, you have to trust me. I think I'm being very good about all this golf you're playing with Elizabeth." She laughed.

Joe smiled. "You are. Of course, I can't think about anyone but you. I've made that clear. I'm still in love with you."

"I never said I didn't love you, Joe. I said..."

"You couldn't feel it," he finished for her. The silence hung between them for a minute. Joe parked the car and got out. He opened the trunk and got out her bags. "I'll miss you, Victoria."

"I'll miss you too," she said. They walked in silence to the gate. Jeff was waiting for her. It was time to board. Joe pulled her aside and kissed her.

"Keep your hands off my wife," he said to Jeff.

Jeff smiled at him. "I'll try, but you know it won't be easy."

Victoria laughed, but it wasn't really fun anymore. Something had changed in the relationship, but she wasn't sure what. She watched the two men shake hands, and it dawned on her. They had really become friends. There was a sinking feeling in the pit of her stomach. Was she jealous of that, too? She shook off the feeling and walked up the ramp to the plane.

"What's wrong, Vic," Jeff asked. "You haven't said a word since we left the ground. Are you already missing Joe?"

"No, I'm just mad at myself. I'm becoming very selfish."

"How so?"

"I felt a stab of jealousy, back there when you

and Joe shook hands. You've become good friends. Do I have to share everything with him?" She laughed.

Jeff laughed too. "I guess you do." He looked out the window. "You know when I came up with this idea I was planning to seduce you on this trip."

"Really, Jeff?"

"Yes, I fell for you the first time I saw you, when you rolled up your sleeve and showed me your muscle." He laughed. "I've loved having you in my life." He paused, frowning. "But I know we can't be anything more than friends. You're still in love with your husband."

"Is that the only reason?"

"No, I couldn't do that to a friend. I think Joe made a point of being my friend for just that reason." He laughed. "But, just the same, I like him. I respect him. He's a good man and he's good to you."

"Yes, he is. I wish I were sure how I felt about him. I mean I do care about him. How could I not? But, sometimes, I still feel like there's something missing."

"I'm sure you'll figure it out." Jeff patted her knee.

"So, you're not going to seduce me?"

"No."

"Shoot." She laughed. "It's funny, Lillian always said you had a thing for me. I didn't believe it. I mean I'm old and clumsy. I'm not really pretty anymore. I really thought I'd lost my appeal. I'm glad you told me that, Jeff. I don't know why it's important, but it is."

"You're still very appealing, but it's not the way you look."

"Oh, thanks," she said sarcastically.

"I didn't mean you're not attractive. You are, but it's more of a vitality that attracts men to you. You are just so determined."

"Joe calls it stubborn." They both laughed.

Victoria found herself caught up in the excitement of the garden show as soon as she walked through the door. They had a day to set up. Their spot was on the end of one of the aisles. It was a good spot. The weather in Washington was still cold and it was raining, but inside the convention hall it was warm. There were fluorescent lights on the ceiling that would help the plants and Jeff had brought grow lights and fixtures for their display.

The bustling activity all around her gave her an excited feeling she hadn't ever experienced before. This was fun.

"You look like you're enjoying yourself," Jeff said standing beside her. They were looking at their progress on the display.

"I am. I'm so glad I came along. This is so much fun. Can I be involved next year, too?"

"Of course, I'd like that," Jeff said.

"What do you think about the display?"

"It looks good. After we get it set up, I want to walk around and get a look at the others."

"We'll do that. Let's get this finished." They started in to work. Joe had two of the gardeners who worked for him helping. One had driven the truck and the other had ridden along. They were just excited that they got to spend a week in Washington, D.C. The work was tiring, but it was the kind of work that Victoria loved. When they got finished, it was 5:00 p.m.

"I can't believe that took us all day." Victoria stretched her tired muscles. "What time do we get started in the morning?" she asked.

"Eight o'clock. That's when they open the doors, but we'll have to be here a little before that. Why? Are you too tired?"

"No, just making my plans. Let's take a look at the other displays," she said.

They spent an hour wandering through the conference hall. Some of the displays were very elaborate. One had a Statue of Liberty in it draped with flowering vines. It looked ridiculous. Several had fountains and water gardens in them.

"All in all, I think we compare pretty well," Victoria said.

"I think so too. Anyway we need to set up a table with cards and pictures in the morning. Let's go get some dinner," Jeff said, and started for the exit.

They had a nice dinner together in the hotel restaurant, and then retired to their own rooms for the evening.

Victoria was exhausted. Her muscles ached from the hard work, but she felt good. She took a shower and washed her hair. Coming out of the bathroom, she caught sight of herself in the full-length mirror. She stopped and looked again. "I've done this before," she said to herself. She looked at her body. Her breasts lay against her ribs, they were a little bit lower that they used to be, but not too bad, maybe not as full. Her waist was bigger. There were little pockets of fat on her hips, and her belly, though firm from running and the hard work of gardening, was not flat.

"My belly used to be so flat. I run, why isn't it flat, now?" she asked herself.

Her legs were muscled, but the tops of her thighs still had dimpled flesh. "I guess you can't escape age."

The phone rang and she picked it up. "Hello."

"Hey," it's me. "How're you doing?"

"I'm okay, Joe. I was just looking at myself naked in the mirror."

"I wish I was looking at you naked."

"I don't think I'll ever let you see me naked again. I'm not pretty anymore."

"I think you're beautiful."

"You have to, otherwise you'd be depressed."

"No, I really do think you're beautiful."

She studied her face in the mirror. There were lines at the corners of her mouth and circles under her eyes. "There are wrinkles on my face too," she said.

"You are fifty-five years old, Victoria. You're not supposed to look like you did when you were twenty. You're still beautiful, just not in the same way."

"Really, Joe?" She looked back at the mirror. "Maybe you're right. I'm just using the wrong standard. I need to learn to appreciate the changes of age."

"There you go." Joe laughed. "How'd the day go?"

"It was great. Oh, Joe, I've never enjoyed anything so much, all the excitement of the show, all the people. Some of the displays are beautiful. I'm having so much fun."

"How's Jeff doing?"

"I think he's enjoying it, too. It's not new to him, like it is to me, but I think he likes it. How's Patricia?"

"She's doing fine. They found an apartment. Since she doesn't have any credit, they want me to cosign with her. I think I'll do it."

"Yeah, I think she'll pay her rent."

"And if for some reason she can't, we'd help her anyway." He paused. "She told me she wants to see a therapist."

"She did?"

"Yes, she said Bob talked her into it. He told her she had to work through her trauma or she'd never be free of it."

"I wonder if she'll ever be free of it anyway?"

"No, probably not, but I'm glad she'll see a therapist."

"Me too." She paused. "She doesn't talk to me." Victoria sounded sad.

"She doesn't need to, Victoria. Her relationship with you is sound. She needs to talk to me, learn to trust me."

"I guess."

"Don't get your feelings hurt. I love you, honey. I miss you."

"I miss you, too." They hung up.

"Now, I'm jealous that my daughter goes to her father instead of me," she said to herself. "What's wrong with me? I want to be the center of everyone's life."

She looked in the mirror again. All she saw were the flaws. Maybe that was why she wanted everyone to like her so much. She didn't like herself. "I'll find a way to change that," she said. "But how?"

Twenty Three

"I can't believe the week is going by so fast," Victoria said to Jeff. "It's already Wednesday. It seems like we just got here."

"You're having a good time." He laughed. "I can see it in your face."

"I am, aren't you?"

"Yes. Oh, Vic, I forgot to tell you. The committee that plans this is chosen each year at the show. I got a call from the chairman this morning. He wants us to be involved next year. Ordinarily I'd turn it down. I don't like doing stuff like that. But I thought I'd give you a chance to do it if you want to. You might enjoy it."

"Work on the committee. Gosh, I don't know. I've never worked on a committee before."

"Give it a try. You might like it."

"When do I have to decide?"

"They asked us to attend a meeting this evening after the show. I thought we'd go and see what it's like. You don't have to give them an answer until the end of the week."

"Okay." They were sitting in folding chairs at the display. There was a lull in the crowd, so they had time to relax.

"Jeff, do you like yourself?" Victoria asked.

"That's a funny question."

"Well, do you?"

"I guess so. What's not to like?"

"Do you like the way you look?"

"I'm not bad looking. Why, don't you like the way I look?"

"It's not you. I don't like the way I look."

"What's wrong with the way you look?"

"That's not the point. The point is that I don't like myself. Remember when I told you that it seemed like something was missing in my relationship with Joe?"

"Yes, I remember." He was looking confused.

"Well, I figured out what it is. It's me."

"You're missing from your relationship with Joe? Vic, this is too deep for me." Jeff laughed.

"No, listen. When I look at myself in the mirror, all I can see are the fat parts and the wrinkles, but when Joe looks at me, he thinks I'm beautiful. No," she said, and frowned. "That's not right. I guess it's too deep for me, too." She laughed.

"No, I see what you mean, but I'm not sure the problem is that you don't like yourself so much as you don't know yourself."

"What do you mean?"

"Well, like when I asked you if you wanted to be on the garden show committee. You didn't know, because you'd never done it. I've never done it either, but I just know that I wouldn't enjoy it. I've done other things like that and I didn't like it. It's not the kind of thing I like to do. On the other hand, there are things that I've never done before that I think I would like to do. I just haven't had a chance to do them."

"I see what you mean, but I'm not sure what the solution is."

"I'm not either. I guess you just have to get to know yourself."

"How do I get to know myself? You're right, but I've lived with myself for fifty-five years. Shouldn't I know myself by now?"

"I don't know, maybe you should keep a journal or something."

"That's a good idea. Thanks, Jeff."

"You're so funny. You've always got something going on." The crowd resumed and they had to get back to work.

That evening at the committee meeting, Victoria found that she did enjoy it. It was really exciting to be involved in organizing something like this. She agreed to serve on the committee.

"I can't believe it's over." Victoria frowned. It was Sunday afternoon. They had just packed up the truck and sent it on its way. "I've worked toward it for a whole year and it's over, just like that."

"Just like that," Jeff said. "Well, tonight we'll go to the award ceremony, then home tomorrow. I'm sure you'll be glad to see Joe?"

"Joe? Oh yes, I will."

"Had you forgotten about him?" Jeff laughed

"Of course, not, I was just thinking about the award ceremony. I hadn't thought about it all week. I was so busy with the show. Now, I'm nervous."

"You'll do fine, Vic. What's the worst that could happen?"

"I could throw up."

"You won't throw up. Dinner isn't until after the ceremony, so you'll have an empty stomach."

"Then I'll faint."

"Drink a glass of juice before we go. That way you'll have sugar in your blood."

"You've thought of everything, haven't you?"

"I've given these speeches before, too."

"Do you get nervous when you speak?"

"Not any more, but I did at first."

"I don't think I'll ever get used to it."

They sat side by side in the audience listening to the awards being announced. Victoria was holding her breath.

"First prize goes to Heath's Greenery, from Dallas, Texas."

She breathed deeply and clapped as the smiling man collected the trophy from Heath's. She held her breath again as the crowd quieted.

"Second prize goes to Simon's Garden Shop, from Bangor, Maine."

"Stop holding your breath or you will pass out," Jeff whispered. "We're not here to win a prize."

She looked over at him a little surprised.

"Third Prize goes to Smith's Nursery, in Flint, Michigan."

The crowd quieted again.

"And an Honorable mention to Gregg's Garden of Eden, from Charlotte, North Carolina."

"I'm sorry, Jeff," she said, when the crowd quieted again.

"About what?" He saw the disappointment in her face, and put his arm around her shoulders. "I didn't realize it meant so much to you, Vic. I really didn't come here to win a prize."

"Why did we come here, then?" she asked.

"For exposure, public relations, experience, fun. I like these things."

"Have you ever won a prize?"

"I got an honorable mention once, long time ago."

"Where's the ribbon?"

"I don't know."

"You really don't care, do you?"

"No, I really don't, but if you do, then there's always next year. I thought your garden was beautiful. We got a lot of comments on it."

"Yes, we did." She looked down at her hands. "But you know what? I would like to win a prize. I do care."

"Good, then you'll try again next year." His arm still around her shoulders, he lifted her chin with his free hand and kissed her mouth. "Now, listen to the speaker," he said, as he turned back to the platform.

Victoria looked at him. The kiss had been sweet, but not passionate. She smiled.

"Get ready, Vic. You're next. They're announcing you now."

"I'm scared to death," she whispered.

"Your stomach is empty, you can't vomit and you won't faint. What's the worst that could happen?"

"I don't know." She heard her name called and got up to walk to the platform. Her feet were numb. She felt like she was floating. She counted the steps to the platform as she climbed them. One. Two. Three. Oh, no, there was a fourth step. Her foot hit the lip of the top step and she felt herself falling. Her early gymnastic training came back to her and she tucked her shoulder, did a sideways somersault and rolled gracefully onto her back. Her legs were stretched out in front of her, and her arms spread to the side. The audience was silent.

"I wish I could pass out now," she whispered to herself. "Then they could just carry me away." She took an inventory of body parts. Nothing seemed hurt, so she sat up. Her back was to the audience. They were still silent. She slowly stood up, brushed off her pants, turned and walked to the lectern. She leaned toward the microphone and said, "I told my colleague that I was nervous about making this speech and he asked, "What's the worst that could happen?" A ripple of soft laughter went through the audience. "I said I didn't know." This time the laughter was louder. "It's really very appropriate to start my speech that way, because that's pretty much the story of my career in this business." She went on to describe her fall into the compost bin, her accidents with the wheelbarrow. The story about her plunge into the mud brought a round of applause. From there she launched into her speech about their year in Atlanta.

"You were great, Vic. Jeff grabbed her when she returned to her seat. He kissed her again soundly on the mouth. "Are you okay? Did you hurt yourself when you fell? I've never seen anything like that. You looked like a gymnast." He laughed.

"I'm all right, maybe a little bruised. I really did pull myself out of that one, didn't I?" She was smiling.

"You sure did. I was so proud."

"I'm proud, too. I didn't know I could give a speech, and you know what? I enjoyed it."

"See, you're getting to know yourself."

They walked down the ramp from the plane. Jeff was behind Victoria. When she spotted Joe standing in the crowd, she stopped short. Jeff ran into her from behind. "Has he always been that beautiful?" she said.

"I don't think he's beautiful." Jeff laughed and walked over to where Jane stood beside Joe. He kissed her and shook Joe's hand. Victoria followed and stretched up on her toes to kiss Joe. The kiss was wonderful, warm and passionate.

"Welcome back, Victoria." Joe smiled. "I missed you."

"She didn't miss you at all." Jeff laughed. "She really enjoyed the show."

"I did. I was so busy, I didn't have time to miss you, but it was great to see you standing there just now." Victoria smiled back at him.

"I wish you could have seen your wife speak. It was great," Jeff said. "She's a natural."

"I figured she would be. Shall we go?" Joe put his arm around Victoria and guided her toward the baggage claim. They collected their luggage and went their separate ways. Jane had ridden to the airport with Joe, but went home with Jeff.

On the ride home, Victoria told Joe about the week at the show. "I'm so happy, Joe," she said. "It's fun having a career."

"I'm glad you're happy in your work." He was quiet for a minute.

"I'm happy in my marriage too."

Joe glanced over at her. "Really?" He sounded insecure. "You haven't said that you love me in a long time."

"I love you, Joe," she said, reaching over to put a hand on his arm.

"Can you feel it?" he asked softly.

"I can feel it."

They made love that night, moving together in a harmony perfected by time. A year ago, she had wished she could experience falling in love again. It had made her sad, because she knew she wouldn't leave Joe. Now it had happened for her, with Joe. She had fallen in love with him all over again. All of the excitement of first love was there, only better with the comfort of years. She wrapped her arms and legs around him and held him tight.

"Well, that's it," Victoria said, after she poured the ashes that had been her mother's body onto the rose garden. It was a warm April day. The sun was shining, but a spring breeze cooled them. Joe was beside her, Patricia and Bob stood on the right of them, the ever-vigilant Patch beside them. On the left were Alex and Ellen, Benjamin sleeping on his father's shoulder. Jane and Jeff stood across the plot with Lillian.

"Do you feel closure?" Joe asked.

"What exactly does that term mean?" she asked. "Is the gap that was left in my life when she died supposed to close? Because if it is, then no, I don't feel closure. That gap will never close." She brushed away a tear.

"I guess I don't really know what the term means," Joe said. "Maybe a better question is do you feel like you've done what you needed to do for your mother?"

"I guess so." She stood quiet, looking at the roses. They hadn't bloomed yet, but the vines were covered with buds, and they were every color you could find. "And, I guess I'll learn to live with the gap."

"I think you already have, Mom." Patricia said, and kissed her cheek.

"I think we should get back," Ellen said. "I need to feed Ben before the guests arrive for the picnic." They were having a picnic to celebrate Ellen and Alex's marriage, and Benjamin's birth, and Patricia's recovery, and a lot of other good things. It would also be a celebration of her mother's life. They walked to their separate cars and went home.

Victoria carried out a fresh bowl of potato salad. The group had gone through one already. "It's a good thing I made two," she said to herself.

"A good thing you made two of what, dear." Dolores Crisp was standing behind her.

"Dolores, how do you always catch me talking to myself?" She laughed.

"I think you must talk to yourself a lot, dear." Dolores smiled. "That's okay. I talk to myself, too."

"You do?"

"Don't tell anyone." She smiled. "It's a lovely picnic. Thank you for inviting me."

"I wanted all of the neighbors to come. I wanted them to see my beautiful new grandson." She looked over to where Benjamin was sitting on Patricia's lap. Ellen and Alex were across the lawn talking to an acquaintance of Ellen's from high school. She turned back to say something to Dolores, but she had wandered off.

Joe put his arms around her waist from behind and rested his cheek on her head. It was such a familiar feeling. She smiled and covered his hands with hers. "Remember what this yard looked like a year ago?"

"I sure do. It was a jungle." Joe laughed. "You've done a great job on it."

"I didn't do it alone. You helped."

"All I contributed was muscle. You did all the planning."

"I still didn't do it alone." She looked over at Patricia holding the baby. She and Bob laughed as Benjamin batted at Patch when he sniffed his head. Bob leaned over and said something to Patricia. She smiled and he kissed her.

"Do you think they'll end up together?" Joe asked.

"I hope so. He's awfully good for her. I'm so glad he convinced her to enroll in a class to prepare her for her GRE exams," she said. "But even if they don't end up together, they'll always be friends. Friends are important, too."

They looked over to Jeff. He was standing between Jane and Elizabeth. "They are," Joe agreed. "You know, I thought Jeff just had a thing for older women, but he and Elizabeth seem to be hitting it off, too."

"Are you jealous?" Victoria laughed as she turned in his arms and put her hands on his shoulders.

"A little," he smiled, and kissed her.

Susanna Chelton Sheehy:

Susanna lives in Atlanta, GA with her husband of thirty years. She works as a Veterinary Technician, a job which fulfills her requirement to be happy and useful. Living in the same general area is her family, including aging parents, grown children, and siblings, and her friends, both old and young.

www.ingramcontent.com/pod-product-compliance
Lightning Source LLC
Chambersburg PA
CBHW021444240626
47153CB00001B/288